ALSO BY DARRELL DELAMAIDE

THE NEW SUPERREGIONS OF EUROPE

GOLD

DEBT SHOCK

THE GRAND MIRAGE

A NOVEL BY

DARRELL DELAMAIDE

THE GRAND MIRAGE, a novel by Darrell Delamaide

First Edition, September 2011

Copyright © 2011 Darrell Delamaide

Author Services by Pedernales Publishing, LLC.
www.pedernalespublishing.com

Barnaby Woods Books
1630 Connecticut Avenue, NW, Suite 400
Washington, DC 20009
www.barnabywoodsbooks.com

Library of Congress Control Number: 2011916882

ISBN: 978-0-9839958-0-7

Printed in the United States of America

To Andrea

THE GRAND MIRAGE

Prologue

Somewhere in Syria, March 25, 1910

Horst Reinhardt loved this time of day. The cold desert sky hinted at the heat to come as the sun broke over the flat horizon. The scorching daytime made Reinhardt hate this wasteland, tundra that stretched into nothingness in all directions.

But this moment at dawn filled him with energy. He stood outside his tent and began his program of calisthenics, keeping to a routine he had set for himself twenty years ago at Gymnasium – jumping jacks, deep knee bends, pushups, running in place. The workout, and a plain diet, kept him trim and enabled him to survive the punishing work of this project.

Reinhardt looked at the stretch of roadbed that had been finished with such toil. The ground was flat and easy to grade, but the surrounding desert afforded no materials for building. Gravel was hauled from a hundred kilometers away -- this site had been picked because of the relative proximity of a small quarry. A massive caravan of camels and mules had delivered the first ties overland from Lebanon. Rails would arrive by ship at Aleppo and likewise be carried laboriously over a terrain devoid of roads.

The railway was a grand project, the effort of two empires – the German and the Ottoman – joining their might. It was the chance for a low-born engineer from Düsseldorf to make a career for himself.

Something was not right this morning, however. The huge canvas tents that served as barracks for the Kurdish workers remained silent. The men should be bustling around by now, preparing breakfast, getting ready for work. It was vital to get as much accomplished in the morning hours before the afternoon sun forced them to seek shelter.

Reinhardt noticed for the first time that the Turkish guards were not at their posts at either end of the camp. A contingent of a dozen Ottoman soldiers was assigned to the site to ward off bandits. Reinhardt heard his two German colleagues stirring in the tent, somewhat set apart from the workers and the main camp.

Uneasy, Reinhardt strode along the roadbed towards the two large workers' barracks. The door flap of the first one hung limply open. Where was everyone? The Kurds generally were quite disciplined and reliable, they had found. This tardiness was not at all normal.

Reinhardt reached the first tent and ducked to enter it. To his astonishment, the two dozen cots were still occupied with the inert forms of the workers. An odd disarray met his eyes – blankets tossed carelessly on the ground, arms hanging over the edge of the cots. As his eyes adjusted to the dim light, Reinhardt saw two of the workers actually lying on the ground. At the same moment, he became aware of a sweetish smell he recognized from his work in the slaughterhouse at home – the smell of blood.

He strode quickly to the first cot and shook the man in it by his shoulder. The movement turned the man over and revealed a wide gash across his throat and a pair of open dark eyes that saw nothing.

Reinhardt recoiled, then stepped to the next cot. More sightless eyes, another gashed throat. Blankets soaked in blood.

He looked quickly into the shadows of the tent corners. Who had done this? He dashed out of the tent and back towards his colleagues, who were emerging from their own tent with a vague look to the silent barracks.

"They're dead," Reinhardt shouted to them. "They're all dead." The two men reacted immediately, running back into the tent to fetch their rifles. They came back within seconds, arms at the ready. But there were no enemies to shoot.

Together, watchful, the three Germans returned to the first tent and determined that indeed all twenty-five Kurds had been killed in identical fashion, slit across the throat. They approached the second tent slowly, already certain of what they would find there. Eighteen more Kurds, some of them mere boys, had been murdered in their cots.

The soldiers' tent was on the other side of the roadbed. The engineers found eight corpses there. Two of the soldiers apparently had put up a fight. How had it happened so quietly in the silence of the desert night? The Germans had heard nothing as the intruders, evidently numerous, had wreaked mayhem on their camp.

"What kind of barbarians would slaughter men in this fashion?" one of the German engineers asked aloud. He had read of Oriental cruelty, but the scene before his eyes surpassed his most vivid image of what that could mean.

They found the other soldiers dead at their posts.

"Why were we spared?" Reinhardt voiced the question in their minds.

"Have we been?" asked another in a quiet voice.

An enemy that could strike so silently and so ruthlessly could return at will to dispatch them.

Without another word, the men gathered water and kits, and saddled their horses. They debated some time whether to head for the quarry, only one hundred kilometers away but even more defenseless than their own camp, to strike out across the desert, or to head east toward the mud flats of the Tigris and Euphrates. They did not know who their enemy was and so could not know which direction he came from. In the end, they decided to go west, across the tundra, in spite of the exposure, toward the civilization they knew and away from the barbarous mysteries behind them.

Chapter One

The steamer passed by the Golden Horn and reduced speed to navigate its way gingerly through the ferries and fishing boats that thronged the Galata dock. Along the quays, baskets of gypsy mackerel glittered in the sun like a harvest of diamonds. Stevedores wrestled with bales of cotton. Crowds of men swarmed along the docks, their red fezzes bobbing through the shadows of the afternoon sun.

Lord Leighton regarded the scene dreamily. He wasn't paying attention to the individual players; he simply absorbed the energy they generated. He looked up at the massive dome of the New Mosque, guarded by the minarets spearing the skyline. In the background loomed the silhouette of Hagia Sophia.

"Hello, Sophie," Leighton murmured to himself. He loved the old basilica, now used as a mosque. Her arms reached out to him like those of a welcoming mistress.

The Englishman was tall, nearly six feet. His dark blond hair framed a large forehead. His eyes were blue or gray, depending on the light. He had high cheekbones and a strong, tapered chin. Usually clean-shaven, he had allowed his beard to grow on some longer expeditions. His nose betrayed Norman ancestry, strong and straight; his thin lips looked severe until he smiled. He was slender in build, though there was nothing delicate about him. His tailored suit suggested a well-proportioned body; in his mid-30s, he was still largely free from middle-aged flab. At Eton, he played rugby and cricket, and as a young man had been an avid polo player. He also enjoyed the ride of a weekend hunt.

Leighton stood alone on this section of the railing. Other passengers were still below-decks busy with last-minute packing. He enjoyed this grand entry to Constantinople, storied capital of Byzantine and Ottoman empires. The city rose majestically in graded tiers, the low sun creating a halo of golden light behind the domes and towers that spilled down the hills of the metropolis. Cries from hawkers at the bazaar wafted through the air, carrying above the din on the quay.

The steamer, a small 2,000-tonner, drifted to the dock, thumping against the padding of hemp as thick ropes were looped around the stays and the anchor slid into the water. A larger steamship moored at the neighboring dock. Leighton discerned a dhow lurking in the shadows of the bigger ships. Traders from Lebanon plied the eastern Mediterranean in the primitive sailing vessels, carrying olive oil, wine, dates – produce of a timeless husbandry. Skiffs ferrying small groups of commuters wove their way through the traffic.

Leighton spotted a motor-car at the end of the dock. As he walked off the gangway onto the dock, a young blond man in a brown suit approached him.

"Lord Leighton?" he asked.

"In the flesh."

"Curtis, from the embassy. His Excellency asked me to meet you."

"How very gracious. Totally unnecessary but a nice gesture."

"We have a motor-car," the young man said, evidently used to impressing locals with the luxury of the embassy car.

Leighton, thinking how motor traffic in London had already gotten out of hand, only nodded in acknowledgment.

"My man will be along shortly with the luggage," Leighton explained.

Broome was at that moment steering a dolly down the cargo gangplank, loaded with their steamer trunks and valises. Leighton waved to the Welshman as he patiently maneuvered the luggage along the crowded dock. Broome favored his left leg, limping slightly, a legacy of his service in the Boer War. He was thoroughly sensible and Leighton had grown quite dependent on him.

They followed Curtis to the car. The driver, a swarthy local dressed in a black suit and fez, strapped the trunks on the fenders. He seated Leighton and Curtis in the back seat and offered a wool blanket against the late afternoon cool; Broome took a seat in the front. The driver expertly started the car, slipped it into gear and started threading his way through the crowd.

Turning for a last look at the packet that had been his home for two and a half days, Leighton was surprised to see a fakir standing just behind the car. He wore a black headdress and a dark brown robe. The scarf was pulled across the lower half of his face, but the eyes staring straight at Leighton startled him – they were as blue as the sky above them. Leighton turned to tell Curtis just as the car lurched to a halt to avoid a train of three donkeys laden with baskets of grain. When Leighton looked back again, the fakir was gone.

They proceeded up the hill into Pera. The roads in the European quarter were mostly paved, unlike the rest of the city. The buildings, too, were modern, built in stone on European designs.

Because his visit this time was quasi-official, Leighton felt obliged to stay at the Pera Palace, the grand hotel of the European quarter. On previous trips, he had preferred to stay in Stamboul, at the Hotel Istanbul. This elegant hotel overlooking the Sea of Marmara also catered to foreigners. While it could not boast the bath and privy in each room like the Pera Palace, it was tasteful and clean. It had also proven sufficiently discreet two years ago for Leighton's trysts with Elena.

Where was she now? Ensconced in a marriage to a prominent bureaucrat or perhaps even a pasha? Leighton indulged in the glow that Elena's memory brought him now. Richard Leighton, 9th Baron Leighton, was a bachelor, moderately wealthy and reasonably handsome, and had his share of experience with women. His travels in the Orient had exposed him to diverse opportunities. In England, there were the dalliances that country weekends fostered. When he was in Paris, friends offered him actresses, and he played the man-of-the-world role expected of him with more or less enthusiasm.

Elena was different. She was his first real passion, the only time he truly lost his heart. She was Armenian, with raven black hair in thick curls down her back. Her skin was olive burnished to a copper sheen; her eyes at times shimmered like dark pools, at times glowed like amber. He had lost himself in those eyes.

"How long have you been out?" Leighton asked Curtis.

"Six months, sir."

"Quite a mission."

"Yes, my first foreign posting," Curtis said, his face and voice shining with eagerness.

Leighton knew most of the Foreign Office mandarins thought Constantinople a backwater. The treaty with Russia three years ago, in 1907, answered the Eastern Question for Whitehall, and brought an end to the Great Game that had pitted the two empires against each other for control of Central Asia. Still enough concern remained for Edward

Grey, the Foreign Secretary, to dispatch Leighton in the matter of the Baghdad Railway.

"His Excellency would be happy to receive you at 10 o'clock tomorrow morning, if that suits milord," Curtis said.

"A perfect time. Again, most considerate," Leighton said automatically. He would need Lowther, the ambassador, as well as some of his attachés, no doubt. It was delicate, this bypassing of official channels.

The hotel was efficient if not warm in its welcome. So many princes and pashas stayed here that they didn't make a fuss over an English peer. The bellhop discreetly inquired whether his lordship would like a "pillow" for the evening. Leighton tipped him generously but declined this traditional offer of female companionship. He had found the custom congenial on occasion on previous trips, but this return to Constantinople was arousing too many emotions in him.

Broome quickly unpacked the trunks – he had so much practice lately – and retired with a murmured good night to the smaller of the two bedrooms in the suite. Leighton ordered his dinner in the room. Afterwards, he poured himself three fingers of Dewar's whiskey and settled in with Burton's Arabian Nights. He carried several volumes of the work with him when he traveled. Tonight he had chosen the "The Porter and the Three Ladies of Baghdad." Three "ladies" indeed – Britain, Germany and Turkey.

The trip, though relatively comfortable, had exhausted him. One of the ladies in the tale quoted Ibn al-Sumam:

> Hold fast thy secret and to none unfold
> Lost is a secret when that secret's told.

Sound advice, thought Leighton, and as ever, so apt. A good one to sleep on, he decided. He laid the book aside, turned off the lamp and slept within minutes.

~

The next morning, as Leighton mounted the steps to the British Embassy, he recalled his meeting with the Foreign Secretary, just last month. It had been overcast in London, with a cold drizzle that never stopped. The splendor of the Foreign Office dispelled the outer gloom, however. As a subaltern swept him through the arched entrance hall and up the grand staircase to Grey's office, Leighton had to pause at the magnificence of George Gilbert Scott's vision. The gleam of the ormolu and bronze chandeliers dazzled him, as did the sweep of the marble balustrade, the gilded capitals of the columns, the glittering tessera of the mock antique mosaic in the floor. Scott had envisaged it as a national palace to impress foreign potentates visiting the capital of the British Empire. It never failed to impress Leighton, at least.

Grey, dour as ever, quickly brought Leighton back down to earth.

"Don't trust the Germans, never have," he grumbled. "Damn Kaiser is crazy as a loon, don't care who his grandmother was."

Kaiser Wilhelm, son of Queen Victoria's daughter Vicky, constantly proclaimed that Britain and Germany were "natural allies," racially superior to the rest of the world. The British royal family had been imported from Germany in the 18th century. Of course, most of their subjects — descended from Angles, Saxons and Normans — likewise were of German origin.

Leighton knew that Grey expected no response to this tirade. The minister's brows jutted out like crags on a cliff face, creating dark caverns pierced by his intense gaze. Grey was known to be rabidly anti-German.

Leighton supposed it was the narrow focus of statesmanship that turned Grey against the Germans.

Leighton himself had largely positive impressions of the Reich. He had visited the Museum Island in Berlin and shopped for Oriental carpets in the red-brick warehouses of Hamburg, where rugs from Persia and Central Asia awaited shipment to points throughout Europe.

"We must stop them," Grey was going on about the Germans. He motioned Leighton over to a map he had unrolled on the table across from his desk. "See here," he said, pointing to the mountains and desert between Ankara and Baghdad, "they want to build a railroad across this godforsaken stretch. There's even talk of taking it down to Basra."

Basra had direct access to the Persian Gulf. Grey didn't need to spell it out. The Gulf gave directly into the Arabian Sea, the waterway to the coast of India. The Baghdad Railway was the missing link in a military transport route from Europe to the jewel of Britain's imperial crown.

"They're bloody fraternal now, but we can't have the Germans knocking on our door in India, or the Turks either for that matter," Grey muttered. Perhaps it was the constant need for diplomacy that made him mumble everything, Leighton thought.

"Certainly not," Leighton said, shaking his head for emphasis.

"Up to you. Can you do it? Can you help us stop this railway?" Grey's eyes stabbed at Leighton out of those caverns.

Leighton paused. "Well, it seems the Turks and Germans themselves are doing a fair job of mucking it up, without any help from us."

The initial leg from Constantinople to Ankara and Konya had been finished two decades ago, with German assistance. The two empires had been unable to agree on further work since then.

"These Young Turks have ideas, though," Grey said. "They dream of resurrecting the Ottoman Empire, making it great again. God forbid."

Britain had shored up the Ottoman realm to keep it from collapsing and creating a vacuum in the Orient, but the last thing it wanted was a resurgent Great Power next door to India. It had skirmished too long with Russia in Central Asia to countenance any threat from the region to the south. For that reason, the Foreign Office had closely monitored the Young Turks since they seized power in 1908.

"The Porte keeps telling us the railroad will be built only with our consent and cooperation," Grey said, referring to the Sublime Porte, the government of the Ottoman Empire. "Balderdash, of course. But they can't afford to be caught out in their lie. That's where you come in. I need you to spy out the situation for me," he said, gesturing again at the empty space on the map northwest of Baghdad. "Any sign of surveying, building, massing resources?"

It was, of course, an assignment for the military. But the sultan's spy network knew the British army personnel and London did not want to risk offending the new regime. The Turks would be dubious about Leighton's trip, but unable to pin anything on him or Whitehall. Leighton had served in South Africa and still carried a major's commission. When Leighton met the Foreign Secretary at a dinner party a few years earlier, Grey had shown great interest in Leighton's travels. The minister had asked Leighton to deliver messages to Arab leaders on two occasions. Another time, he had requested an account of Leighton's trip to Aden.

Leighton felt ambivalent about these assignments. Am I a spy? Leighton asked himself. An agent of His Majesty's government, yes. A secret agent, formally, though his role would be fairly transparent to the Ottomans and the Germans. He was to gather information for the Foreign

Office and, where possible, act on its behalf to further the Government's policy. What better definition of a spy could there be?

Leighton thought of himself more as a soldier, an officer in His Majesty's Army. A patriot, as must be any member of the aristocracy, by definition. Noblesse oblige. What would his grandfather have thought of his assignment? Approval, Leighton reckoned. It was for the Crown and for the country. What other loyalties could a young British peer have?

Yet spying seemed to betray the code of a gentleman. It was deceitful and in some respects cowardly. How to reconcile the two roles? Leighton wished he could talk to someone about it. Grey would simply widen his eyes in astonishment if he raised the issue.

The Foreign Secretary was looking at him sternly. "This is the biggest job I've had for you so far, Leighton," he said. "If the Kaiser gets his Berlin to Baghdad railway, he could become even more aggressive in Europe. It could lead us all to war."

Leighton knew that many in Asquith's cabined feared war with Germany. Such a war, with the modern firepower that now filled Europe's arsenals, would be a disaster for the continent.

"Well, yes, I'll do what I can. I will join a caravan to Baghdad and scout out what I can," Leighton said. A simple plan. Perhaps.

Curtis met him in the embassy lobby and led him up a wide marble staircase to the reception room. Three men were conferring in low voices as they entered the room. The tallest of the group turned to Leighton and stepped forward to greet him. He was a barrel-chested man with a classic mutton chop mustache, now gone completely white. He was dressed, as was Leighton, in formal morning coat. Leighton didn't know much about Sir Gerard Lowther except that he'd received a hero's welcome when he took up his ambassador's post two years ago in Constantinople after the Young Turks seized power.

"Lowther," he said simply, with exactly the right amount of deference. It was calculated, Leighton thought, doled out in just the right quantity, as though from a limited and rapidly diminishing supply. There was no trace of reticence, let alone hostility, toward an emissary from the government with mysterious instructions.

"Good of you to receive me," Leighton said.

Lowther only nodded at this, and turned to his companions. "Maitland, our military attaché," he gestured to a man in regimental uniform, similar in bearing to Lowther, with somewhat more color in his hair. Turning to a short, nervous man with flaming red hair and mustache, Lowther said, "Fitzmaurice, our esteemed first dragoman."

"Ah, the famous Fitzmaurice," Leighton said with real enthusiasm. "Your reports on the Armenian massacres were brilliant." Fitzmaurice had made his name as a young diplomat by writing eyewitness dispatches of the atrocities visited on Armenians in the period 1894 to 1896. Dragoman — one of those terms that made the Orient so deliciously mysterious, Leighton thought — was an official interpreter, a guide not only to a foreign language but to a foreign culture. Despite his Celtic features, Fitzmaurice, who had been raised by a Turkish nanny when his father was stationed at this very embassy, spoke fluent Turkish and Arabic.

Fitzmaurice smiled uncomfortably and said something unintelligible. His eyes did not meet Leighton's.

"How was your trip out?" the ambassador said.

"Splendid," Leighton said. "I took the steamer from Bari and we had glorious weather."

Lowther did smile at this. "Ah, yes, an astute choice. For all the dithering about the Orient Express, it is a tiresome trip by train. Much more refreshing by sea, indeed."

Further polite inquiries established that Leighton had settled into his suite at the Pera Palace, was suffering no ill effects from the trip or change in climate, and was pleased to be back in this magnificent city.

"So, the Baghdad Railway," Lowther said finally.

Leighton nodded.

"Whitehall is worried about the Germans, we know," Lowther continued. The railway had been on his agenda since he arrived two years earlier, though not near the top.

"Deutsche Bank is the big financial backer, and German manufacturers are eager to supply the project," Leighton said. "The Germans are selling the Porte on the advantage of rail for trade."

"An easy sell, I should think," Fitzmaurice chimed in. "A caravan — with its camels, mules, horses and the carts they draw – can manage only two or three miles an hour and a maximum of twenty miles a day. A railroad can transport goods ten times as fast for a fraction of the cost."

"But once a railway is built, it can transport anything – including troops and munitions," Leighton continued. "It creates a supply line across the desert."

"India," Lowther said simply.

The vast territory of the Raj, an entire subcontinent, had been under British control for a century. In 1877, Queen Victoria was granted the title Empress of India by Parliament. Britain's whole objective in the Great Game had been to preserve the mountain ranges to the west of India as a buffer against any attack from that direction.

While the 1907 treaty allayed worries about Russia, Whitehall was growing concerned about Germany. The Reich had come late to the colonial land-grab in Africa and other parts of the globe. The king of the Belgians had more overseas territory than the Kaiser.

"We've represented the concerns of His Majesty's

government to the Porte on several occasions," Lowther said.

"Grey thought that I could perhaps, unofficially, scout out the terrain and see how honest the Porte has been about the state of the project," Leighton said. "My thought was to join a caravan."

"Yes, our Orientalist," Lowther said, betraying no hint of irony. Leighton was an accomplished scholar in Oriental studies – the languages and culture of the Near and Middle East. He had presented monographs on Syria and Egypt to the Royal Geographic Society. He was currently at work on Koranic commentaries from Baghdad and had been there once before. If Lowther was disturbed at the idea of a meddler, he seemed determined not to show it. Fitzmaurice, however, was markedly quiet.

"Fitzmaurice, perhaps you can help our distinguished visitor find a reliable merchant to accompany on a caravan," Lowther said, turning to the dragoman. "Also you said you have some useful information about the railway."

Fitzmaurice smiled. "Yes, there's been some interesting meetings between our friends at the German Embassy and some of the Young Turks here," he said. The so-called Young Turks had wrested control over the Ottoman Empire in 1908 while keeping the sultan as a figurehead. The group exercised control over the government through the shadowy Committee on Union and Progress.

"Unfortunately, I have some meetings now at the Porte," Fitzmaurice said. "Perhaps we could meet here for tea this afternoon and I'll fill you in on what I know."

Fitzmaurice took his leave with a nod to the other two men.

"Young Turks," Lowther's neck flushed red. "Pretending to control everything without showing their faces. They want power without responsibility. Jews and Freemasons looting the empire, all it is."

Though Fitzmaurice had left the room, his ideas could not have been better expressed than by the ambassador. The peculiar take of the Irish dragoman, a Roman Catholic, on the Young Turks and their motivation was well known in the Foreign Office. It was also well known that Lowther had fallen completely under Fitzmaurice's sway.

"You think it's money that motivates them?" Leighton asked.

Lowther now looked amazed. "But of course," the former businessman said, "doesn't money motivate everyone?"

Leighton quickly decided not to argue the point and Lowther caught a warning in Maitland's glance.

"We have another distinguished guest from London in two days," Lowther said, changing the subject. "The Home Secretary, Winston Churchill. He's actually on a holiday, yachting in the Med."

Leighton knew Churchill, though not well. They were exact contemporaries, both born in 1874. But Leighton had gone to Eton and Cambridge, and Churchill to Harrow and Sandhurst, so they had met for the first time in South Africa, Leighton with his regiment and Churchill a war correspondent. Their paths had crossed more often as both became active in Parliament, Churchill in Commons and Leighton in Lords. Leighton knew the politician to be strong-willed and ambitious; he also had great wit and was amusing to be around.

"He will be meeting with the sultan and will bring up the railway," Lowther said. "Obviously it won't do for you to attend, but I'm sure Churchill can fill you in afterwards."

Lowther spoke about the nice weather, a signal that their audience was now over. As Leighton took his leave, Maitland indicated he would walk out with him.

"Curtis tells me Sturm was hovering around your car

when you arrived yesterday," Maitland said when they were in the hallway.

"Was he the blue-eyed chap all done up as a fakir?" Leighton said.

"Yes, he masquerades constantly, damn fool."

"German then?"

"Yes, with all the usual German subtlety," Maitland said, not smiling.

"Seemed harmless enough."

"Not to worry," Maitland said. "I'll make certain he doesn't bother you any further."

Leighton was pondering exactly what that could mean as Curtis arrived to escort him out.

~

"He seems safe enough," Lowther said. He was fussing with a huge cigar that had arrived for him on the same steamboat as Leighton.

Maitland only grunted. He had long since expressed his aversion to Grey's plan. "Meddler," he said finally. "Amateur."

"Come, come, Maitland," Lowther said, as a flaming match enabled him to release the first gray clouds of smoke. "He's a good soldier. Served with distinction at Ladysmith."

They'd had this argument before. Maitland had gone into a rage when Lowther first told him of Leighton's mission. The ambassador had been surprised at the force of Maitland's opposition. It seemed too much for simple bureaucratic resentment over one's turf being invaded.

"Even there he registered a complaint with the High Command," Maitland said. "Thought our soldiers were too rough with some of the kaffirs."

Lowther grunted and puffed. "Well, true, you can't have

too much conscience in war." He smiled. "But there's no kaffirs here."

"Well there's no question he's soft on the Muslims. Speaks the bloody language, goes to the mosque – he's practically a heathen himself."

Lowther seemed to be in silent communion with his cigar.

"And there's the history of the woman," Maitland said, whispering, though the two men were alone in Lowther's vast office. Lowther rested his cigar in a huge obsidian ashtray and listened.

"Armenian." The soldier warmed to his subject now that he had the ambassador's attention. "Absolutely torrid, four or five afternoons a week in a seedy hotel room in Stamboul. Beautiful woman, if your taste is for that dark, Oriental type."

Lowther reached for his cigar again.

"She's married to Talaat Bey," Maitland said.

"He was fucking Talaat Bey's wife?" Lowther was truly shocked. This was more than a breach of protocol, it bordered on treason.

"No, he left Constantinople and she married Talaat later," Maitland said.

Lowther retrieved his cigar, puffed it back to life. "Why would an Armenian marry a Turk?"

"It happens all the time," Maitland said drily. "Her father subsequently got a cushy appointment at the university."

Lowther's frown and creased brow seemed to be a comment on women and their motives.

Maitland was silent for a time. "His meddling could be dangerous. Dangerous for us, perhaps fatal for him."

"Well it wouldn't do to have a dead English peer in our patch, now would it," Lowther said. "Security is your department, Maitland. Hold you to it."

Maitland sensed his dismissal, but he sat still, his brows knitted. Finally, he rose without a further word, nodded, and left the room. Lowther was re-lighting his cigar.

Maitland maintained his serious demeanor as he walked down the hall to his own office. He did not want Leighton to die, he just wanted him gone. He would take care of the visitor while he was in Constantinople, but once he was on a caravan to Baghdad, he was on his own. Then, Maitland smiled to himself, Leighton would be gone.

Chapter Two

Leighton walked down the hill and across the Galata Bridge. It was a glorious day, sunlight gleaming off the white domes and minarets under a vault of blue sky. He had decided to use his free afternoon to visit the Turkish bath in Stamboul. He had changed to a touring suit after lunch and now, with the aid of his walking stick, was ready for a brisk promenade to the heart of town.

The bridge teemed with the full range of Ottoman subjects. There were the Turks in the their dark suits and fezzes, a Greek from the Aegean sporting silver tassels and glittering buttons on his coat, a swarthy specimen from central Asia wearing a leather cap and flowing tunic, a young Balkan man in an embroidered vest and fur-edged hat.

There were turbans of all shapes – bands of simple white muslin wrapped around a cap, domed turbans of silk pinned with decorative jewelry, and one cone rising nearly two feet above the head of its wearer.

On the other side of the bridge, a string of charcoal braziers grilled mackerel and bluefish. A loaf of warm bread stuffed with sliced onion and grilled fish cost a pittance and made one of the best meals to be had in the city, Leighton thought. Vendors pulled wagons loaded with cucumbers that they pared in the twinkling of an eye for buyers.

At 36, Leighton still possessed a boyish regard in a face free of signs of age or responsibility. He enjoyed his whiskey and a good claret, but avoided tobacco. His wealth, modest by the standards of the industrial age, was sufficient for him to live more than comfortably on his income.

When in London, he attended the sessions in the House of Lords. He had known the prime minister, Asquith, since childhood, so his connections with the current government were quite close. He had come very near to courting Violet Asquith, but found the field rather too full for his taste. He supposed the time for him to marry was coming soon. He would dutifully take the steps necessary to propagate an heir and continue the line. In due course.

~

The quarry. Sturm watched the Englishman stroll across the bridge. The way he carried himself, the way he regarded everything he saw with detached amusement – it all said this is mine, I own this, I rule this. The arrogance of the man offended, no, enraged the German.

Today, Sturm wore the brown caftan of a wandering dervish. He shrouded his head in a white turban around a black cap. He knew his blue eyes told everyone this was a disguise, but the beauty of Constantinople was that it didn't matter. Dervish, spy, Turk, Arab. Live and let live. The sultan's secret service knew who he was and left him alone. Other intriguers interfered with him at their own risk. The Ottoman subjects had long since learned to stay out of anything that didn't concern them. So he was free to stalk through the city at will, wearing whatever camouflage he chose. At a distance, the caftan obscured him perfectly, allowing him to track the Englishman's movements.

"Stop him," Hoffenberg had said. The pompous little Swabian was his chief.

~

Leighton came out into the main bath, a large, cavernous room dimly lit by sunlight coming through small windows along the top of a huge dome. Tiles covered the wall to a height of ten feet, surmounted by bare granite. The temperature was mild and the room was largely empty. A masseur worked on a client opposite him and two other men lounged in stone chairs, white towels wrapped around their waists.

Leighton moved through the smaller rooms surrounding the main bath. The temperature rose a few degrees each time he passed from one into the other, following the circular trail. Leighton headed straight for the hottest room, for him the whole point of the bath. White vapor filled the room and Leighton's body grew slick with sweat and steam. He sat on one end of a bench occupied by a dark figure he could hardly make out. It was quiet. A fountain burbled in the adjoining courtyard, soothing like a nearby brook.

After some time, when the steam had relaxed him, Leighton gestured to a boy that he wanted a massage. Within minutes, an olive-skinned man, bald on top with a thick mustache, clad only in a white loincloth, appeared in front of him and motioned him to a bench. The man donned a rough mitten and began to rub Leighton's back and limbs. The mitten formed white rolls of dead skin as the masseur worked on the Englishman. After this exfoliation, the Turk poured a bucket of warm water over Leighton and began kneading his back and shoulders with great force. Leighton gave himself over to the massage and entered the state of well-being that this treatment always induced in him.

As Leighton made his way slowly back to the dressing room, he felt someone's stare from the central courtyard. He looked over and thought he saw a flash of blue eyes as a shadowy figure moved away from the column there. Though it all did seem harmless, Leighton was glad at the thought of Maitland finding a way to distract Sturm, if that's who it was, from spying on him.

Leighton left the bath thoroughly refreshed. The narrow streets of Stamboul were dim already in the late afternoon as he made his way downhill toward the bridge. The smell of seared lamb and grilled onion wafted through the late afternoon air.

He turned into a narrow alley and had gone several steps before he became alert to changes around him. The buildings reaching up on either side of the passage scarcely left room for two people to pass. There were no doorways or windows on the ground level. No other pedestrians were in the alley and the buildings muffled the hum of the crowd. The farther end of the alley was shrouded in darkness. A cul-de-sac?

Though he was confident of his orientation, Leighton had decided to retrace his steps to the main road, when he heard some shuffling behind him and turned just in time to see a robed figure lunging at him with a long, curved dagger. Without thinking, Leighton thrust up his cane to parry the blow. He struck out at his assailant and felt the solid maple stick connect with a skull. Leighton turned and ran down the alley, grateful that the hard-packed earth was dry. He looked back over his shoulder and saw there were two, maybe even three men chasing him down the dim passage. He had no weapon. His walking stick would be no match for several foes armed with daggers.

He plunged into the shadows at the end of the alley. A canvas roof strung along posts in the wall created the gloom. To his dismay, Leighton saw more robed figures ahead, blocking his way to the street. He raised the cane, gripping it with both hands, as he prepared to batter his way through the blockade.

The new adversaries surged forward. Leighton felt himself pressed against the wall as strong hands grasped his wrists and held them over his head. He was smothered in the woolen robes of his attackers and he waited for the sharp, hot thrust of a dagger into his abdomen or chest. He felt nothing, though, and stumbled as the men plunged past him into the alley and left him behind. Amazed, Leighton saw this second group throw themselves on the assailants from the other end of the alley. He didn't wait for the outcome, but dodged into the street and ran until he was in the midst of the usual throng of people in the city's crowded streets.

Had he just stumbled into the middle of a clash between two violent sects? Constantinople was rife with small factions of religious fanatics--Muslim, Christian, Jew. Bodies were fished out of the Bosphorus daily, victims cudgeled or stabbed to death in the internecine warfare.

As he brushed himself off, looking again at the miracle of his unharmed body, Leighton thought it unlikely that this was a chance encounter. He had no idea if one of his assailants had blue eyes, and even less of a notion who his rescuers might be. It was preposterous that the Germans would try to assassinate an English aristocrat in daylight in the city. But who else would have attacked him? And who were his unexpected allies?

Chapter Three

It was shortly after five when Leighton arrived for his meeting with Fitzmaurice. The dragoman had ordered tea in one of the ground floor parlors and he sat reading a dossier when Leighton entered.

"Sorry to be late," Leighton said. "Had a bit of an adventure on my way back from town." He related the encounter in the alley. Fitzmaurice frowned.

"Have you told Maitland?"

"I've only just arrived."

Fitzmaurice reached behind him to a velvet bell pull and tugged it once, firmly. They heard a distant clang, and almost immediately a steward in white livery appeared at the door.

"Can you see if Colonel Maitland is in the embassy," Fitzmaurice said to the steward. The man, whose mouth was all but invisible behind a thick black mustache, nodded and left.

"A spot of tea should calm your nerves," Fitzmaurice said, getting up and serving Leighton a cup of tea from the silver service. It was dark, more like a breakfast tea than light evening fare. It did hit the spot and Leighton was glad for the smoky, rough edge to the drink.

They sat silently, waiting to see if Maitland was coming. The parlor, Leighton noticed, with its green velvet armchairs and chintz curtains, could have been in a parsonage in England. In a few moments, the steward reappeared.

"Colonel Maitland has departed the embassy," he said in a slightly guttural accent.

"No matter," Leighton said. "I'll see him in the morning."

Fitzmaurice was thoughtful. "Is it possible you were the object of the attack? I mean you personally, not just a European who wandered into the wrong alley," Fitzmaurice asked.

Leighton thought of his own suspicions, but shrugged. "Who would want to attack me?" Then he added, "And if that was the case, what was the other group? Who would want to save me – in the absence of our devoted Colonel Maitland?"

Both men were silent as they deliberated these questions.

"Would you prefer some whiskey?" Fitzmaurice said abruptly.

Leighton shook his head. "The tea is just the thing, thank you."

"We have," Fitzmaurice said, putting down his tea, "good connections to the customs service, and this helps us enormously keeping track of Europeans here.

"We know that two railroad engineers arrived from Frankfurt am Main last week. The Holzmann building firm, which worked on some of the earlier railways here, is located in Frankfurt. Last week, one of the top executives from the Krupp steel company arrived in Constantinople. He has already had several meetings at the Ministry of Interior."

Aside from anything else, the Baghdad Railway was a great commercial opportunity. The construction, the rails, the rolling stock all represented valuable overseas contracts. Germany and Britain, along with the United States, were the leading railroad builders. As to capital, London was the preeminent global market, but the booming German economy had masses of private capital to tap.

"And a Deutsche Bank representative has been more

or less permanently attached to the German Embassy," Fitzmaurice said, as if reading Leighton's mind.

"The Interior Minister is Mehmet Talaat, one of the key C.U.P. members in the government," Fitzmaurice continued. The Committee on Union and Progress, a group whose full membership was known only to the initiated, was the executive body of the Young Turkey party, which controlled the empire. "Churchill will meet with Talaat when he's here, and perhaps we'll learn more. I'll accompany the Home Secretary."

Leighton knew that Fitzmaurice had a wide brief at the embassy. The little man's blue eyes were alight with enthusiasm for his role.

"It certainly seems something is afoot," Leighton said.

"Yes, that's our feeling. We need to know whether work has actually started," Fitzmaurice said. "You know the route, I take it?"

Seeing Leighton's hesitation, Fitzmaurice rose quickly and motioned for Leighton to follow him. He led the way up the marble staircase and entered the ambassador's office without knocking. Lowther was absent and Fitzmaurice went over to a large table opposite Lowther's desk and extracted a roll from a map case along the wall. He spread it out on the table.

"You see the Germans originally wanted to go along here, east of Ankara," Fitzmaurice pointed to the map. "The so-called northern route. It's shorter, and cheaper to build."

Leighton looked at the map and followed Fitzmaurice's tracing of the route through the mountains via Kayseri, Sivas and Dyarbakir.

"But the Russians didn't want the line that close to their new border," Fitzmaurice pointed to Kars, "so the Porte backed off and settled on the southern route, even though it is longer and costlier."

Fitzmaurice pointed to Konya, due south of Ankara.

"The line has been completed to here, and is projected to continue eastward through the Cilician Gates," Fitzmaurice pointed to the famous pass in the Taurus mountains, which Alexander the Great had taken on his march to conquer Persia, "to Adana, and then through the Anamus mountains to Fevzipasa."

Fitzmaurice paused. "The Ottomans insisted the route had to remain inland, out of range of our ships' guns, and that means building a very long and expensive tunnel between Ayran and Fevzipasa." Leighton saw the small space on the map and translated it into tons of dirt and stone that had to be moved.

"The line descends to Aleppo, then continues mainly eastward to Nusaybin," Fitzmaurice traced the route along the map through the steppes north of the Syrian desert, "and from there bears southwards along the Tigris River to Baghdad." Fitzmaurice pointed to the river's meandering route to Baghdad. "The eventual plan is to continue the line to Basra," he pointed to the port atop the Shatt-al-Arab waterway, "and there was even talk of going to Koweit, directly on the Gulf."

Leighton studied the map. His travels had not taken him that far inland in Syria and Mesopotamia. Seeing the route on the map aroused his sense of adventure and for the first time he found himself enjoying the prospect of this journey. The stretch across the steppe would be similar to his trips through the desert in Arabia.

Leighton had grown to love the desert. It had not been love at first sight, however. He reveled in the lush green of England, its damp, its chill. His home, which he cherished, represented the polar opposite of the desert, with its barrenness, its heat. And yet that dry, parched landscape, swept by wind and baked by an unrelenting sun, held its own beauty. Not a charming beauty that invited, but a brazen, austere beauty that dared.

"How can you stand to spend so much time in that godforsaken desert?" a dinner companion had asked him once at a country weekend in England. It had been one of those glorious fall days when riding was sheer joy and they were all full of good spirits from the earthy smells of autumn.

"The desert makes you forget time," Leighton heard himself answering. "You don't feel like you are spending time, you are simply there."

His companion, the young wife of a Foreign Office mandarin who was away on a mission, was intrigued.

"Isn't it dreadfully uncomfortable, so hot?"

"It makes you forget the discomfort, too."

"How can it do that, make you forget everything?"

"I'm not sure. Perhaps because it is so vast and empty. It makes you feel smaller, less significant. It is totally indifferent to your concerns, your comfort."

The woman laughed. He found out later her name was Georgina. "I don't think these woods care much for my comfort either," she said, "but I feel more comfortable here, I'm sure, than I would in some desert."

Leighton looked at her for a while. "It's true," he said at last. "I dare say someone raised in the desert would find life here too cold and damp." His philosophy withered before her guileless sincerity. "I think it's just something you get used to."

That night, he and Georgina got more used to each other in the comfort of clean linen with a coal fire warming the room. They never met again, and yet Leighton invariably saw her green eyes when he returned to the desert. He had gotten used to it and the person he became in the absence of his home comforts.

~

Fitzmaurice had some cost estimates for the railway construction. Deutsche Bank played a key role in providing the capital – the Ottoman Empire was essentially bankrupt. The French had taken over management of the imperial debt in the 1870s. The Porte truly was at the mercy of the European Powers. The Germans had sought international capital for the Baghdad Railway, but the British banks had boycotted it and the Americans had no interest.

Leighton had little banking experience, but some understanding of public finance from his work in Parliament. Also, he did understand power, and readily saw that it would not do to underestimate Germany's financial strength in this gambit.

"Do you want one of the guard to escort you to the hotel?" Fitzmaurice said as they parted.

Leighton brandished his walking stick. "I have my trusty bat here," he said with a smile.

He arrived at the hotel without any incident and dined alone in a nearly empty restaurant. He would talk to Maitland in the morning about his brush with potential assassins. It was a potent brew — the Kaiser, the Young Turks, Britannia — but a poisonous one? More Dewar's, more Arabian Nights, and sleep smothered his worries.

~

"Good Lord!" Leighton exclaimed.

Broome popped out of his room. "Milord?"

"Nothing, Broome, sorry, just something in the paper."

Leighton sat in his dressing gown over breakfast, reading the Levant Herald.

"A German attaché has been murdered," he explained to Broome.

Friedrich Sturm, described as a commercial attaché to

the German Embassy, had been fished out of the Bosphorus yesterday evening, the paper reported. He had been stabbed and mutilated, said the brief, front-page story, obviously a late insertion. The paper did not detail the nature of the mutilation.

Broome served some tea to Leighton and retired without any comment. The valet had learned when to speak and when to hold his tongue, a talent much appreciated by his employer.

Leighton went to the phone in his room.

"Hello, can I call the embassy from here?" he asked the operator.

"Sorry, sir, our telephones are only internal," the male voice replied.

"Right," Leighton said, ringing off. "Broome," he summoned the valet, "I need to go to the embassy immediately." Broome, who had already laid out Leighton's suit, helped him dress quickly, and he rushed off.

Maitland was crossing the lobby when Leighton arrived.

"You've heard about Sturm?" Leighton asked.

Maitland's face remained devoid of expression. "Yes, I saw the papers."

Leighton stared at the military attaché for a moment. "Yesterday," he said at last. "You said you would take care of Sturm."

"Good Lord, man," Maitland said, his expression now between a laugh and a curse, "you don't think...." His face snapped back to neutrality. "I sent a note up to the German Embassy, that's all. We had an understanding about Sturm's activities and I reminded them of it." He looked impatient. "The Gendarmerie is here."

"May I?" Leighton said, moving to accompany the colonel.

Maitland muttered under his breath in annoyance, but

could hardly rebuff this well-connected visitor from London. Leighton walked with the Maitland to the parlor he had sat in the previous evening. To his surprise, the police official awaiting them was European, not in uniform but in a plain dark suit.

"Deedes," the man said.

Leighton knew the Gendarmerie has been established recently with European assistance to reinforce the rudimentary policing in the Ottoman capital. He was nonetheless surprised to find an Englishman leading a murder investigation.

"We are called in for any crime involving diplomatic personnel," said Deedes, whose accent betrayed Northumbrian origins. "Sir," he said, addressing Maitland, "you sent a note regarding Sturm to the German Embassy yesterday?"

Maitland said Sturm had apparently been spying on Leighton's arrival two days ago, in breach of the understanding the two embassies had reached. Maitland introduced Leighton, offering no explanation of his status. Deedes, a tall, gawky young man whose suit fit badly, examined Leighton for a moment, and then just nodded. "I see," he said.

Leighton kept silent about his glimpse of Sturm in the bath, unsure whether he'd actually seen the German spy or a phantom in the dim, vaporous steam bath. Nor did he see any relevance for the attack in the alley. He would say nothing of that at any rate before he had a chance to discuss it with Maitland.

So the conversation was brief. Deedes elicited some information from Maitland regarding earlier incidents of Sturm's spying activities.

"Any clues pointing to a perpetrator?" Leighton asked as Deedes put away his notebook.

Deedes deliberated and then spoke slowly. "The nature of the wounds...," he stopped. "It was a goddamned butchery," he said with feeling. "All the extremities were removed - hands, feet, ears, nose, and —" Deedes interrupted himself, inhaled and exhaled, and in a calmer tone continued, "— and his member."

None of them spoke. Deedes was in his 20s. The two older men had seen many things in battle in the far reaches of the British Empire. The physical violence did not shock them. That such was visited on a diplomatic attaché in peacetime was of much greater concern.

"Does it appear politically motivated?" Maitland asked. His expression indicating that he did not really expect Deedes to have the answer. Rather, he wanted to make sure the question was part of the investigation.

"Herr Sturm was very active in gathering intelligence for the German mission here," Deedes said. "He investigated many of the sects."

"Religious fanatics, you think?" Leighton asked.

"We're just beginning our investigation," Deedes said. "The Porte is extremely anxious because of the diplomatic implications." The Kaiser was very sensitive to real or imagined slights against the Reich. He would want to know why a German diplomat was the victim of such a murder in a friendly capital. France, which controlled Ottoman finance and had designs on Morocco, or Britain, which had prised control of Egypt from the Porte's frail grasp, seemed much better targets for fanatic reprisals.

Deedes promised to keep them informed of the investigation's progress and departed.

"Bizarre," Maitland said.

"You know, Maitland, I thought I saw Sturm in the bath yesterday afternoon," Leighton said. He told him about the glimpse of blue eyes in the steam bath.

"You didn't mention it to Deedes."

"I wanted to talk to you first," Leighton said. "Also, it was hardly a positive identification of Sturm."

"Yes, indeed."

"I have something else bizarre for you, Colonel." He described the attack in the alley.

"Did you see how they were dressed?"

"It was dim in the shadow. All I really saw were those dagger blades. They were covered head to foot in these robes, not black, not white, but I couldn't really say. The group at the other end wore dark robes but I saw even less of them."

"Do you think you just stepped in the middle of a sectarian conflict?" Maitland asked. First Sturm, now this. The colonel was openly skeptical of what he implied was Leighton's paranoia.

Leighton shrugged. He had not expected much help from Maitland.

"Are you armed? Do you need a pistol?"

"I have my service pistol with me." Leighton had no intention of carrying it on the streets of Constantinople but wanted it with him on the caravan.

Chapter Four

Leighton was reflective as he walked back to the hotel. Spies were everywhere. Embassies were full of them. Leighton knew this was the nature of diplomacy, especially in the tense atmosphere of the early 20th century. Intrigue was the very stuff of diplomacy, and intrigue required spies.

It had always been that way and always would be, he told himself. What was spying, anyway, except an attempt to find out what was going on that might affect your interests. A legitimate pursuit, no question. And yet it seemed underhanded, ungentlemanly to covertly gather intelligence.

Empires, especially, required spies, Leighton mused. The cynic would say to keep down subjugated peoples. Truth in that, for sure. But a more important reason was that empires extended beyond the boundaries of a single nation. That extension created added needs for information.

Spies enforced authority. The sultan, for instance, spied on his own people in Constantinople. He had his spies in London and Berlin, but his main concern was ferreting out any conspiracies in his own capital. The Young Turks had their spies, tracking the sultan as well as potential opponents.

Many a brave officer had suffered a painful death in the Great Game, played out between Britain and Russia in the vast steppes and mountain ranges of central Asia – yet they were more soldiers than spies. One unfortunate Cambridge Orientalist, Edward Palmer, had undertaken a dangerous mission to the Bedouin along the Suez Canal during the Egyptian unrest and was shot and thrown off a cliff for his gold – a victim of common theft rather than espionage. Sir Richard Burton had at times been a spy. Even on his own, infiltrating the Muslim holy places, he had been a spy for Western civilization. Few, however, would call Burton, knighthood notwithstanding, a gentleman.

Leighton had met the great Burton once, in the summer of 1888. Leighton was 14, home from Eton for the holidays. Burton was making a triumphant passage through the home country. He was restless, spending little time in any one place. Leighton's grandfather said he seemed to be running from death. He came to tea at the Leighton estate. Leighton's grandfather was a regular correspondent of the great man, researching odd passages for him as he labored on his translations in Trieste. He was the British consul there and flitted from desk to desk in his study, working on his projects.

Leighton knew of his grandfather's admiration for Burton. The older man had spoken of Burton's exploits constantly – the trip to Mecca, disguised as a fakir, when discovery meant death for an unbeliever; the search for the source of the Nile; the translation of the Arabian Nights. The older Leighton had a portrait of the explorer in his prime, fierce with his dark eyes and sweeping mustache, his gaze like a bird of prey.

It was a shrunken version of the explorer who stepped out of the carriage on that summer day. He was stooped and walked stiffly. The handlebar mustache had turned white and he wore a goatee. His eyes were no longer fierce, sunken in his face. His lips were bluish white, his cheeks flushed red. He panted with the effort of walking.

The young Leighton stood respectfully behind his grandfather and the invited guests. Richard had shot up in the past year, his voice had changed. He watched as Burton slowly, formally shook hands, rarely lifting his head to look his interlocutor in the eye.

This shuffling old man, Leighton thought, had performed the dance of swords with Sufi dervishes. He had partaken in secret erotic exercises in dark corners of India. He had learned 120 languages and dialects, written and spoken, and explored cultures on every continent.

Burton had already walked past the young man, ignoring him. Then, without warning, he turned back and looked directly at Leighton. A glimmer of the earlier flame lit his eyes.

"You must be young Richard," he said. His voice was a rasp. "Your grandfather has great hopes for you." The old man extended his hand. It seemed to Leighton almost transparent. It was dry, surprisingly soft to the touch.

"Honored to meet you, Sir Richard," Leighton managed to say his rehearsed greeting.

Burton grunted. "Remember, boy, we must respect other cultures. Without respect, empire is lost."

Leighton flushed. "Yes, sir," he stammered.

"Don't ever forget it," the old man said. He turned away from the boy as abruptly as he had first turned toward him, and shuffled on as if the encounter had never taken place.

That was more than twenty years ago. For Leighton, it was like yesterday – those eyes still burned into him, that soft, dry hand still tingled in his, that admonition still made him flush in excitement and confusion.

Leighton had asked his grandfather what Burton meant. The elder Lord Leighton had only smiled at him and patted his arm. "You heard him," he said. "It was clear enough."

Burton died only two years later, in Trieste. The papers were full of tributes to the great man, a grand service was held in London. Leighton resolved to pursue Oriental studies at Cambridge. He wanted to advance the British Empire with his respect for the culture Burton had embraced so fervently.

Leighton modeled himself on Burton, but with somewhat less ambition. Leighton's scholarship was accomplished, but not brilliant. He traveled into exotic corners, but only where white men had tread before him. He experimented sexually, but never with abandon. He felt the same lust for life, but found it tempered by the aristocratic reserve of his upbringing.

~

Leighton met again with Fitzmaurice the next morning. The Irishman, dressed in a three-piece tweed suit that seemed warm for the climate, escorted his visitor to the embassy garden, where cypresses shaded them from the heat.

"I've sent inquiries to several of the merchants who trade in British goods," Fitzmaurice said immediately. "I expect to have a caravan for you in just a few days."

"Splendid," Leighton said. "Thanks for your help."

The men walked some time without speaking. Leighton felt that small talk about the weather or the garden would be wasted breath with the dragoman.

"It is a dangerous time for us," Fitzmaurice said, breaking the silence. Leighton waited for him to continue. Fitzmaurice stroked his mustache – one of his many nervous mannerisms – but said nothing more.

"London is clearly worried about the railway," Leighton said at length.

Fitzmaurice looked sideways at him as they walked. "The railway is not the greatest of our worries, however. A power vacuum in the Orient could unleash a world war – and that's where the Young Turks are taking us."

Leighton truly admired Fitzmaurice's work on reporting the Armenian massacres at a time when no one wanted to believe them. Yet he shared the Foreign Office view that the embassy dragoman had grown too close to the old sultan and could not assess the situation in Constantinople with any objectivity. In fact, London increasingly saw the dragoman's role as pernicious.

"The so-called Young Turks, while young and clumsy enough, are not even Turks," Fitzmaurice said. "Jews, Freemasons, atheists, adventurers – the lot of them."

In truth, many of the Young Turks had joined Masonic lodges and a number of them were Donmeh – Jews who had converted to Christianity. However, Fitzmaurice's fixation on these incidental attributes seemed excessive.

"Turks or not, they are decidedly in control here," Leighton said quietly. Sultan Abdul Hamid had backed a counter-coup the previous year, which the Young Turks had successfully repulsed. They forced the sultan to abdicate and retreat into exile. His brother, Mehmet Resat, an obese dotard, was made sultan purely as a figurehead for the Young Turk regime.

Fitzmaurice gazed coldly at Leighton. "So it would seem, but they do not have the people behind them," Fitzmaurice said. "There is much fanaticism here, and the Young Turks spurn religion. They are vulnerable and it would be folly for us to cast our lot with them."

"They don't seem to receptive to our lot, in any case," Leighton said with a smile.

Fitzmaurice's cheeks, already quite ruddy, turned almost purple. He started to say something and then bit off his response. Instead, he stroked his mustache furiously.

"This dynasty has survived for centuries," he said. "The sultan is the high priest of Islam. He will win in the end."

Leighton wasn't so sure. The history of Islam, as Fitzmaurice must well know, was filled with rejected caliphs. History also showed that all empires declined and fell. The Ottomans, at five centuries, had lasted longer than most. How long would Britannia survive as an empire, he wondered.

"Still, the present reality is that the Young Turks are in control," Leighton insisted. "London is worried about an alliance between them and the Germans."

"We are not at war with Germany," Fitzmaurice said. "They are our natural allies."

Leighton said nothing. Many, including the Kaiser, subscribed to Fitzmaurice's conviction. Leighton, however, shared Grey's unease over a land link to the Persian Gulf.

Fitzmaurice kept his blue eyes focused ahead, not looking at his interlocutor.

"Tell me about your Koran commentary," he said suddenly with a big smile. Leighton saw some of the charm so often attributed to the dragoman. He launched into the details of his project. Fitzmaurice surprised him with his knowledge not only of the Koran but of the vast literature of exegesis. Leighton was translating some of Al-Tabari's voluminous commentary from the 10th century. Fitzmaurice pointed out that Zamakshari's abridged version from the 12th century actually helped clarify some of the original work and might be an aid in translation. Leighton was sincere in his gratitude.

The sun had risen toward its zenith, making it warm even in the shade of the garden. Fitzmaurice excused himself to attend a lunch in Galata – the dragoman kept a busy social schedule.

"Good luck in your researches, Leighton," he said in parting. "I look forward to reading your monograph."

Leighton felt his stomach muscles relax as the diminutive Irishman went into the embassy. As amicable as the conversation had appeared, he had been tense. He wondered why.

~

Churchill had dominated the dinner conversation. He was as Leighton remembered him – a young man in a rush to be middle-aged. He bristled with energy, talking and moving constantly. His brimming self-confidence often spilled over, drowning the timid. He had opinions on every subject and proclaimed them as the final word. One London socialite had wittily observed that you became acquainted with all of Churchill's faults on your first meeting with him and got to know his virtues over time.

Now, over cigars and port, Churchill continued to be the center of attention. He was not an imposing figure – he was half a head shorter than Leighton, slender, a bit lost in his smoking. He made himself larger with his grand gestures, brandishing his cigar in his right hand and port in his left. He was expounding on the need to curb the fiscal power of the House of Lords.

"You can argue the history of it till you're blue in the face," Churchill was saying. "We must look to the future and we have no future unless we remove this obstacle to progress."

The assembled embassy staff knew better than to offer any serious challenge to Churchill's position.

In due course, Lowther steered the Home Secretary to the corner where Leighton was standing.

"Leighton, delighted to see you," Churchill said, advancing with hand thrust out. "Can't keep you away from your Orient, I see."

"Good to see you, Churchill. I trust your vacation has been enjoyable."

"A yacht is a wonderful place to get some work done," Churchill said, with no trace of irony. "No interruptions, no one pestering you." Churchill was notorious for his fixation on work. Besides his government duties, he produced a prodigious amount of writing on various subjects.

"To business," he said, seating himself and striking a match to relight his cigar. "The sultan is useless. Talaat is something else again. He truly has a mean look in his eye."

One colorful dispatch from a first secretary in Constantinople had described Talaat as having a yellow gleam in his eye that one rarely saw in a human but more often in some animals at dusk.

"Would not give me a straight answer about progress on the Baghdad Railway," Churchill continued. "Instead, wanted to sell me on the idea. I told him His Majesty's government is opposed to the project. We want to protect our Basra concession." A British riverboat company had the license to serve Baghdad from Basra. It was the fig leaf Whitehall used to hide the true reason for their opposition to the railway.

"He wasn't buying it, of course. He did make the usual protestations of friendship, implying that London is a vastly more important relationship to them than Berlin. Sly fellow."

Churchill paused to puff his cigar back to life. He leaned forward and fixed Leighton in his gaze. His gray eyes turned to steel. "Richard," he said, "it's vital that we stop this railway. We must prevent German expansionism from reaching the point where it will provoke a war."

Churchill was known for being less pessimistic than his cabinet colleagues regarding the possibility of war with Germany. He saw a genuine risk of war, but was convinced it could be avoided. His attitude irked the military experts, who had replaced France with Germany as the principal enemy in their minds.

Leighton shuddered at the thought of a European war. With imperial ambitions at a high pitch and with the damaging capacity of modern technology, such a conflict would be a cataclysm. It could reduce Europe to rubble, literally, and worse, culturally.

Leighton's face reflected his distress. Churchill offered him no comfort.

"There's one other thing, Richard, that I'm sure Grey did not mention to you," the Home Secretary said. He looked quickly around him and lowered his voice when he resumed. "There are those in the Navy who insist we need to replace the coal-powered engines in our fleet with oil-fired engines, to keep ahead of our rivals. We have found oil in Persia but we know that there is petroleum in Mesopotamia as well. The Germans already have the concessions along the route of the railway. We do not want them to have this resource in the event of war."

Leighton had followed the news of the Anglo-Persian finds and knew that oil was becoming a fuel for engines as well as for heating and illumination. It was, however, the first he had heard of petroleum as a consideration in the Baghdad Railway project.

"The Foreign Office is playing this close to the chest," Churchill said, as though reading his mind. "The embassy here is not aware – at least not officially – of our interest. We deal directly with an Armenian who lives in London and keeps us apprised of policy at the Porte. We will act at the appropriate moment."

Leighton remained silent, absorbing what Churchill had said. The Home Secretary puffed on his cigar a moment, keeping his eyes on Leighton.

"We must meet more often, Leighton," Churchill said at last, breaking the spell. "Come see me at my club when you've returned to London." Not waiting for a reply to this command appearance, Churchill nodded, stood and went to join the group around Lowther.

Leighton waited a moment, pensive. If Churchill was right about the risk of war, his mission took on greater importance. He believed in the task because it served the

Crown – Churchill had certainly driven that point home. In his heart he felt as well that a railroad carrying Turkish soldiers and German products to Baghdad would bring harm to a culture he had grown to love through his studies and his travels. It was a civilization of the spirit, free as the wind that blew across the desert, and there was no place in it for iron rails fixed into the earth.

Chapter Five

William Morrison told everyone to call him Bill. He introduced himself as William Morrison, then added, "But you should call me Bill." He was a big man, lanky, with long, rough-looking hands. He had a florid complexion, which, along with the twinkle in his eyes, made him look the picture of health. He was invariably polite, with a studied attention to good manners, as though he had cribbed his Eleazar Moody etiquette guide just the night before.

He came from Buffalo and was a big booster. "It's the coming city," he'd say. "We rival New York and Chicago in terms of commerce and have them beat in beauty."

Morrison had worked on the hydroelectric plant at Niagara Falls and was in the Orient to drum up some interest in this new technology.

"There are no falls here," Leighton observed.

"Easy enough to simulate if we can build a dam," Morrison said cheerfully. He was trying to talk to authorities in Constantinople and planned to go on to Baghdad. The thought of a dam on the Bosphorus, let alone on the slow and muddy Tigris or Euphrates rivers was a testament, Leighton reasoned, to what they called American optimism.

Morrison made good company, though, and could always be found in the bar at 5 p.m. He was full of epithets from Mark Twain, an American writer who had traveled abroad and wrote about it at length, apparently with some humor.

"He did a 'Slave-Girl Market Report' for Constantinople that reads just like the daily cattle report in the Buffalo Evening News," Morrison said. "Hilarious. 'The new crop of Circassians is looking extremely well.' Hell, that's funny." Morrison actually slapped his knee at the recollection.

One day over drinks, Leighton broached the subject of his caravan.

"It could be a good way for you to get to Baghdad," Leighton said.

"For all the reception I'm getting here, I may as well," Morrison said, and laughed. "Be better off trying to build a hydroelectric plant in a desert as trying to get anything out of this lot."

Morrison was not the first to discover that the Ottoman Empire was slow to take up new ideas, Leighton mused to himself.

Leighton thought Morrison would make the caravan look more legitimate. He also considered the American would be a good man to have in a tight situation. He had fought with Teddy Roosevelt's Rough Riders in Cuba during the Spanish-American War and this vied with Buffalo as his favorite subject.

Leighton found his war stories immensely entertaining. Morrison was modest as to his own exploits, but his accounts couldn't disguise that he had been in the forefront of the action.

"What a man will do to defend the interests of empire," Leighton remarked at one point in passing.

"Hold on," Morrison said. "You Brits are the ones with the empire. The U.S. of A. is a republic. We were just defending our own interests against Spanish aggression." He had put his drink down on the bar and turned to Leighton as he said this to show that it was an important clarification.

"A republic cannot have an empire?" Leighton chided. "What about Venice? It was a republic, it had an empire."

"Venice is a tiny city in a swamp, of course it needed to have possessions," Morrison said. The engineer was proud of his education. He had gone to a technical school in Boston, the Massachusetts Institute of Technology, and had absorbed a smattering of history and literature along with his scientific studies. "England ain't that big either. The United States, on the other hand, has a whole continent and doesn't need any colonies abroad."

In the face of such conviction, Leighton abandoned the discussion about America's imperial designs. Just as well, he thought, if the giant remained asleep. There were enough Powers chasing new territories and little good land left to be had.

~

The days passed quickly. Leighton actually got some work done on his translation. The manuscript was in the British Museum collection. He'd hit upon the idea of photographing some of the pages so that he could continue his work while traveling. Expensive and laborious, it was nonetheless better than copying, which was difficult and fraught with error. The manuscript contained numerous passages that were incomprehensible to Leighton and he needed to consult the Islamic scholars, the ulema, in Baghdad. There were also some contemporary writings available there that he wanted to work on as well. The commentaries, applying the principles of the Koran to daily life, gave a detailed picture of social customs in that golden age of the Abbasid caliphate.

Leighton persisted in his promenades, keeping to the thoroughfares of the city. Crowds presented a certain risk, too, of course. An assassin could easily slip a dagger between his ribs without it being noticed until he was well away. The assault in the alley remained a singular affair, though. Perhaps it had been a coincidence, bad timing on his part. Or perhaps Sturm had been behind the attack, hard as that was to accept. Who, then, had done in Sturm, and why? Could Maitland be so devious?

Leighton remained alert but otherwise kept these questions at bay as he strolled through town. One afternoon's walk took him along the site of the old sea wall, mostly gone now to make way for the railroad. This brought him, not totally by chance, past the Hotel Istanbul. It was the place more than any other in the city that he linked to Elena. He counted the floors, looking for the fifth-floor window to the room that had been his. Shutters covered the window, as they had when Leighton and Elena held their afternoon trysts.

They had met at a hookah party in the early summer. It was at the house of a high official in the Ministry of Culture, a lovely stone building with a terrace overlooking the Bosphorus. The fragrance of blooming jasmine bushes suffused the air. Literati and artists of various sorts attended. Leighton was there because Lady Hester Stanley, a sculptor and certainly the most Bohemian spirit of Leighton's acquaintance, had insisted that he accompany her. It was a small gathering of twenty or so free spirits who met regularly in this home, an oasis of culture in the desert of Ottoman repression. They sat ranged along divans and overstuffed leather footstools, a hookah before each group of four or five. Elena came with her father, a translator of Persian verse. Herself a poet, Elena was demure and hardly spoke. She did boldly take her turn on the water pipe, inhaling the cool smoke and letting it escape her mouth in a languid flow. Leighton, no expert at this, was happy if he could inhale and exhale without choking. He realized only as the evening progressed that the hookahs were filled with hashish, not tobacco. The gathering took on a warm glow even in the feeble light of the lamps and candles illuminating the room. The conversation took place largely in Turkish and ranged over Persian and Arabic writers scarcely known to Leighton. Occasionally, in deference to the English guests, their host asked questions in English. As he responded to a question about his own work on Koranic texts, Leighton saw Elena's eyes – those dark brown liquid eyes – regarding him. He felt then a stir of arousal that surprised him. Later, as her father read from his latest work, she glanced at Leighton again and their eyes met, a brief moment that seemed to him in his drug-induced euphoria to last hours.

Two days later, he called on the father, Armik Krikorian, and expressed an interest in his new translations. The older man, immediately grasping the real purpose of the visit, expounded at considerable length on Persian poetry before suggesting, as if it had just occurred to him, whether the English scholar would like to hear his daughter's verse. Leighton confessed that he was a true aficionado of poetry in all languages and Elena was summoned. So it began.

Leighton had puzzled at the time over the father's acquiescence in a transparent ploy to seduce his daughter.

"He is an atheist," Elena told him in the course of one of their afternoons in the hotel. "He has been so saddened by what is done in the name of God he has turned away from religion."

Leighton knew hardly anyone excited enough about religion to turn toward it or away from it, save for a Roman Catholic convert he had met at a dinner party. She had proselytized him unrelentingly through seven courses.

Elena, it turned out, was fond of smoking and always carried cigarettes with her in a carved silver case. She took out one and lit it with a hotel match. She inhaled deeply and blew out a plume of smoke. It was a heavy Turkish tobacco with a sweet smell. Elena was propped in a sitting position on the pillows, a damask silk sheet covered the lower part of her body. Her breasts and belly and shoulders remained exposed, full curves of unbridled carnality, Leighton had discovered. The black curls of her hair tumbled across her breasts, hiding one brown aureole. The other nipple, still partially erect from their lovemaking, poked through. The shutters, closed against the afternoon heat, threw bars of light and shadow across her. She smoked silently.

"For him, love is everything," she said finally. "Human love, not divine love."

"He doesn't seem the type," Leighton observed. He sat in the armchair, a silk gown pulled over his shoulders.

"Now his passion is totally in his poetry, he has escaped the flesh," Elena said.

A week later, Elena told Leighton how her mother had been lost in a pogrom in 1890. Elena, an infant, was at home with a Turkish nanny when her mother was seized in the marketplace in Garin. Her father was away in Constantinople, talking to a publisher. Two dozen Armenians in this village alone perished under the clubs and blows of neighbors, Turks and Kurds, they had lived together with all their lives. The battered corpses were shoveled into a mass grave and the government bureaucracy refused to acknowledge the incident had taken place.

"My father was inconsolable. My aunt, who also was away during the pogrom, tried to take care of his household needs, but within the year he moved with me to Constantinople. He felt we would be safer in the capital, amongst the Armenian community here."

Armenians made up close to one-tenth of the population in Constantinople, the largest group after the Turks and the Greeks. Leighton had never fathomed the animosity of the Turks toward the Armenians, which erupted at times in the provinces in cruel acts of hatred. It was undoubtedly religious, Muslim against Christian, but there was some fierce ethnic rancor as well.

"He has taught me to believe in love as I find it," Elena said. "I was baptized, but my Christian education was purely for form. My father considers middle-class morality to be a sham."

They didn't venture out much in the daylight. They drew too much attention, she with her striking beauty, he with his aristocratic European bearing. Yet, one sparkling summer day they had to get out of the hotel. The sky was so blue it almost hurt to look at it. The city glowed.

They went to the Galata Tower. The stumpy, grimy construction had been a landmark in the city since the 14th century. It was used as a fire observation post but it was well known that a few piastres would encourage the "observer" to go for coffee while visitors enjoyed the view.

It was this view that stopped them. The giddiness of being out together after making love gave way to a feeling more like awe. The sea, the sky, the city glittering in the reflected sun, simply was unmatched for its beauty. Far more than even so magnificent a structure as Hagia Sofia, this panorama was a temple to the glory of creation.

They stood, wordless, not touching. Yet Leighton was more aware of Elena's presence than at anytime except at the peak of love, when they merged and became truly one. His eyes focused on the Sea of Marmara before them, he saw her glowing beside him, sensed her quiet breathing and felt with a stab of anguish that he wanted this woman always with him, wherever in the world he went.

She turned and smiled at him, suppressing a giggle in the face of his intensity. They risked a kiss and her warmth chased his conceit away.

The affair had come naturally to Leighton. It was driven of course by his bodily urges, but normally he had sufficient strength of will to check those urges when he wanted. His will, however, melted in this instance. He desired this woman, more than he had ever desired a woman before.

It was from the beginning an affair that had an ending. There was no chance of marriage – both of them knew that. Their worlds were too far apart, their needs in society too different.

~

Leighton felt ambivalent about a family. He knew it was his duty to establish his own family, to generate children, carry on the family legacy. It was duty alone, though, that pushed him in this direction. His own situation growing up had estranged him from the notion of family, or at least that narrow sense of husband, wife and children. He could understand being a grandfather, but had little comprehension of being a father. He had no one really to talk about these feelings with.

Would he ever be able to settle down? Was there another Elena waiting for him somewhere in the gardens and bazaars of the Orient? On some trip back to England would one of the young society women appropriate to his station suddenly appear to be a good match? Or would he retire to his English estate with his whiskey and his memories, like others in similar situations who were never discussed but known to everyone.

He had never really gotten over Elena. During the voyage home after they parted, he had fallen into a deep despondency. He had kept to his cabin, shades drawn, lying silently on his bed for hours with no thoughts in his head. Emotions were largely strangers to him. He knew passion when he was with Elena and he knew longing when he was separated from her. Grief had visited him when his grandfather died. Enthusiasm animated his Oriental studies.

But most of the time it was duty or propriety that motivated his actions.

His bad mood continued upon his return to England. He retreated to the country and rattled around the huge home, a specter among the servants. He felt hollow mostly. Yet sometimes deep in his gut there was a wrenching, almost like the retch of nausea, that occasionally doubled him over and made him seek refuge in the privacy of his room. He shed no tears.

He turned down most invitations. Once he accepted a weekend in Kent and regretted it as soon as he arrived. The others were down from London, full of city bustle still, alive with intrigue and purpose. Among them, Leighton felt dead. They quickly learned to leave him to himself. He excused himself from Saturday dinner, pleading relapse of a vague desert malady, and departed early Sunday.

He occupied his time with some translations, but he achieved little. He was unable to apply himself to the task for any length of time, some days not at all. He rode, as in a trance, seeing nothing of the countryside.

Whiskey had tempted him for a time. Its narcotic dulled the pain, which in fact seemed to reside in his belly. He was surprised to discover that he was finishing a bottle in less than a week. He never lost his senses or his sense of control, nor was his reason dimmed. It eased the pain, what was the harm?

However, he noticed the narcotic effect wearing off sooner, and the next drink coming at a shorter interval. He began to feel he was not in control. He stopped drinking whiskey and abstained from wine.

In time – it seemed a long time, but in the end was less than a year – the pain eased on its own, not healing so much as simply subsiding. He felt it there still, only calm now, having mercy, for a time at least, like an ulcer, ready to flare up again if provoked.

He resumed his nightcap, took a glass of wine or two at dinner. The wine brightened the meal, the whiskey helped him sleep. His fifth lasted him now the right length of time, as it always had.

Only after some months did any sense of inner calm return to him. He went up to London for lectures at the Royal Geographic, visited his club and renewed some acquaintances. Once he even accompanied his cousin Gwendolyn to the theatre and surprised himself when he laughed at the comedy. His translations took on greater momentum and he found himself more often at the British Museum for research, able to engage in intense conversation with some of the experts there. He felt more at ease with his friends, accepted invitations to dinners in town.

The hollowness was still there, but now it was confined to a corner of his soul and life went on around it. He resumed his sexual adventuring but avoided any serious relations with women of his own class. If not for the niggling responsibility to produce an heir and carry on the title, he felt he could die a bachelor. The vast passion Elena had aroused in him appeared to belong to her and remained in her possession.

His English friends, who had never known Richard Leighton the secret lover, saw little change in him. Only his old teacher, Mahfoudh, a visiting lecturer at Cambridge that year, seemed to look upon him differently. The three or four times they met during the year, Mahfoudh said nothing, asked no questions, but a softness came into his glittering brown eyes when Leighton took longer than normal to respond. Leighton himself seemed unaware of these moments of distraction. His thoughts didn't go to Elena, they simply wandered off into his private wasteland. Mahfoudh understood. The old man had been young once himself and physically vibrant. He pitied and envied his young protégé for the pain and bittersweet pleasure his grief gave him.

Leighton eventually resumed his travels, though he steered clear of Constantinople. He visited Berlin, Cairo, Beyrouth and finally Venice, before he boarded the steamer to the Bosphorus. In Alexandria, on his way back to Europe, he had entered into a brief liaison with a woman, a young widow. It was an affair without passion on his part, but sweet and comforting nonetheless. Amani, herself hungry for male companionship, had been sensitive to his reserve, gentle and giving, and had succeeded in drawing him out of himself.

When he thought about it – and he tried not to think about it – Leighton decided that he had found the love of his life and lost her. It didn't seem possible to him that he would feel this kind of passion again.

Chapter Six

Leighton talked little during his morning shave. The lather and razor discouraged his opening his mouth or moving his jaw. Broome shaved him so adeptly that the whole process lasted scarcely a quarter of an hour. Broome would sometimes fill the void, talking about whatever issue happened to preoccupy him at the moment. Leighton had learned to pay attention. The Welshman was shrewd in a way that defied the best education. Broome, for his part, had found it easier to overcome the reticence natural to his station and by now did not hesitate to discourse with his master as a peer.

So it was not really a surprise that one morning, as he shaved Leighton, Broome ventured, "It seems they should make natural allies, the Turks and the Germans."

Leighton had been wondering aloud as they began at the seeming inconstancy of the Young Turks, siding now with the British, now with the Germans.

"How so?" Leighton asked, keeping his head straight forward as Broome scraped the razor along his neck.

"Pogroms," said Broome. "They both like pogroms." He started on the other side of Leighton's face. "The Turks bash the Armenians. The Germans bash the Jews."

Leighton reflected. There had been reports during their sojourn in England of a pogrom in Breslau in Silesia. Three men were killed and several Jewish shops were destroyed. The travails of the Armenians in Turkey were rarely reported in the press, but were a staple of conversation in the European community in Constantinople.

"Like the Boers," Broome continued stolidly as he wiped Leighton's face clean of the remaining traces of lather. "Boers bash the Hottentots. Possessed of a streak of intolerance, the lot of them."

Leighton bit his tongue. He had seen numerous examples of intolerance among his own countrymen.

"More than other nationalities, you think?"

Broome wrestled with the steaming towel, placing it carefully on Leighton's face and removing it, before speaking again.

"More vicious, I'd say. Seems to get right down to the bowels of the common folk." The tone of Broome's voice signaled this was his final word on the subject. He finished wiping Leighton's face dry, applied the talc, and began putting away the utensils into the kit.

An interesting distinction, Leighton thought. In India and in South Africa, Leighton had seen British troops subjugate native populations, sometimes brutally. It was a military strategy, however, not a visceral hatred. There was no doubt that Brits looked down upon the native peoples as racially inferior, but there was no irrational persecution of them.

Leighton nodded at Broome as he stood. Turks and Germans, natural allies? Perhaps Broome was on to something.

~

Broome's bedroom was virtually a small alcove in their suite. The bed was just a cot, with a thin mattress and rough linens. Broome didn't mind. He had slept on the ground often enough that any bed was a comfort to him.

He had only one dim bulb overhead. He was too tired anyway for any reading. He reached into his daub kit for a glass bottle with a stopper in it. He opened the bottle and carefully measured a few drops of the clear liquid into a glass on his bedside table. He added some water from a pitcher, swirled the glass to mix its contents and held it for a while in both his hands.

He reckoned the master knew about his laudanum. He had never commented on it or given any indication, but Broome knew by now that not much escaped his attention. The cannonball that had left Broome with a limp had also left him with a wrenching pain in the lower back that medical science apparently had no remedy for. During the day, when he was busy, he managed to forget the pain, though it never really went away. At night it was simply there, implacable. The laudanum let him sleep.

Broome rationed his opiate with great rigor. He knew that it would gradually lose its effect if he was not careful. So his dosage did not eliminate the pain, it only eased it to the point that with his discipline of mind he could will himself to ignore the residual pain and sleep.

Fortunately, laudanum was easy to acquire in Constantinople. Turkey produced much of the world's opium from its vast poppy fields. Broome had smoked opium when he was in India, but he was not interested in the narcotic effect itself. Only some help for his pain.

The cannonball had been a mistake. Ladysmith had actually been relieved and Broome was marshaled with other infantry troops outside the walls. Suddenly the cannon, part of the town's defense, exploded and shot the ball into the troops, killing the man in front of Broome and smashing into his thigh. The fuse on the cannon had been improperly doused and had burned slowly even after the siege was broken. The surgeons set Broome's broken bone as well as they could in the field hospital, but it grew back unevenly and pinched a nerve in his spine, leaving him in constant pain.

Broome wasn't bitter about his fate. The man in front of him was killed, the man behind him was unhurt. He had simply been the man in the middle. But his injury decided him not to return to his father's farm, nor to his betrothed. He wrote home that he had decided on a life of domestic service in the city. His father had two other sons and had no need of the third to take over the work on their small farm. Broome's betrothed in fact married the youngest of the sons. Her brief note announcing the marriage, written by the village postmaster, wished him well in his new life.

And his life had gone well. He was comfortable, well taken care of. His work, by comparison to the grueling life of the farm, was easy, undemanding. In London, he had his pub. A few other old soldiers congregated there and they had a pleasant time together, though none of them talked much. Beyond asking where he'd been, they evinced little curiosity about Broome's travels and he volunteered no details. The men preferred to keep their horizons short. They'd seen enough of the world to last them.

When he came to Leighton two years ago, his life improved. He read his master's books and learned much about the exotic locations they visited. Best of all, though, he found he could talk to this well-educated aristocrat, not, perhaps, as an equal, but somehow on equal footing as an observer of life. It was a rare affinity, which Broome had not encountered in domestic service before, and it brought him great consolation.

So sleep came to him, the pain in his back dulled to a gentle throb, almost soothing.

Chapter Seven

The German Embassy invited them all to a reception. Lowther declined. He felt it would send a wrong signal to the Porte if he were too fraternal with the Kaiser's representative. With the first secretary in London, Maitland was the ranking embassy official. The invitation had specifically included Leighton, "the visiting member of the House of Lords." Fitzmaurice, who had many dealings with the Germans, also came.

They rode together in the embassy motor-car. Leighton and Fitzmaurice wore white tie, tux and top hat. Maitland was decked out in full military regalia. The reception was at the villa on the Bosphorus, in that stretch of verdant shoreline just north of Constantinople where most of the delegations maintained a small palace. It was a Bosphorus night, heady with the smell of sea and jasmine. Stone walls and iron grills fronted the road but thick vines of papery bougainvillea blossoms spilled over the top, covering the hard gray edges.

"Cheer up, it's a beautiful night," Leighton said. Maitland wore a scowl – Leighton had never seen him without one – and Fitzmaurice was pensive. Leighton had grown to enjoy parties. His scholarly pursuits kept him alone so much of the time, he now relished the glitter and wit of a good party. In London, he had to choose his parties with some care. But here, real parties were few and he was determined to enjoy this one. "I suppose it's old hat to you fellows, but I'm looking forward to an embassy party here."

"It's true, the Germans do know how to throw a good party," Fitzmaurice said. "Unfortunately, there's always so many Germans there." He chuckled at his own joke. Leighton smiled good-naturedly and Maitland kept his scowl.

"Do you suppose the Sturm business will put a damper on the affair?" Leighton asked.

Maitland grunted. "Good riddance to bad rubbish. Think even the Germans will be happy to be quit of him," the colonel said.

"Still, the brutality, must bring a chill to things," Leighton mused. Sturm's cold, wet end seemed far removed from this warm, silky evening. Sweet odors of lavender and jasmine mingled in the air, with an occasional bite of peppery tamarind or jacaranda. The clatter of horses' hooves and carriage wheels, the rumble of motor-cars along the exclusive drive mixed with snatches of conversation and bursts of laughter from the terraces of the villas or passing travelers.

"I think the uncertainty about the railway will be weighing more heavily on His Excellency," Fitzmaurice said, with the barest hint of smugness. The German ambassador, Marschall von Bieberstein, had invested his entire prestige in the Baghdad Railway. The coup by the Young Turks and the sultan's loss of power had been heavy blows for him. His diminished standing at the Porte had immediate consequences in Berlin.

The man himself showed little trace of diminishment as he greeted them in the reception line. Tall, with the erect shoulders of a military man, he exuded a sense of power, as if the Kaiser, the infantry, Krupp and Krauss and Maffei all stood immediately behind him, ready to unleash the might of the German Reich.

"Lord Leighton," he boomed, laying the emphasis on Lord and gripping the Englishman's hand in a vise. "So good to meet you. I've heard so much about your work." The ambassador's English was good, if accented.

Leighton murmured the appropriate polite responses. Bieberstein held him by the hand a moment longer.

"I hear you will make the overland trip to Baghdad," he said in a lower voice. "You must come back in a couple of years and we will take you there in the luxury of a railroad car." The steel in his voice softened. "Almost as good as a flying carpet," he said, laughing in a quick bark and releasing Leighton.

Leighton nodded and moved down the reception line, absently shaking hands with the other embassy personnel. A man to be reckoned with, Bieberstein. Leighton was hardly away from the line when a stout figure in a blue uniform accosted him.

"Lord Leighton," the man said. "Hoffenberg."

Leighton shook the proffered hand. The man was short and powerfully built, his wiry black hair brushed across a bald pate on the top of his head.

"I am Colonel Maitland's counterpart here at the German Embassy," Hoffenberg explained. Leighton figured him for Sturm's master.

"I was sorry to hear about Sturm," Leighton said.

"Barbaric," Hoffenberg said. "The legends of Turkish cruelty have not been exaggerated." His English, too, was thickly accented but fluent. Must be the training. The British Foreign Office was never so careful when it sent its emissaries out into the world.

"You think the murder was done by Turks?" Leighton asked.

"Can you imagine a Christian perpetrating such a barbarity?" Hoffenberg asked, genuinely horrified.

Leighton thought of some Christian actions in South Africa, that Afrikaners perpetrated on native Hottentots, that Brits perpetrated on Afrikaners. The Turks had no monopoly on cruelty or barbarity.

"It seems almost an act of war," Leighton ventured.

"War? We are not at war," Hoffenberg exclaimed. "It was the cowardly act of a base, heathen criminal." A frown of deep disgust gave way to something approaching a smile. "Sturm was a good soldier and his Fatherland will remember him. Soldiering is such a dangerous profession." He looked at Leighton slyly. "How fortunate for you that you have turned to scholarly pursuits."

To this, Leighton mustered his haughtiest, "Indeed."

"But we are here to enjoy the party," Hoffenberg exclaimed. "Have you some champagne?" he asked, looking at Leighton's empty hands. Hoffenberg snapped his fingers in the air without so much as a glance to see if any waiters were in hearing distance. A waiter in a white coat and gloves appeared with a tray of full champagne saucers. "French," he said, handing a glass to Leighton, "not our poor German version." Leighton took the comment, which would have been gauche from a fellow Brit, in stride. The Germans always had something to prove, he had observed. The two men toasted the Kaiser, then the king.

Leighton recognized no one as he circulated through the vast rooms, gaily lit with hundreds of candles reflected in the crystal chandeliers. Damask silk covered the walls above the polished wainscoting. Most of the guests were Europeans, with the occasional darker features of Turk or Arab floating by in the whirl. There were few women, and they seemed to be the matronly, gray-haired spouses of senior embassy personnel.

Leighton had just helped himself to a portion of caviar, the salty Persian type, when he heard her voice. Unmistakable, throaty and musical at once. He shuddered as a wave of feeling swept over him. His throat tightened and he put down the plate of caviar, picked up his glass and slowly sipped some champagne. The voice, again, curiously demure and bold at the same time. How did she do it? So typically feminine, yet so different. He turned slowly. He couldn't see her, but heard her voice a third time. Then a tall blond man stepped away to greet someone and there she was, in a dark-blue sequined gown, her hair up in Western fashion, dangling earrings and necklace glittering, radiant, a visitation of the gods to earthly mortals. Leighton had scarcely recovered his breath, when Elena glanced casually in his direction, betraying nothing. Another figure came between them as Elena turned back to her conversation.

Leighton stepped through the crowd and approached her group, to all appearances the bemused man of the world, even as the beat of his heart threatened to paralyze him. He paused outside the circle. With no affectation, Elena interrupted herself. "Richard, how wonderful," extending her hand as the circle widened to take him in. He took her hand, gloved in blue silk, raised it formally to his lips. Even through the thin fabric, the heat and pulse of her hand excited him. "Elena," he said, "more beautiful than ever." Hollow, formal words, but in this case so true.

Elena introduced him to her circle, a commonwealth of diverse countries. "Lord Leighton is an admirer of poetry," she said. "He and my father are great friends." She smiled to hide the irony that unwittingly crept into the remark. Leighton nodded as Elena pronounced their names, paying attention only to a barrel-chested man with iron-gray hair who was introduced as the representative of Deutsche Bank. Leighton smiled at the banker, getting only a blank stare in return.

A burly, dark-complexioned man, bullet-headed and sleek, stepped up to the group, placing a proprietary hand on

Elena's elbow. She smiled up at him. "Darling, look who's here. The friend of my father's that I told you about, Lord Leighton." She turned her smile to Leighton. "Richard, my husband, Mehmet Talaat." Automatically, Leighton extended his hand. So this is the famous Talaat Bey, he thought. Elena kept her smile, but Leighton saw a flash of pain in her eyes, a glisten she quickly controlled. He also saw that yellow gleam in Talaat's eyes as he displayed his teeth. "Lord Leighton," he said with a nod. "Gentlemen, you'll excuse us," he said, with a glance that took in the group. Elena smiled evenly as Talaat swept her away.

"A fine-looking lady," Morrison said. The American had quietly come up on Leighton's left. Leighton turned and smiled at his new friend. "You know her?" Morrison asked. Leighton smiled again. A new appraisal came into Morrison's eyes. "Like that, eh. Well, well," the American said. Leighton made no comment. "You sure communicate volumes without saying much," Morrison said with a laugh. "You'll have to teach that trick to me some day."

Leighton was watching Talaat and Elena to the door. Talaat paused to have a word with Hoffenberg. The German nodded vigorously. It seemed to Leighton that the German stole a glance in his direction. Talaat shook Hoffenberg's hand and rejoined Elena, who was standing at the door, pointedly not looking in Leighton's direction.

Leighton was stunned. Of course he had expected Elena to be married. The reality hit him harder than he expected. He had never contemplated marriage to Elena. The passion and carnality of their relationship had never fit into his picture of drawing rooms and tea in rainy England. His relations with Elena were wild, sensuous – Oriental. Not connubial in any sense that Leighton had ever given to marriage. But he found now that he could not imagine her married to anyone. Her temper seemed too full of fire for the docile role of helpmate, her nature too feral for the domestic state.

Three adversaries. Everyone had been very polite, but Leighton saw that he had three formidable opponents ranged against him in Bieberstein, Hoffenberg and Talaat. Here in the ballroom of a Bosphorus villa, it was all very civilized. Out in the vast treks to Baghdad, the railway could become a savage affair.

Chapter Eight

The next day, Leighton sat at a café along the old Byzantine wall and ordered a samovar. He liked tea and had grown to like this Oriental fashion of drinking it, so different from his native England. There, the tea was brewed fresh and laced with milk. Here the concentrated tea, already saturated with sugar, was kept warm and diluted with hot water for drinking.

Fitzmaurice had sent Leighton a note this morning, saying that he had found an Arab merchant to sponsor him on a caravan. It was to leave from Konya next week. That gave Leighton five more days to fill. But he was accustomed to the caprices of travel and rarely grew impatient.

He sat with his sheaf of papers and slowly sipped his tea, replenishing it from the samovar as he read through a typed report on the Young Turks. It was sensitive material to be carrying outside the embassy, but not secret in any sense and not compromising if it somehow escaped his possession.

Leighton read the sections on Mehmet Talaat with particular interest. The paper, written by the political attaché, provided some biographical details. It mentioned a marriage when Mehmet was a young man – though he was still only in his early 30s – but gave no details of the woman or her fate. It was possible Talaat had simply taken a second wife – it was not encouraged but permitted under Islam – though it was more likely the first wife had died, perhaps in childbirth, or had even been divorced.

Was Elena only interested in safeguarding her father? She was complex and difficult to fathom. As intimate as they had been, Leighton knew there were whole sides of her personality that remained a mystery to him. Her feigned docility suggested some ulterior intent, but one that was hidden to Leighton.

That she should end up with Talaat of all men. Unfortunate, really, for his mission. Leighton believed that Talaat had immediately sensed that there was something between Elena and him, and that it made him aware of Elena's English friend in a way he might not have been otherwise. So strange the way lives intertwine, Leighton thought. The Indian notion of karma sometimes seemed to have a surprising relevance.

Since the attack in the alley, Leighton kept to wide avenues and public places when he went out unaccompanied. He looked around from time to time to see if he could spot anyone following him or observing him. No doubt true spies would know how to make themselves invisible, he thought. But at least he would be able to spot of band of dervishes with drawn knives, Leighton reasoned.

~

Elena picked up the charcoal with the tongs, struck a long match and held the flame to the black lump. It sparked and glowed and she placed it in the holder. She lifted the lid of a small tin sitting next to the brazier and, using a silver spoon, sprinkled some dark grains of ambergris from the tin onto the charcoal. She set the brazier carefully on a tile in front of her on the silk carpet, then stood quietly as a thin spiral of gray smoke rose, infusing a sweetish fragrance into the closed room. She carefully raised the hem of a cotton veil from her head, unfurling it into a shroud held by her extended arms, capturing the wisps of smoke. Her skin and hair absorbed the animal scent. Her beauty, she knew, aroused men. It was the elusive fragrance of this mysterious product from the bowels of a whale that drew them under her sway. She inhaled the smoke, letting it coil through her throat deep into her lungs, prickling, tingling.

Perfume would mask the potent fragrance, allowing it to work its magic undetected. Elena lapsed into a trance. Ambergris contained no narcotic, but she lost herself in the scent, falling into the memory of Richard's embrace.

~

They met at the Café Bellevue in Taksim Park at the end of the Grande Rue de Pera. It was the place to see and be seen and as innocent a venue as possible for a young married woman to meet a single man. The park was an innovation in Constantinople. The sultan had lavish gardens, and the beys had their well-cultivated grounds. A public park, open to everyone, was a new concept, more or less forced on the Ottomans by the Western "nations" in Pera, who demanded this accouterment of civilization.

Leighton had been surprised to find the note from Elena waiting for him yesterday at the hotel. What was the point? Why torture themselves with a meeting? Yet his trepidation quickly gave way to anticipation about seeing her again, talking to her again, even if it would have to be in public.

A waiter in black jacket and silk waistcoat brought a samovar to their table, outside in the shade of a plane tree. Strollers, mostly in Western dress, crisscrossed the paths around them. Many Europeans observed Sunday even though it was a workday in the Muslim calendar.

"It happened only six months after you left," Elena explained to Leighton. "The price was high. My father has a good salary as an official whose office exists only on paper. We have a house in Pera. We are safe."

"And the quest for love your father preached to you?"

"He said to take love where I could find it. He never suggested it was to be found in marriage." Elena stopped. She wanted a cigarette, but would not smoke in a public place. "My father did not recommend it. He only relayed Talaat's terms. The choice was mine."

It was not really a choice, Leighton knew. The protection of Talaat in these uncertain times was worth much to an Armenian. His enmity could have been fatal.

"Richard, you must be careful with these people," Elena said.

Leighton thrilled at the warmth in her voice. "They don't seem to know what they want," he said. "They want to revive the Ottoman empire, yet they foster Turkish nationalism. They distrust the sultan's allies, especially Germany, yet they are trying to play the Powers off against each other."

"They know one thing," Elena said. "They want power. They have it now, but it could slip from their grasp. There are many who resist change. They do not like this new goal of making everything modern." Leighton shuddered as a chill passed over him.

"Why are you going overland to Baghdad?" she asked. "It's so much easier by sea."

Leighton yearned for her, the odalisque of his afternoon trysts, and cherished their bygone intimacy. But he was guarded in his answer.

"You know better than I that this culture is not founded on the sea," he said. "It is rooted in the steppe, the desert. I don't want to be just a tourist."

A flash of hurt crossed Elena's face. She saw his deceit

for what it was. It grieved her that politics came between them.

"It's a grand adventure," he said, trying to lighten her mood with a smile. "I'm growing too sedentary in my middle years."

Elena flushed, deepening her complexion. Her eyes flashed. "Richard, what are you doing here?" she asked.

"The Orient is my life, my work," Leighton started to answer.

"No, I mean you, the British, why are you here?"

"We have an empire," Leighton said. "We have interests to protect."

"So far from home?"

"History has assigned us a role," Leighton said stolidly. "Our interests are global."

Elena was silent.

"Is it possible that history will take away your role?" she asked finally.

Leighton paused. "No empire has lasted, and nor will ours."

"Perhaps the age of empires is at an end," said Elena. "Perhaps it is time for people to rule."

Leighton thought he understood. Nationalist movements stirred throughout the existing empires, agitating for self-rule among people speaking the same language and practicing the same religion.

"Do you want an independent Armenia?" he asked her.

"Why not? We are a people with a long history."

"And an independent Arabia, and Kurdistan and a thousand other splinter nations?"

"Yes, yes, why not?" Elena's answer was almost a cry.

Leighton paused again, to let her emotion subside.

"Our modern industrial economy requires a global exchange of goods to function and empire is the most effective way to ensure that exchange of goods," he said. "And to ensure the peace. Think of the prosperity that the Pax Britannica has brought to the world."

"Peace," Elena spat out the word like a bitter pill. "Richard, how much war have you seen? Was your father not killed in battle?"

"Peace has its price," Leighton continued doggedly. "We settle local skirmishes to ensure world peace and trade."

Elena turned away. "If empire is good, why do my people suffer so."

Leighton yearned to take her into his arms. He leaned forward on the table.

"Your people have prospered under the Ottomans, they are a vital part of the imperial economy," he said. "It is only when nationalism gains ground that other peoples are persecuted. Nationalism is based on exclusion. It is Turks who persecute your people, not the Ottoman Empire."

A dreamy, bitter look came into Elena's eyes. "Ah, Richard. You know so much and yet so little. Because you rule, you have no understanding for those of us who are ruled."

She looked away. A man in a dark suit sat in the recesses of the café. A group of European women occupied a table near them. Leighton was keeping an eye on the man in the café. Talaat had any number of minions he could call on to spy on his wife, or on the visiting member of the House of Lords.

Elena faced Leighton and smiled, dismissing the argument. "I've written poems," she said. "About us," lingered in the air, unspoken. "I show them to no one." Mischief gleamed in her eyes. "They will discover them after my death and marvel at my depravity." Her look included Leighton in this conspiracy to shock the world. Leighton wondered at her beauty. He ached for her. They sat in silence, reliving together the hours of tenderness and passion they had enjoyed, happy to be so near to each other again. Leighton refilled their cups from the samovar, adding hot water to the sugary concentrate. The sun cast a circle of white heat around the shade of their tree. It was a wonder of Constantinople that the waters surrounding it bathed the city in cooling breezes. "Perhaps I will burn them," Elena said. "But not yet. They will comfort me when I'm a wrinkled old crone." She laughed her throaty laugh, bit her lip at the thought. Leighton said nothing, lost in the poetry of his own recollections.

Chapter Nine

Morrison ordered his usual "bourbon and branch."

"Great bar here, carries Jack Daniels," he said, smacking his lips after the first sip. "Best whiskey in the world."

Leighton quietly sipped his Scotch and soda. "Why do you have the water on the side?" he asked.

Morrison looked at the tall glass of water next to his tumbler of neat whiskey. "Don't want to dilute the taste," said Morrison, pronouncing it die-lute in his American accent. "I should ask you why you dilute or pollute your whiskey with that fizzy water."

Leighton shrugged. He always drank his whiskey with soda before dinner and neat after dinner.

"Don't get me wrong," said Morrison. "I like water." He drank a gulp of water to demonstrate his point, and smacked his lips again. "Nothing like water." He paused, and cast a knowing glance at Leighton. "Water is power," he said with a grin.

Leighton laughed. "You mean hydroelectric power?"

"That's one type of power," Morrison said, "but water is powerful in many ways. You Brits know that. How else could such a tiny little island wield such immense power in the world – it's surrounded by water."

"There are many islands that don't rule the world. It's Britain's ships and cannons and men who rule the world, not the water around it," Leighton said.

"True enough, but without the water to transport those men and cannons, Britain would never have an empire 'where the sun never sets,'" Morrison said. "Without that moat of water, Britain would never have fended off Napoleon."

"Well, there you are," said Leighton. "France must have nearly as much coastline as Britain and yet this proximity to water did not make it all-powerful."

"I didn't say water conquers all, I said it has power," Morrison said. "Look at these vast deserts here. Whoever controls the oasis that has the water controls that desert. Water is power."

He sipped his bourbon, his eyes focused on something beyond the Pera bar.

"The United States must be a great power, then," said Leighton.

"Well that's my point, my friend," said Morrison with a slight curve of his lips. "Why do you think Roosevelt started out in the Department of the Navy? Why do think he's pushed for a bigger navy? Why he thought the war for Cuba was so important? Why he championed the Panama Canal? It's all about water and it's all about power. Teddy has a great sense understanding of and taste for power. Your man Churchill is a lot like that. Mark my words, he'll be sniffing around the navy too on his way to the top.

"But I digress," Morrison said. "Yes, the United States is already a great power. I would expect it to be one of the greatest powers in history."

Leighton sipped his whiskey. The conversation seemed a stretch from the simple glass of water on the side. Morrison at times seemed to have a secret agenda.

Transport certainly was another power. Germany, mostly landlocked, had to look to land transport to impose itself. That's why the Berlin-Baghdad Railway was so important to them, Leighton thought.

~

On another evening, Morrison was alone in the bar, nursing his whiskey, looking idly out the window. By profession, he was an engineer, and had spent several months working on the power plants at Niagara Falls. But he didn't live in Buffalo, he lived in Washington, D.C., where he worked for the Office of Naval Intelligence.

Morrison had fought at Roosevelt's side in Cuba. When Roosevelt moved into the White House, he summoned Morrison to work for him. The engineer became Roosevelt's chief agent in Panama. When Colombia refused to let the U.S. build the canal, Morrison helped organize dissident elements to throw off Colombian rule and establish the Republic of Panama. The new republic quickly acceded to Roosevelt's plan for a special American zone to build the Panama Canal.

Morrison was an odd secret agent, but oddly effective. With his long, lanky form, his loud and uncompromising accent, he certainly didn't blend into the background. His very insouciance protected him from suspicion. He seemed too simple and open to be harboring any secrets.

In Panama, the Colombian authorities had dismissed him as a naive and ignorant Yankee. They didn't know he understood Spanish and they sometimes unwittingly betrayed useful information by talking in his presence about problems with the rebels.

In secret, Morrison had met with rebel leaders and relayed their requests for material and money to Washington. His futile quest to persuade the Colombians to grant a canal concession made an ideal cover for his activities.

And now he was on another mission for Roosevelt. True to his pledge, Roosevelt had declined to run for a third consecutive term of office and had left the White House in 1909 as the most popular politician in U.S. history.

After a year in Africa shooting big game and collecting plant specimens, Roosevelt had summoned Morrison to London as the ex-president made a triumphant tour through Europe. At a late-night dinner at the Savoy with just the two of them, Roosevelt had entertained Morrison with stories of his safari. Over cigars, he became serious.

"Lieutenant," Roosevelt said, addressing Morrison by his rank from the Rough Rider days, "I need a favor."

A favor for the man who talked softly and carried a big stick was a command performance.

"I want you to find out what the Germans are up to in Mesopotamia."

Morrison knew that no comment was expected or needed.

"They are locking horns with John Bull over that Berlin to Baghdad railway," Roosevelt continued after some reflective puffs on his cigar. "Lot of trouble brewing there and no telling what the consequences will be."

Morrison knew that Roosevelt worried about the inevitable clash between Europe's Great Powers, as each followed its imperial ambitions. The Office of Naval Intelligence from the beginning had included in its intelligence-gathering activities any facilities foreign governments had for transporting troops and materials, whether on land or sea. The agency had closely monitored German activities in the Caribbean during Roosevelt's administration.

"I'm just a private citizen, of course," Roosevelt said, giving Morrison a deliberate wink, "but I'll have a word with Rodgers and square it with him." Rodgers was the head of ONI and Taft, Roosevelt's handpicked successor as president, was not likely to override any suggestions from Roosevelt, private citizen or not.

"Mr. President, I'll do my best," Morrison gave his ritual reply to the man he had served for 12 years and whose orders he would follow no matter what his title.

Roosevelt bellowed his distinctive laugh, throwing back his head and clapping Morrison on the shoulder. "By God, I know you will, Lieutenant. We're counting on you." He gave Morrison's back a parting slap as the two returned to their rooms.

~

Leighton took his American friend to John Pasha's place in Stamboul. A grocery store run by an Armenian who had anglicized his name, it also sported a restaurant and bar. Leighton had come here occasionally after his visits with Elena and greeted John warmly.

The two men took a table, the only customers at what used to be a bustling time. Tables dotted one side of the store, apparently at random. Shutters opened onto a rough verandah where further chairs were scattered, all empty now. The smell of cloves and turmeric from the grocery shelves pervaded the space. "John, why so quiet?" Leighton asked.

"Politics," said John, shrugging his shoulders. Something fatalistic in his mien suggested that he was more comfortable with his new failure than his previous success. "The CUP is much stricter than the sultan," John said.

Leighton laughed.

"This place used to be popular with students from the War College," Leighton explained to Morrison. "They would come here and order their whiskey served in a lemonade glass. The worst rabble-rousers could sit here at John's and have a drink with the sultan's top spy. The Ottoman bark was always much worse than its bite."

"A good thing to keep in mind," Morrison said.

"Well, the CUP includes those very officers who used to carouse here and they seem intent on giving their orders some teeth," Leighton said.

Morrison only nodded at this, and pensively sipped his whiskey.

It was dark when they came out. Leighton took the way along the sea wall and led Morrison down a cobblestone road in need of repair. Little of the city's lantern light penetrated this far. A half-moon offered them some illumination, though, and Leighton knew the path well. Morrison picked his way with care, stepping around patches where the stones had crumbled or been removed for other projects. The stones glistened in the moonlight, wet from the evening dew and the nearby sea.

Leighton was embarking on more tales of the Young Turks when Morrison gripped his arm and gestured ahead. The two men saw movement in the shadows. Leighton looked back from where they had come, but could see nothing in the darkness. The railroad track lay to their right, yielding a faint odor of pitch.

Neither of them was armed. As they stood there, the movement ahead ceased. Moving slowly, Morrison began to remove the thick leather belt he always wore. Leighton had noticed it often – heavy cowhide, tanned but untreated, wide with a big metal buckle. American fashion, Leighton had concluded. As he pulled the belt from his pants, Morrison nodded at the loose paving stones at their feet. They had crumbled into jagged rocks of various sizes. Leighton grasped Morrison's meaning, and bent over to pick up some hefty pieces.

Three men emerged from the shadows, advancing toward Leighton and Morrison. A glint of steel flashed from hand of one of the men. Rather than wait for their approach, Morrison ran at them, swinging his belt in an arc over his head. Leighton ran after him, a stone held up in his right hand. As they neared the intruders, Leighton hurled the stone with all his momentum behind it. It struck the man on the right full in the chest, knocking him backwards and down to the ground. At that moment, Morrison's buckle, whipping at the end of the belt, struck the middle attacker on the side of the head, knocking him into his companion on his right. Leighton hurled another stone, hitting the middle man in the knee, making him crumple on the pavement with a cry of pain. Morrison let his momentum carry him past the attackers, then whirled, swinging the belt around and lashing at the man still standing. The man ducked, but tripped over his companion and fell on top of him. The first man hit by Leighton's stone scrambled to his feet, but did not come after them. Instead, he turned and ran back into the shadows. Leighton and Morrison stood before the other two, breathing heavily, Morrison poised to flog them again with his belt and Leighton with his last remaining stone held in both hands over his head. The two attackers disentangled, rose warily to their feet, and backed into the shadows.

Leighton and Morrison heard their sandaled feet retreating along the retaining wall.

"Who the hell was that?" Morrison said, as he gulped for air.

Leighton threw the stone down in front of him and bent over with hands on his knees, likewise drawing deeply to catch his breath. "Beats me." He looked at Morrison. "A belt!" Leighton exclaimed, gasping for breath. "I don't believe it. You beat them off with a belt."

Morrison laughed. "Genuine buffalo hide," he said between gulps of air. "Old Mexican trick. Learned it in a couple of bar fights down in San Antonio, when we were down there for Riders' drill." He strapped the belt back on, not bothering to pull it through the loops in his pants, and buckled it with a flourish.

He came over and slapped Leighton on the back. "Pretty good throwing, though. Have to get you for our Buffalo baseball team."

They laughed, relief making them giddy. Still, they remained alert as they took the next road up to a brightly lit main street.

Leighton wondered if this had been a random attack on two white men in the dark. Was it related to the attack in the alley when he first arrived? But if Sturm was behind that attack, and Sturm was dead, who would have mounted this new attack? Morrison looked at Leighton sidelong a couple of times as they walked back through the city, but he asked no questions.

Chapter Ten

The night mist glistened on the cobblestones of the quay. It was the quiet hour just before dawn, when even miscreants take a rest. Packers and tugboats rocked gently in the swells; the water slapped against the stone. Leighton walked along the quay, dressed in a Burberry coat and tweed hat against the damp. He was paying little attention to his surroundings, but saw a bulky object floating in the water below a mooring rope. He knelt on the edge of the quay and reached for the object, which was wrapped in cloth. He tugged at the cloth, and realized it was woolen caftan. As he pulled the object out of the water, he knew it was a body and he cast a glance quickly around to see if a gendarme or anyone was there to help him. The sodden mass showed no signs of life. A whitish lump protruded from one end of the woolen garment and Leighton saw with horror that it was the stump of a leg. He turned over the lifeless form and felt rather than saw both arms ending in stumps as well. But the face, as the hood of the caftan fell away, threw him back as if propelled with great force. His stomach wrenched and he felt the vomit gushing through his mouth and nose. The face, puffy and swollen from the time in the water, was also mutilated. A purplish hole was where the nose had been. The unmistakable shape of a penis dangled from the mouth, which was stuffed with what appeared to be the scrotum of the corpse. The greatest shock, though, was the recognition of the victim's face. Barely discernible through the mutilation, Leighton nonetheless recognized his own features, his gray eyes wide and sightless.

Leighton awoke in a sweat, nausea still gripping him. He breathed in sharp, quick gasps, only gradually feeling the comfort of the damask sheets, the warmth and closeness of his hotel room. His pulse was racing still from the nightmare. He reached for the glass of water on the bed stand and slowly sipped it. He turned on the lamp and saw the time was 4:30. He leaned back in his pillow and let his breathing and heart rate return to normal. So vivid, this dream! He had not felt such a fear even in war. Here his enemies were not visible, the battle lines not clear.

Leighton lay awake in the comforting glow of the lamp. A light fragrance of baking bread drifted through the closed shutters. Otherwise, there was no evidence of human life in the silence of the night. Broome no doubt slept on in his drug-induced slumber. Leighton brooded – about his mission, about the cruel and hostile environment he was entering, about the lost certitudes of his life.

He thought about his father, a shadowy figure in his memory, dim and blurry. He knew from photographic portraits how his father looked, but in his recollection the face was always out of focus. A deep rumble of sound echoed in his mind when his father spoke, yet he could distinguish no words.

Only one incident stood out clearly. His father was in full dress regalia of the Hussars. His tunic shone a brilliant blue and his helmet gleamed golden. The white leather bandolier, the kid gloves, the saber in its shiny black sheath made his father look like a god of war, an unearthly apparition of martial force.

This clanking fearsome figure knelt on one knee before his small son. He smiled and his waxed mustache came briefly into focus. "You like my uniform, young man?" the voice rumbled and a hand, surprisingly gentle from such a warrior, ruffled his hair. "You can grow up to be a brave soldier, too, someday, my son. Serve the queen." The teeth, the mustache were in front of him; he could not see the eyes. Suddenly strong arms pulled him against the wool, the leather, the shining brass. He smelled talcum powder, hair wax, a trace of tobacco clinging to his father. "Be brave, boy," his father rumbled. And he was gone and Leighton never saw him again.

He remembered his grandfather's death. He was 19. The Michaelmas term had just begun at Cambridge when the carriage arrived to fetch him. He had ridden in silence, his eyes dry, but open, blank. No memories flooded his consciousness, no concerns. His mind, too, was empty, his heart numb. The only father he had ever really known lay dying. There was nothing to say, nothing to do. No tears would stop it. Grief, the feeling of loss – those would come later. Just now, life stopped as the old man put up his final struggle against death.

The smell of the disinfectant made Leighton throw up. The odor permeated the house as servants hurried quietly about their duties, tense with fear of the death that roamed the halls. The physician, a relatively young man from the village, emerged from time to time from the dying man's room, his eyes blank and his mouth turned down in a frown.

All knew these last-minute ministrations were futile. The cancerous growth was too widespread, had infiltrated too many organs. The old man, who had turned 85 the previous summer, was on his deathbed.

Leighton had spent the previous evening, after his arrival, sitting in the room with his grandmother and mother. The dying man, drugged, lay insensate rather than asleep. He had been unable to speak, acknowledging their presence only faintly through his glazed eyes. His withered figure scarcely raised the blankets that covered him.

Leighton's grandmother had gone into a trance of her own, as if her soul had joined that of her husband in whatever hell it was suffering. Leighton's mother spared only an occasional glance for her son, a look that sought support rather than gave it. Leighton realized he was becoming the man of the house, the source of strength, the pillar. He would inherit the title and the estate, and the responsibility for the family.

Death is a terror, Leighton felt, particularly this slow, wasting death. His father, killed by a tribesman's spear in the Kashmir, met perhaps a happier fate, though far too young. Maybe this slow death was the punishment for living so long, enjoying so much of life, Leighton reflected.

When they were admitted to the old man's room again, a calm descended over Leighton as the inevitability of his mentor's death came home to him. He watched the drama serenely. After only an hour, the old man ceased to thrash. Before the doctor himself could react, Leighton stood, walked over the bed, and gently closed his grandfather's eyes.

There had been other men to take the place of his father and grandfather, mentors to the aspiring Orientalist.

He went to study at al-Azhar University in Cairo with the revered alim, Ahmad Mahfoudh. He had expected an old, stern fanatic, immersed in the strict codes of Islam. So great was Mahfoudh's reputation for scholarship that Leighton imagined him slipping into his dotage. He hoped only for some crumbs of wisdom from the failing mind before it expired.

Mahfoudh was in fact only in his 50s when Leighton first met him, seemingly decades away from senility. He normally dressed in the traditional robes and turban of the ulema and observed all the Islamic precepts, including abstention from alcohol. But he was in fact an urbane, sophisticated man whose flawless English betrayed his many years at Oxford. He would don one of his Savile Row suits for a night out and, to Leighton's amazement, he was a convivial companion.

"You expected a mummy, perhaps?" Mahfoudh teased Leighton.

His heavy glasses, with lenses like the bottom of a whiskey bottle, betrayed his scholarly calling. When with friends, however, he would slip them into his pocket and, virtually blind, trust in his surrounding company to take care of him. He slicked his hair back in the English style when he went without his headdress.

But it was the brilliance of his teaching that most enthralled Leighton. He spoke rapidly and it took Leighton some time to catch everything. His eyes were animated and his hands in motion, whether he was discussing the medieval perception of Allah or the significance of an upturned tail in an 18th century manuscript.

"Discernment," he told Leighton in the weekly meeting he consecrated to the Englishman by himself, explaining in English the essentials of what had been discussed in his teaching sessions that week. "We must discern the meaning in these old texts. And discernment requires two things – inner peace and a sense of the spiritual." At that point, Mahfoudh would fix his eyes, magnified through the powerful lenses, on the young Englishman. Do you possess these qualities? the eyes asked.

Leighton asked himself that question as he sat in the far corner of the mosque when it was empty – he was not permitted in during the prayer time. His practice of his Christian faith was casual at best. The Church seemed to him a human institution, a segment of the social construct. Personal piety seemed a remote quality, appropriate for widows and young children perhaps.

He had the feeling that inner peace and spirituality were not things he could learn from a teacher. And yet, sitting with Mahfoudh he felt that man's inner peace emanating to those around him. Listening to Mahfoudh decipher the medieval texts, he felt the sense of spiritual that was embedded in the script.

The daily sessions with Mahfoudh were attended by half a dozen others, but Leighton was the only European. He spent altogether three years in Cairo, learning from Mahfoudh, making only one trip back to England in that period, for three months over Christmas, and found his view of home altered. He felt at home there still, but somehow detached from it in a way he could hardly describe. He brought the North African desert back with him to England. In the quiet, muffled sounds of England, he heard the piercing babble of Cairo on a crowded morning. Most telling, for him, were the services in church. What had been for him a comforting ritual that held little meaning beyond the sense of fellowship it conferred, came alive in a new way. For the first time in his studies of Islam, the Allah of his Arabic texts took on the identity of the Christian God worshiped in his country vicarage. He had always known that the object of adoration in both religions was a single one. After all, there cannot be two one and only Gods in the universe. Oddly, this recognition made him feel at peace, at least for those moments he was in church. He attended services more dutifully than he had since childhood. He was in some senses a child in religion once again, rediscovering a sense of awe that he had lost along the way. He hesitated to call it faith because even in his peace he held back, the rationalist in him observing this curious folk religion. He wondered if religion could help him discern texts if his mind refused to accept it.

The vicar, who had baptized Leighton and despaired of his ever returning to the fold, beamed when he saw the young scholar.

"Lord Leighton, so good to see you on a Sunday morning."

"Reverend," Leighton said, doffing his hat.

"Thought we had lost you to the pagans," the vicar said, his jowls quivering in a broad smile.

Leighton smiled in return. "Actually it was my time abroad that brought me back to the church," he said, amiably. He did not feel obliged to enlighten the pastor about those "pagans" whose faith in one God and his justice would shame most of these country parishioners.

"But of course," the vicar's smile broadened even further. "The gift of faith must appear so much greater in a land bereft of it."

Leighton bit his tongue; this was almost too much. At that point, an older couple, who Leighton recognized as shopkeepers from the village, greeted the vicar, and Leighton moved silently away.

The vicar was ignorant and yet ensconced in a grand tradition of ignorance. Crusades and jihads had been fought between heathens and unbelievers, both of whom believed in a beneficent, protective God. Leighton hoped his work making some of the great learning of Islam accessible to his countrymen would finally, in time, dispel this ignorance.

Mahfoudh himself was absent part of his final year in Cairo, off in Paris on a guest lectureship. It was like a great beacon had been turned off. Leighton felt lost in his studies. Doubts assailed him about his scholarly calling. Mahfoudh's assistant turned every text into a dry, lifeless shred of history and Leighton had trouble paying attention.

Mahfoudh returned eventually and Leighton regained some of his enthusiasm. But he realized he needed a break from his studies. He had a commission from the 13th Hussars and decided it might be time to take it up. Rather than take the weeks to conduct his correspondence from

Cairo he decided to return to England and take his chances on a rapid call.

He went out with Mahfoudh the night before his departure. It was just the two of them and few words were spoken.

"A soldier now," Mahfoudh said, "for the great British empire." There was no reproach, only a hint of futility that his hard-earned learning was being set aside.

"I will return to my studies."

Mahfoudh looked at him for some time, then nodded. "Yes."

Leighton didn't feel as sure as he said he was. He didn't know where his commission would take him. India was not without its dangers, as he knew from his father's fate. There was unrest in the Cape Colony from the Boer settlers.

They finished the meal mostly in silence. Mahfoudh in fact demonstrated no curiosity about possible postings, the demands of an officer in Her Majesty's Army. The British, despite the protection they extended to Egypt, were suspect. An infidel power that inserted itself in the heart of Islam. Mahfoudh didn't say it, but it was as though Leighton was betraying him and going over to the other side.

Leighton sensed it. He knew, though, that he had always been on the other side. Mahfoudh knew it as well. The scholar usually succeeded in keeping secular politics out of his lessons, but occasionally his anti-British feelings boiled over.

One morning he had come seething to a meeting with Leighton. He had attended a reception hosted by the British consul general and effective ruler of Egypt.

"Your Lord Cromer has a low opinion of 'Orientals,' you know," Mahfoudh snapped at Leighton. "He says they are not very accurate, that they are vague."

Mahfoudh fixed him with his brown eyes, brighter even than usual. Leighton was at a loss for words.

"He should meet my cousin Ibrahim," Mahfoudh said at last. "Ibrahim could tell him exactly how many sheep he has, their ages, when they were last shorn. Very accurate." He paused. "He could tell Lord Cromer how many date palms are on his land, what they yielded last year, or any of the last five years, down to the last peck. He could tell him the ages of each of his twenty grandchildren, very accurately."

Leighton frowned.

"Lord Cromer talked at the Queen's birthday celebration. He spoke to his people, as though none of my people were there, though I was not the only Egyptian there. He spoke of how vague Orientals are. He implied that Europeans, being more accurate, are a superior race, worthy of ruling such a vague race as my own.

"You understand, my dear Richard, the Orient is a creation of the Occident. It is a concept imposed on a subject peoples. Yes, Europeans rule now, for many reasons, though I don't really believe that accuracy is one of them. For many centuries, Orientals ruled much of what was then the known world. These vague Orientals invented mathematics, created urban systems and infrastructure that only just now are perhaps being matched by modern technology. If they are vague with Lord Cromer it is because they have no respect for his authority."

Leighton thought of the history of Granada, Cordoba, Seville - great lights of medieval Arab culture, with well-lit streets and functioning sewer systems while the rest of Europe lived in mud huts.

"The nomads of Arabia are not lesser beings simply because they prefer to live free in the desert rather than cowering in a dirty city. The people of Egypt are not a subject race just because Britain has imposed its administration on a corrupt regime. England has seen its share of unworthy rulers and but for the fact that it is an island would have seen other conquerors than Caesar or William."

"Lord Cromer is certainly aware of this," Leighton protested. "He no doubt hoped to boost patriotic spirits with his remarks."

Mahfoudh smiled, though his eyes remained sad and bright. "He has published his remarks in the London newspapers. He is going to write a book of his profound thoughts to instruct the British people on what he has learned in his years of ruling such a poor people as mine."

Leighton felt a slight wave of nausea. His eyes pleaded with Mahfoudh; he could not muster a response. "I'm feeling very vague myself right now," Leighton said, attempting a smile.

This time, Mahfoudh's eyes smiled, too. But he quickly became serious again. "Richard," he said, "don't ever forget. I am an Oriental because you are an Orientalist."

Chapter Eleven

Julius von Hoffenberg strode through the anteroom to his office, nodded curtly at the young lieutenant who served as his assistant, opened the double door and entered the large corner room where he worked. As he closed the door behind him, the stiff posture he maintained in public left him. His shoulders sagged, his belly assumed a comfortable, paunchy shape, his Prussian strut became a Swabian amble, a rolling gait that suited his hilly homeland in southwest Germany. The Prussians were the most military race on earth, and keeping face in their army was a demanding task.

Worth it, though. Hoffenberg relished his prestige in the Kaiser's Reich. It meant spending more time in dirty, crowded Berlin, and, now, abroad. His theater of action, though, was infinitely larger than it had been for his military forebears, confined until his father's generation to the comic opera Kingdom of Wuerttemberg. Yes, the Prussians strutted, but it was a march of power and purpose, not a popinjay's vanity. Hoffenberg was happy to keep in step.

There was a sharp rap on the door, and his assistant, a serious but slightly anemic youth from East Prussia, announced Captain Ernst.

"Ernst," Hoffenberg said in greeting. "Take a seat."

Ernst was anything but anemic. His large square face bore the pockmarks of childhood disease, a dueling scar creased his right cheek. He saluted and sat.

Hoffenberg scowled at him. "Have you replaced that idiot Sturm?" The report to Berlin on Sturm's murder had pained Hoffenberg. How did the English put it in their ever quaint fashion: It blotted his copybook. Hoffenberg blamed Ernst for the botched agent.

"I have found other ways to keep track of the Englishman," Ernst said. Hoffenberg bit off his question. Better not to know, perhaps.

"And Sturm's assassins?" Hoffenberg asked.

Ernst scowled. It was the permanent set of his face. "Muslim fanatics, I'm sure," he said.

"Yes, but which fanatics? Who?"

"Fanatics who oppose all foreigners in this sacred land of theirs," Ernst said, spitting in his contempt.

"So you have no clues," Hoffenberg said. He had learned quickly to see through Ernst's machismo. The captain masked his failures with surliness, like the low-born infantry private he was at heart.

"I have met the Englishman," Hoffenberg said. "He is clever. Do not underestimate him a second time." Leighton had impressed Hoffenberg more with what he didn't say than anything in their actual conversation. Also, he had that easy confidence of the English upper classes, comfortable after generations with the wealth and power that made them rulers of the world. Well, they should enjoy it while it was still left to them, Hoffenberg thought.

"He shall be dealt with," Ernst said. He bristled, angry at the embarrassment this meddling fop had caused him.

"When? Where?"

"He shall not leave the Taurus mountains alive," Ernst said with conviction.

"He must not. He will ally Britain with our enemies in Mesopotamia and we cannot afford further damage to the railroad."

The railroad, Hoffenberg thought. The brilliance of it, Berlin to Baghdad, to Basra, to India. Yes, the British were right to oppose it. But they would fail. Their day, their century, was past. The new century belonged to the Reich. Already the Reich's army was bigger, its economy more powerful than Britain's. Now the Reich would have a navy to rival theirs, turning England into a vulnerable little island. And India, their precious jewel, their Raj. A small stone for the German crown – Africa, the Near East, the Far East, all ripe for German dominion. The English had grown soft. That debauchee Edward VII could not stand up to the Kaiser nor would his stupid son, the Prince of Wales, be up to it. Could polo-playing officers match the Prussian military machine?

Ernst waited patiently during Hoffenberg's momentary reverie. The man was tougher than he appeared, Ernst knew first hand. The two had served together in Morocco. Ernst had seen Hoffenberg all but sever a man's head with his saber in one hand-to-hand battle.

"See to it," Hoffenberg said in dismissal. Ernst saluted, bowed and left.

~

The light in his office had grown dim, but the barrel-chested man in the leather chair did not call for the lamps to be lit. He pressed his seal into the wax and waited patiently for it to cool. Yet another letter to Berlin, to Arthur von Gwinner, the head of Deutsche Bank, the most powerful financier on the Continent. His predecessor, Georg von Siemens, had always believed in the railway. But von Gwinner now had many claims on his attention and von Bohlen's current task was to keep the Baghdad Railway in front of Deutsche Bank's director.

Erich von Bohlen was a believer. He believed in progress, he believed in capitalism, and, above all, he believed in the Baghdad Railway. He had spend twenty years of his life proselytizing government officials, financiers and industrialists in Berlin, Düsseldorf and Constantinople. And he had made many converts. He was completely Jesuitical in his mission – preaching empire to the politicians, military strategy to the soldiers, dividends to the bankers. The end justifies the means, oh yes, he was convinced. His own vision was something else. Von Bohlen saw a Mesopotamian plain rich in grain, a peasantry living in comfort, an economy raised above subsistence to plenty. History would chronicle his long campaign to get the railway built, and honor him as one of the great imperialists, a Rhodes for the Orient.

The room was virtually dark now, and still von Bohlen sat, his jaw thrust forward, his iron-gray hair slicked back. He had lived in Constantinople for more than two decades. He would die here. He loved this place, these people – it was more home to him than cold, dreary Düsseldorf, or even Berlin. Von Bohlen recognized early that he was not brilliant and could not hope to match the business geniuses drawn to Berlin toward the end of the century. No, he had different qualities – tenacity, stamina, and a kind of selflessness unknown to successful men. Then he found his mission. He had volunteered for the Constantinople post thinking only that it was new territory for the bank and a chance for him to pull away from the crowd. Once he arrived in the Ottoman capital, however, he saw a special, historic opportunity – a railway to bring this sprawling, primitive domain into the industrial era. Von Bohlen knew the railroad business from his family's steel firm. Germany had built more railways than any other country and German engineers were the best in the field.

The door opened and a man carrying a taper mumbled an apology as he moved quickly to light the lamps on the desk and the wall. Von Bohlen did not reply. The phone on his desk rang.

"Bohlen," he said. Then he listened and said nothing. It was Hoffenberg. The color rose along von Bohlen's neck and jowls, but still he said nothing.

"Rubbish," he said finally. "The British may join the project. I personally have spoken with a number of City figures who are interested in the railway."

These politicians and their intrigues! They could not grasp that a new era had arrived. Capital made it possible for nations to collaborate. There was no longer a need to beggar thy neighbor, for capital created wealth enough for all. Germans, French, British, Turks – all stood to gain from the railway. The more the merrier!

Von Bohlen held the receiver away from his ear as Hoffenberg ranted in response. More Prussian than the Prussians, this peasant from Wuerttemberg. Thank God it was the von Gwinners of the world who made the decisions and not simpletons like this bantam straight out of a musical comedy.

The British understood profit. They had built an empire on profit, and would see the value of co-opting the railway, if these meddling soldiers did not upset the delicate balance of interests it represented.

Von Gwinner had asked him about oil. An Armenian, Gulbenkian, had predicted that Mesopotamia would have as much oil as Persia. The man had never even visited the place. He had talked to the railroad engineers and determined from what they told him, and the similar geology, that oil would be found. Von Bohlen was unconvinced, but if it piqued von Gwinner's curiosity and gave him another reason to support the Baghdad Railway, the banker would use it. His letter to von Gwinner encouraged the bank to enter into negotiations with Gulbenkian and join the consortium he was putting together to search for oil in Mesopotamia. The railway had acquired mineral rights along the route almost as an afterthought in the 1903 concession to complete the railroad to Baghdad. It would be natural to broaden this prospect with an investment in Gulbenkian's Turkish Petroleum Company. It all worked to the good of the railway, and that worked to the good of the German Reich.

~

"We're set for day after tomorrow, Broome," Leighton said. The Welshman was lathering Leighton's lower face.

"Very good, sir. I'll have the laundry done and everything packed," he said. He stropped the razor on a dark leather band and began shaving his master.

"We'll leave from Haidar Pasha, on the Asian side, and take the Anatolian Railway to Konya," Leighton said. "There we will meet a caravan returning to Baghdad."

Broome finished the right side of Leighton's face and moved over to the left side.

"Mehmet Ali is our sponsor. He imports British woolens and will be sending a shipment on the caravan," Leighton continued, pausing as Broome finished up with his upper lip.

"Mr. Morrison will accompany us?" Broome asked.

Leighton could only nod in assent as Broome wrapped a steaming towel around his face, Leighton's favorite moment in the morning ritual.

"A new experience for both of us," Leighton said as Broome removed the wet towel and dried Leighton's face. "I've never gone overland to Baghdad." Using a puff, Broome powdered Leighton's face and neck with talc. "Should be quite an adventure."

"Will we have rifles?" Broome asked.

"I'm sure the caravan will be armed," Leighton replied.

"And of course I have my service pistol. It will be a trek. The mountains, then the desert." Broome had crossed the Transvaal on foot and was unfazed by the physical challenge of the journey.

"Good to get out of the city," was all the Welshman's phlegmatic temperament allowed him to say.

~

The ambassador saw Maitland in the hall and took him aside by the arm.

"So will you have someone with him?" Lowther asked the soldier.

"My orders are very strict, sir," Maitland said. "Absolutely no official involvement."

Lowther looked at the other man. Maitland showed no expression, his eyes glittered blankly.

"But you must have agents, natives who can't be traced to us," the ambassador said.

Maitland shook his head slowly. "I'm afraid most of our agents are known."

Lowther grunted in exasperation. What a fool game they were about.

"Do you know what the Germans are planning?" Lowther asked.

Maitland hesitated. "They are having him followed."

"Followed? That's all?"

"Nothing else has come to our ears," Maitland said, no hesitation this time.

Lowther felt uneasy. Things didn't add up. The ambassador had learned to live with this ambivalence.

~

Maitland met Fitzmaurice in his office. The colonel kept his windows shuttered and the drapes drawn against the afternoon sun. The gloom, relieved only slightly by the low-wattage ceiling light and a desk lamp, suited him. The still air was thick with stale smoke from his cigars. Fitzmaurice coughed nervously when he entered this den, fighting off the panic the closeness of the room inspired in him.

Maitland motioned to the chair in front of his desk and Fitzmaurice sat.

"Well, he's on his way," Fitzmaurice said in a quiet voice.

"Chances don't look too good," Maitland said. His voice was neither quiet nor loud and betrayed no emotion.

"Grey's a cynical bastard to send him on this mission," Fitzmaurice said, more loudly. "It's suicide."

Maitland shrugged. The Germans may have invented the word Realpolitik, but the British had practiced it for centuries.

"He's a soldier," Maitland said. "He served at Ladysmith. He knows what's expected of him."

Fitzmaurice, who had spent his youth as an apprentice in a counting house, felt little appreciation for Maitland's words.

Maitland smiled. He saw the other man's confusion. "It's about empire," he said.

This Fitzmaurice could understand. Yes, the mandarins in London were moving the pieces across the chessboard of the globe. Sacrificing a pawn here, a knight there, even a lord, to protect their king and check the opponent.

Maitland and Fitzmaurice thought Leighton's mission useless at best, and potentially embarrassing if things went wrong. In either case, the failure of the mission would vindicate their skepticism and discourage London from bypassing the embassy in the future. Too bad if Leighton suffered the consequences of this ill-advised venture.

Chapter Twelve

They took the ferry from the Galata bridge across the Bosphorus to the Haidar Pasha station on the Asian side. A stiff breeze made the water choppy and the ferry splashed a steady spray onto the deck as it forged its way across the strait.

The station loomed ahead of them like an outpost of the Teutonic Knights, its round towers designed by German architects to make it look like a fort. The monumental building, which had just been completed the previous year, was a gift from the Kaiser, his contribution to making the Baghdad Railway a reality. The sandstone facade gleamed in its newness. The station extended into Kadikoy Bay on more than a thousand timber piles. It had its own dock, with flights of marble steps leading up to the main entrance facing the water.

Their train was easy to spot, the large sleek European cars eclipsing the local suburban trains. Metal plaques on each of the cars as well as the locomotive proclaimed that this equipment had been manufactured at the Henschel-Werke in Cassel, Germany.

"So this is the famous Baghdad Railway," Morrison said as walked along the platform.

"Actually it's the famous Anatolian Railway," Leighton said, "at least for the time being."

"Well, if the Germans get their way, this train will end in Baghdad in the not-too-distant future," Morrison said, glancing sideways at Leighton with a curious look.

Leighton did not rise to the bait. He kept silent.

"How does Britain feel about that?" Morrison insisted, his usual bantering tone gone.

Leighton reflected. "My understanding from the embassy staff is that Britain is concerned about their shipping concession from Basra if the railroad is extended that far."

Morrison just grunted at this. Leighton was spared any further inquiry as the two men jostled their way through the crowd on the platform. Most were in simple pilgrim dress, with a scattering of merchants and a small contingent of khaki-clad soldiers. A couple of European gentlemen were standing outside the first-class car. Leighton could not determine their nationality, though he was reasonably sure they were not English. When one of the men turned to step into his compartment, however, Leighton saw a dueling scar on his cheek that marked him as a graduate of a German university.

"Aha, here are our seats," Morrison said, holding the door open for Leighton to step up into the first-class sleeper compartment. Leighton had just time to see that the two men boarded separately before he climbed into the train.

"I'll warn you that I fall into a bit of a daze in a train," Morrison said. "Something about the motion makes my mind a blank. I'm not very good company."

Broome directed the porters to get their steamers checked and took his place further back in the car, in a second-class compartment.

There were actually very few passenger cars on the train and all but the one containing their compartments were third-class cars filled mostly with peasants returning to their homes in Anatolia or pilgrims under way to visit the Mevlana shrine in Konya.

Leighton settled into the plush upholstery of the first class cabin and felt like he was back in Europe. The burled walnut paneling and thick carpeting fashioned a cocoon for the travelers. When the train pulled out of the station with much shrieking of whistles, the know-how of the German engineers made itself felt in the smoothness of the ride.

"You gotta hand it to the Germans," said Morrison, placing his boots on the upholstered footrest in front of him, "they sure know how to build a railroad." Again a sidelong glance at his companion.

Leighton nodded, looking out the window at the profusion of new housing in the Asian quarters of the city, little more than hovels, as primitive and shoddy as anything in an Anatolian village. Children ran naked or clad scantily in rags along roads of packed dirt. Donkeys pulled makeshift carts filled with wooden planks scavenged from building sites and junk heaps.

"So poor," he commented, more to himself than Morrison. And yet Byzantium had been one of the most prosperous cities in the history of the world.

The train plowed ahead, ascending slowly from sea level to the plateau of the Anatolian steppe. As the train moved away from the coast, the landscape became increasingly arid and signs of human habitation disappeared.

So here I am on the Baghdad Railway, Leighton thought, or at least the first stage of it. He settled back and opened the volume of Rumi poetry that he had acquired the previous day at the bazaar. The Sufi mystic, revered as Mevlana by Turkish Muslims, had lived and taught in Konya, the current end station for the railway. That was a day and a half away.

Shrubs with thin creepers clung to the rocks and sand of the hard-baked terrain. The train rumbled at a slow pace past an occasional cluster of huts, where bent figures swathed in dark robes herded fat-tailed sheep. Leighton briefly considered the German traveler he had seen and speculated whether his presence was a coincidence. Just one man, he concluded, and hardly a threat even if he was following them.

They were shunted around in Eskesehir, with part of the train continuing east toward Ankara, and their car hooking up with the Konya train. Soon afterwards the porter arrived to make up their beds for the night ride through the steppe. Morrison, fell quickly asleep, snoring softly. Leighton, after locking the door as a precaution, lay awake reflecting on the lines from Rumi:

> If love were only spiritual,
> the practices of fasting and prayer would not exist.
> The gifts of lovers to one another are,
> in respect to love, nothing but forms;
> yet, they testify
> to invisible love.

Civilizations had risen, prospered and vanished in this arid land -- the ancient Hittites and Phrygians, the Greeks, the Seljuk Turks, and now the Ottomans. The Armenians. Leighton thought of Elena, her gift of love. Had it vanished like those lost civilizations?

~

They debarked at Konya. An ancient city, once the capital of the Seljuk Turks, it had fallen predictably into ruin as an Ottoman provincial center. As in Stamboul, most of the old city wall had been removed to make way for the railway and other "modernization" projects. The citadel on the hillock in the center of town had crumbled and a mosque now dominated the peak.

"Thought you said this was an imperial capital," Morrison said as they emerged from the station.

"Yes, well, somewhat the worse for wear after six

hundred years," Leighton responded dryly. He had seen no sign of the German in the black suit as they left the station.

It was a short walk to the hotel and the two men passed several stalls displaying lustrous pastel-colored carpets with intricate geometric designs.

Amidst the squalor that greeted them in Konya, Leighton detected signs of prosperity. The Anatolian Railway, completed little over a decade ago, had proven a surprising success, and the volume of traffic and trade to Konya had surged. Now that harvests could be transported to the capital and other population centers, canals long since fallen into disuse were repaired, extending the arable land beyond the confines of the oasis itself.

The drab hotel near the station evidently catered to pilgrims more than European tourists. However, it would be more comfortable than the hard ground that was to make their bed for the next five to six weeks, Leighton thought.

~

Horst Ernst held back after the train stopped in Konya. He did not want to pique the interest of Leighton and his companion. He finally emerged from his compartment and retrieved his small trunk, which he consigned to a porter. Outside the station, he took one of the waiting hansoms to the villa of the railway director in Konya, a German engineer who also functioned as honorary consul.

The captain wore a civilian suit. He had lasted at university only a couple of semesters, just long enough really to obtain the dueling scar that had gotten him expelled. His father, a prosperous entrepreneur in Berlin who was exhausted after years of the young man's rowdiness, had urged young Ernst to pursue a military career and backed it up by threatening to cut off his son's allowance otherwise. Ernst found, somewhat to his surprise, that he liked the military. The discipline irked him at first, but he appreciated immediately the emphasis on force, the training to hold violence in check – until that moment when it could break out and wreak its destruction.

Ernst's military superiors had quickly assessed his explosive potential. He was reassigned to a rifle division, a group of specialists schooled in sharp-shooting and other deadly skills. Ernst thrived in this environment. He proved himself adept and became one of a select number of officers set aside for special assignments.

The young lieutenant-adjutant's first mission was in Germany's colony in South-West Africa. As Germany sought to subdue the Herreros tribes there, Ernst was ordered to assassinate a recalcitrant chieftain. The young officer worked alone, with no official support. He was successful and returned to Berlin as a full lieutenant. Then he was dispatched to Morocco, where he fulfilled a number of delicate assignments for the ambassador. His only brush with failure was on a foray in the Atlas Mountains, when he lost most of his commando unit in an attempt to break a Moorish tribe that was abetting the French. However, what he failed to do in battle he succeeded through treachery, when he induced a rival of the chieftain to slay the tribal leader.

His current assignment seemed relatively easy, though more politically sensitive than usual. Ernst had murdered British agents before. However, these were usually local snitches in the employ of the British government, not actual British subjects and certainly not a member of the aristocracy. This posed no problem to his scruples, but it did constrain his tactics.

It made much more sense to handle the matter here in the wild rather than in the capital, Ernst thought. He regretted ever having listened to Sturm's harebrained scheme. Of course, Sturm had paid for his mistake.

Ernst already knew what hotel Leighton was staying at. He knew of Mehmet Ali's sponsorship for the caravan, and he knew the caravan. The presence of the American perplexed him, however. Who was he? What was his game? Before setting out on his own trek across the steppe the next day, Ernst wrote a cable for the director to send to Constantinople. He wanted to know more about this Morrison.

Chapter Thirteen

At dusk, the chant calling believers to prayer pierced the evening. Leighton, who had returned with Morrison to the carpet stalls, motioned to his companion to follow him through the city's dirt streets. He led the American to an imposing walled mosque with an arched gate where the faithful had gathered in response to the muezzin's summons.

They followed the crowd into the courtyard. The chant from the minaret ceased. A thin, wailing melody arose from a small group of musicians next to a formation of white-robed dervishes wearing tall red fezzes. Slowly, one, then another, and finally all of the robed figures started spinning in place. The robes, fitted like a high-waisted petticoat, billowed around them. Their heads fell back, only white was showing in their eyes. The dancing figures increased the tempo until each was a blur in the twilight, the flash of the face and those white eyes marking several revolutions a minute.

Morrison's jaw had dropped. "Whirling dervishes," he whispered in awe. "It's not a fairy tale."

Leighton nodded quietly. The Konya mosque was the center for this Sufi practice. The dervishes entered a trance, induced by their religious fervor and an abundance of narcotics, and spun in place in an acrobatic feat that no circus act in Europe could hope to match.

The men met Mehmet Ali in the hotel lobby the next morning. His dimensions bespoke prosperity in his business.

He wore a striped silk robe over a European riding suit. A fez perched above his beaming face.

"Lord Leighton," he bowed. "So happy to be of service."

Leighton muttered the appropriate thanks for his courtesy in allowing them to join his party in the caravan and the obligatory praise for Fitzmaurice's good offices.

The merchant again bowed and continued to beam. Leighton asked Morrison and Broome to wait for them in the carriage. When he and Ali were alone, he pulled out his porte-monnaie and counted out several bills. Ali's hand appeared from beneath the folds of his robe, accepted the money without counting it, and disappeared again into the robe, the smile remaining fixed the whole while. Leighton now smiled as well, and, business concluded, the two men joined the others in the carriage that would take them to the caravan waiting at the edge of town. Ali had arrived earlier in the week to see to the transport and proper loading of his goods. He had two assistants with him, one of whom, Leighton soon determined, was his son.

The caravan was in full commotion when they arrived at the camp site just east of Konya. There were more than three dozen camels, single-hump dromedaries. Mehmet Ali's bolts of cloth burdened a half dozen of them, strapped in even bales across the humps. The drivers strung a heavy rope through the nose-rings of the camels, forming three trains that could plod along abreast of each other or in single file as the terrain permitted. The animals, well-rested and watered after their week-long sojourn outside Konya, were docile and even playful as their tenders secured their burdens.

The dusty, fetid odor of camel hair pervaded the camp. Several wagons, drawn by mules, carried the camping equipment and other supplies needed on the trip, which would take about five weeks. There were a number of caravansaries along their route, but most evenings would be spent in tents.

Two large horses, a chestnut and a roan, were given to Leighton and Morrison. Broome received a dappled mount, much smaller, almost a pony. The leader of the caravan, Abdul Latif, was a Bedouin from Syria. He wore a gray robe and brown burnoose, with a white turban covering his head. The nimble Arabian he rode wheeled and pranced through the disorder and tumult of the packing as Abdul Latif jerked the reins now this way, now another. His dark eyes flashed as he barked curt, guttural commands to his drivers, a dozen men of all ages. One gray-bearded man in a striped burnoose seemed to have a permanent hunch. A bare-headed boy, thick brown curls framing his smooth, hairless face, looked to be in his early teens.

The camels brayed and honked as they were herded into formation. They would set the pace. The wagons clattered into place at the rear of the caravan. Abdul motioned the three Westerners to join him at the head of the caravan. Holding his prod high in the air, Abdul shouted a final command and rode at a trot to lead the train onto the road to Baghdad.

The first leg of the journey was across the flat, dry Anatolian steppe and would be easy going. The Taurus mountain ranges were a different story. The ascent in single file would be slow. While weather should not be a problem at this time of the year, brigands, some in large gangs, would be a hazard. The final stretch would be across the arid steppes north of the Syrian desert and then the mud flats between the Tigris and Euphrates.

An adventure indeed, Leighton thought. Morrison wore a big smile, evidently pleased with the tumult of launching this expedition. He was dressed in khaki and a slouch hat that Leighton surmised dated to his Rough Rider days. "Tally ho!" Morrison waved at Leighton in his best imitation of English aristocracy. Leighton wore his pith helmet with a field jacket and riding breeches. They cantered together to catch up with Abdul, Broome loping along behind.

The cloud of dust kicked up by the movement of men and beasts recalled to Leighton the dry trek across the African veldt to relieve Ladyfinger ten years ago. No camels, then, but troops of infantry followed his regiment of Hussars.

Then, yellow dust rose in thick clouds, turning the sun into a crimson orange ball sinking slowly toward the horizon. The dust choked the men through the kerchiefs they had used to cover the lower part of their faces. Leighton rode unmasked, but wiped his face often with a handkerchief that by now was full of grime. Dust covered their helmets and uniforms, their horses and kit.

The squadron rode single file on the narrow, rutted road. Refugees trudged in the opposite direction, their faces gaunt. They, too, were filthy from the dust and sweat under the burning sun. They carried satchels, or just sheets wrapped around belongings. Two younger men pulled a dogcart loaded with clothing and some small pieces of furniture. The cart had somehow survived the foraging for firewood, but no beast of burden had lived to pull it.

Further up the column, Leighton could see a ragtag gang wearing hats with drooping brims. He heard the clanking of chains and manacles before he saw the iron binding them together. Their clothes were torn and stained, their eyes hollow in the shadow of their hat brims. They made no sound. Uitlander auxiliaries herded the dozen or so captives along, slapping them into place with cudgels if they broke rank. These Boers weren't commandos, just farmers who had tended their crops during the siege. They were being taken now to the concentration camp at Pietermaritzburg.

Leighton led his band at a slow gait. The light was fading as the orb of the sun touched the horizon. A group of auxiliaries emerged from a thicket of trees on their right.

The men held a kaffir, stripped to the waist. The African was slight of build, his arms like a bundle of string. He offered no resistance to his captors. His eyes were downcast and empty.

The Uitlanders raised up a wagon wheel that was a good five feet in diameter. Two of the men held the wheel while two others expertly strapped the kaffir to the rim, facing the spokes. A short, powerful man stepped back and began thrashing the captive's back with a dark leather strap, folded in the middle where he held it and knotted at each end. The flogging created deep red welts across the black skin of the kaffir, who still put up no fight and uttered no sound.

Leighton stopped his horse and looked around for a supervising officer. It was none of his business, but he wanted to reassure himself that this brutality had been sanctioned by some authority and wasn't just a wanton act of the settlers. Had the kaffir collaborated with the enemy? Or perhaps just failed to deliver a dinner on time?

Floggings were common in the campaign, Leighton had already realized. The victims were almost always kaffirs, rarely whites, and never enlisted men.

Leighton clenched his jaw. The British Empire had partly justified its going to war against the South African Boers by citing their brutality against the native population. Yet the British settlers, so far as Leighton could determine, showed the same fierce cruelty against the natives as that imputed to the Boers. War always created an environment of barbarity, but Leighton felt that England had a mission to set higher standards. If the empire truly was about more than profit, Britain needed to have a civilizing effect on savage nations, to impose a moral rule where there was none. What he was witnessing belied all these ideals.

Leighton spurred his horse forward.

"You there! What's this about?" he shouted at the

man who had been giving the commands. No rank was distinguishable in his makeshift uniform.

The man looked around, squinting into the sun as he took Leighton in.

"Who wants to know?"

"Leighton, lieutenant, 13th Hussars."

The man leaned to his right and spat. He turned back around without any further word.

Leighton rode up to the man with the whip and grabbed it from him as he raised it to strike again. "Stop this immediately!" Leighton shouted.

The other auxiliaries looked to their chief, who glowered at Leighton, but shook his head in answer to his comrades.

The victim's legs had given way and he was slumped against the wheel, held up by the straps binding him to the rim. He showed no signs of consciousness. His back was glistening red and pink with blood and slashed skin.

Leighton felt the nausea rise in his throat. Fortunately he hadn't eaten since breakfast, nor had more than a few swigs from his canteen to drink, so his stomach turned to little consequence.

Leighton knew that maggots would soon set into the mangled flesh of the victim's back. Even if he got some treatment afterwards, his chances of surviving such a brutal flogging were slim. Nor were any relatives or friends visible who could take him in charge as the settlers unbound the victim's hands and let him slip to the ground.

"See that this man gets some treatment," Leighton said to the commander. The man, his face weathered and partially hidden by his wide-brimmed hat, muttered, "Sir!"

Leighton clinched his jaw. He turned his horse and cantered back to his waiting squadron, raising his hand for his men to resume their march. A futile effort, no doubt, Leighton thought. A mile further along, he threw the leather whip into the brush. He would file a report, but the kaffir was almost surely doomed, and the auxiliaries unlikely to suffer any punishment.

Chapter Fourteen

The caravan settled into an easy routine – an early start at dawn, a brief pause during the heat of the day to eat and rest, and a camp quickly pitched in the dusky light after sunset. They made good time on the steppe, though winds would rise in the afternoon that covered them with dust and sand and slowed their progress. Vegetation clung to crevices in the hard, arid ground, a gray growth that lent little color to the landscape. The terrain was flat, unbroken by trees or habitation of any sort.

Abdul Latif said little as they rode. He evidenced no curiosity about his companions, their objectives, their lives. His comments regarded the weather, the terrain, the animals. He dismounted five times a day for prayer, spread his rug on the earth, knelt and bowed toward the south, toward Mecca.

Only once did he broach the subject of the railroad.

"The Rumi intend to build a railroad here?" he asked, using the Ottoman name for Europeans.

"There are some Rumi who would like to do so," Leighton said, after a pause.

Abdul rode in silence.

"Do you approve? Would you like to see a railroad here?" Leighton asked.

Abdul looked at him. "I can take my camels halfway across the earth. There is not so much iron to cover the entire world."

Leighton had no answer for that. He could not argue politics with someone who eschewed abstract thought. He suspected, however, that Abdul underestimated the amount of iron Europe was ready to lay across the globe.

Morrison seemed to enjoy the spectacle of it all.

"I really feel like I'm in the Orient now," he said. "Camels and sheikhs, the whole kit and caboodle."

Leighton, bemused by the use of this Americanism, said nothing.

"We had a World's Fair in Chicago years ago," Morrison said. "I was just a youth but I knew I had to go. It was all about American advances in science and technology, but you know the pavilions that got the most visitors were the ones about the Orient."

He rode for a while. "People can't get over those harems. Dancing girls. Fleshpots."

"No fleshpots here," Leighton observed.

Morrison laughed. "These fleshpots may not exist except in the imagination of American consumers. There's a cigarette, very popular, called Fatima – the billboards show a harem girl with a veil covering her face."

"The Orient means much more than harems," Leighton said patiently. "It's more about the spirit than the flesh."

"Well, the distinction doesn't seem to be drawn so sharply in these parts," Morrison said in a more serious tone.

Leighton thought it a shrewd observation. He reminded himself once again not to underestimate his companion. He nodded in agreement but said nothing more. Elena had changed his view of the Orient, enlarged it. Now, he could readily see now the truth of Morrison's statement.

After five days, they reached the foothills of the mountains and ascended the first of several passes they needed to traverse before reaching the flat land on the other side of the ranges.

They spotted the camp as the trail turned downward from the pass on the afternoon of the sixth day – a large barracks tent pitched up against an escarpment, flanked by two smaller tents. A trestle table sat in front of the big tent, which had two flaps open to the mild afternoon air. Several mules were tethered down the slope and a makeshift pen held a few hens and wild turkeys. A uniformed figure suddenly stood up from behind the table. He hastily shouldered a rifle and walked at a fast pace towards them.

Abdul Latif reined his horse in and moved to one side, motioning the caravan to continue its plodding pace. Leighton rode over to join him, taking in the accouterments of the camp.

"Caravan to Baghdad," Abdul Latif said to the sentry.

The figure, dressed in the khaki of the Ottoman Army, made a show of looking over the parade of mules and camels. He stared openly at Leighton.

"What camp is this?" Abdul Latif demanded.

The man examined him suspiciously. Finally, he muttered, "Survey brigade."

Leighton smiled. A good sign. Engineers were mapping the route of the railroad. So they were on the right road. Leighton turned to the caravan leader and whispered, "Abdul Latif, we need to break soon anyway, and this slope is perfect for us. It may be steeper as we descend. Also, there is water here."

Abdul Latif's lips curled almost imperceptibly. He knew that the Englishman wasn't interested in the brook that paralleled the trail. Also, the trail led in a few miles to green spacious meadows. But it was already late and the site here was acceptable. He nodded in assent and turned to shout the command. Then he addressed the sentry again. "If it please you," he said, purely as a formality, "we will share your site. We will take the upper slope." The escarpment split the gentle hill in two. The upper portion was actually somewhat flatter, a small plateau. For the surveyors' small camp, home to the engineers for many days, if not weeks, the proximity of the lower slope to the brook, visible further down the slope, made it more advantageous.

The caravan teams quickly erected their tents. The vista was grandiose – the peaks of the Taurus range caught fire from the setting sun. The gloom deepened in their encampment and the temperature plummeted. They lit the first fires. Leighton saw two horsemen approach the lower camp from the pass. Moments later, three men, two on horseback and one mounted on a donkey, came up the trail the caravan would descend tomorrow.

Shortly thereafter, two of the men approached the caravan camp from below. They were Europeans. The younger, blond man wore a brown leather jacket and a field hat, buttoned up on one side. The other man, older, dressed in a wool touring suit, appeared to be subordinate to the younger man. He followed a step or two behind the large strides of the blond man, his shoulders slightly hunched in deference.

Abdul Latif and Tarkan, the lead camel driver, rose to greet the visitors. Leighton approached.

"Good evening," said the blond man, with the suggestion of a nod and a glance that included Leighton. "Mueller, Georg. This is my assistant, Thomée."

They completed the introductions.

"We are engineers," Mueller said. "We are surveying for the Baghdad Railway." His gaze, seemingly at random, settled on Leighton as he said this.

"Must be very challenging on this terrain," Leighton said.

"Yes, we must determine the best place to tunnel," Mueller said. "It will be a work for years."

Leighton bit his tongue. Outright questions would only arouse further suspicion about his presence.

"We work, even though our whole project has become uncertain because of the political situation," Mueller said. Again, Mueller's gaze stopped at Leighton. They stood still at the fire in front of Abdul's tent. Abdul Latif himself kept silent, watching the sparring between the two Europeans. Morrison had quietly joined the group.

"Yes, the Young Turks, hard to know what they want," Morrison said. "William Morrison," he said, introducing himself to the two Germans. "Hydroelectricity."

Mueller's eyebrows raised ever so slightly, subtly expressing his skepticism about Morrison's veracity, even as he nodded. A slight roll of his head seemed to make the point that water was in scarce supply in this terrain, but he stopped short of actually making a comment, ironic or otherwise.

"You must be careful of bandits in these mountains," Mueller said instead. "There are large bands, quite fierce."

"And yet you have but a single sentry," Abdul said.

"Ah, but we have nothing to steal," Mueller said with a smile, "except a few mules. These thieves aren't interested in our maps and charts."

"Have you had any reports of attacks?" Abdul Latif asked. "We followed this trail from Baghdad a month ago and saw no bandits."

"You are many, perhaps well-armed," Mueller said. Abdul Latif made no gesture, no comment. "The bandits may be seeking easier prey."

Silence again. Finally Abdul Latif said, "Would you drink some tea with us?" He gestured in the direction of a boy busying himself with a pot at the fire.

"No, thank you," Mueller said. "Our work continues even after dark. We must plot today's findings on our charts. And we depart again at daybreak for more surveys."

The two Germans shook hands again and turned down the slope.

~

The next day was uneventful and they picked their way along the mountain ridge. The early morning fog dissipated quickly and left them under a burning sun. Darkness descended suddenly on them at the end of the day. Abdul Latif wanted to reach the caravansary that he reckoned was only two miles further. They pushed on, a half-moon lighting the path, which had broadened to a wide avenue at this point.

Leighton and Morrison rode as usual at the front of the caravan, a short distance behind the guide. Rock formations jutted up raggedly on their left. On the right, a gentler slope, with isolated boulders.

The first bullet hit Leighton's horse in the neck, severing a vein and spraying a dark cloud of blood. Leighton managed to spring free as the horse fell, so that the animal didn't pin him to the ground. Another bullet whistled past his left shoulder as he drew his gun. Morrison rode his horse between Leighton and the rocks on the left, where the shots seemed to originate. He dismounted quickly with his pistol in hand and motioned to Leighton to take cover behind his dying horse, now bleeding and moaning softly in the path. Behind them, Abdul Latif was drawing the camels into a circle.

Leighton and Morrison fired their pistols in the direction of the rocks ahead. Abdul Latif, still mounted, fired his rifle repeatedly. Several of his men, rifles in hand, spread out on both sides of the path. Broome dismounted with his weapon and dashed forward to join Leighton, firing a round even while hobbling in his uneven gait.

Other bullets thudded into the dirt or slapped against the rocks. Morrison continued to use his horse as a shield, holding the reins firmly in one hand while he fired his pistol with the other. There seemed to be several gunmen attacking them, but they did not leave their positions in the rocks to attempt a frontal assault.

The firing paused briefly, then a fresh volley showered over them. Silence followed. The members of the caravan remained still, alert. Abdul Latif, who had stayed on his horse during the attack, edged his mount forward, rifle held level and ready to shoot.

"They have gone," he announced. Having repulsed the attack, Abdul Latif had no interest in giving pursuit. He trotted back to regroup his camel trains.

Leighton sprang up and looked over at Broome, who had flung himself down near the rump of the prone horse. The Welshman was gamely getting to his feet, apparently unscathed. Leighton, his pistol still in his right hand, gave his valet a salute. Broome nodded curtly in return. Leighton waved to Morrison, who waved back to show he was unhurt. Leighton felt he had been right about the American, who showed true gallantry in this attack.

Leighton then crouched down to examine his unfortunate horse. The beast had expired, a lake of dark blood pooling around his head. Morrison joined him as he rose.

"Bandits?" Morrison asked.

Leighton looked sharply at him. Strange bandits who shoot to kill and depart without any attempt to steal.

"Evidently," Leighton said. The two men exchanged a smile.

The guide was riding back in their direction, still slumped forward in his saddle. He had not been so fortunate. One shoulder was torn and bleeding where a bullet had grazed him. Worse, a second bullet had hit him in the thigh. Abdul's men pulled the wounded man from his saddle and the medic, a Kurd with great understanding of bullet wounds, attended him.

Leighton looked up into the hills, but he could see nothing in the dim moonlight.

"Why do you think they stopped?" he asked Morrison.

The American shrugged. "Too much resistance?"

Leighton mounted an unattended horse and started up the incline. Morrison followed, making a sign to Ali that they were investigating the hills.

"Has it crossed your mind that they could still be there?" he asked Leighton.

Leighton didn't reply, but he proceeded slowly and kept a watch for any activity.

"Do you think we hit any of them?" he asked Morrison.

"I kept my eyes closed while I shot," Morrison joked.

They coaxed their horses up the rocky path. Morrison kept his pistol drawn while Leighton leaned over, looking for tracks or traces of blood.

They came around one boulder and stopped abruptly when they saw a dark figure huddled there. It appeared lifeless. Leighton dismounted slowly and drew his pistol as he approached the figure cautiously.

"It might be a ruse," Morrison warned.

The figure was dressed in a dark caftan made of coarse material. His face was not visible and appeared to be turned toward the rock. No rifle or gun was in sight.

Leighton neared the figure and touched it gently with his boot. There was no reaction. With pistol cocked he moved around and gave the form a firmer kick. Morrison kept his pistol leveled at the lifeless figure. Finally, Leighton reached over and pulled at a shoulder to turn the figure over. A dark-complexioned face with a black beard gazed at them with sightless eyes. No marks were visible.

Leighton holstered his pistol and knelt to examine the

corpse more closely. Morrison dismounted and joined him, keeping an eye on the surrounding rocks.

Leighton stretched out the body and probed the front for wounds. Finding none, he turned the body over, and saw now that the cloak was wet. Leighton pulled aside the cloak and uncovered a dark patch in the caftan.

"He was shot in the back," Leighton said, looking at Morrison.

The American looked around at possible lines of fire. Rocks and boulders cascaded down the hill, creating a jagged and irregular landscape that afforded ample cover to a marksman.

"Hell, the shot could have come from a dozen places," he said.

Leighton left the big question hanging between them – who would have fired a shot at their attackers from behind them?

"You remember I told you about my mysterious saviors in that attack in the alley?" Leighton said. "It seems they have followed me here."

Leighton examined the face of the dead man.

"Hard to say whether he is a local tribesman or a hired assassin," he said.

"Richard, is there any reason someone would want to assassinate you? The first shot hit your horse," Morrison said.

"Perhaps someone is hostile to British interests and considers me a target," Leighton ventured. "Or perhaps it was just outlaws who chanced to shoot at me first. I'm more perplexed by the attackers of our attackers."

"It would be quite a coincidence if you stumbled a second time into a random skirmish between hostile parties, I agree," Morrison said, looking at Leighton. "Why do I feel you're not telling me everything?"

Leighton smiled at his comrade, but said nothing.

"We have an expression at home," Morrison said. "'Ask me no questions and I'll tell you no lies.' I withdraw my question."

They clambered over the rocks and found the ground torn up by the movement of men and horses. There were numerous spent bullet casings. One rock bore the brown speckles of dried blood.

"Where did they go, I wonder," Morrison said. "We seem to be using the only serviceable passage through these mountains."

"If they are local, they can make their way through these rocks without a path," Leighton said.

"That means they could visit us again at any time," Morrison said.

Leighton only nodded in response. He suspected who his attackers might be. He could not fathom who his mysterious allies were.

A scrape on a stone behind them made both men spin around with pistols ready. It was one of Abdul Latif's boys, who gestured for them to return to the caravan. They returned to their horses, leaving the body where they found it, and followed the boy back to the camel train.

~

Verdammt, Ernst thought. The assailants had escaped and Ernst had no clue who they were or why they fired upon his band. Was it possible they had followed them? Were they brigands or something else? Ernst thought again of Sturm – could these villains be the same who murdered him? Had the British taken measures to protect their precious lord after all?

They had lost Mahmoud. The rest of them, six in all, had escaped, unscathed except for a bullet that grazed the hand of one of his men. They had not waited for Ernst's order to disperse after the surprise attack.

Ernst had met up with the band two days earlier, after riding ahead of the caravan across the steppe. The men, a ragged pack of outcasts from local tribes, were in the pay of the engineering team, to protect them from bandits. They agreed with alacrity to his offer of gold for an extra service. It would not be the first time they had preyed on a caravan.

The resistance put up by the caravan surprised Ernst. But the mission would have succeeded had their assailants not appeared. Ernst cursed again. The mercenaries would expect their gold in spite of their failure to accomplish their goal. And now he must arrange yet another ambush against the English meddler, who seemed to lead a charmed life. He would attempt nothing now before the Cilician Gates, Ernst decided. The caravan party would be on its guard. Ernst knew how to await his moment.

Chapter Fifteen

The cold gripped them again as they ascended the mountains. The night brought a pervading chill, fueled by icy blasts that seemed to come directly from Russia. A rest day in the Cilician plain had brought some respite and lulled them into a sense of well-being that the mountains just as quickly dashed. In the plain, the air held the silky promise of summer. The peasants, dressed in their baggy pants and leather caps, planted crops in the fields, lighting torches to prolong the day. In untilled fields, they saw flocks of mohair goats, tended by boys in white sheepskin coats and yellow dogs.

The rest day was necessary after the passage through the Cilician Gate. The beasts had to proceed single file along the narrow ridge, masses of rock jutting above them on each side. The camels and mules kept their footing easily enough, though they required insistent coaxing to keep moving along the path. The wagons had more trouble, catching a wheel in a crevice or ditch, skirting the fragile edge of the path at a dangerous pitch, they required as much pushing as pulling through the narrow pass.

Descending to the plain, the caravan had skirted the towns and camped an extra day outside Adana. Morrison came to the camp late. He had ridden into Tarsus, curious to see the home of St. Paul.

"Hard to see it as the home of a Christian, let alone one of the apostles," the American engineer told Leighton that night. "Mosques everywhere, and that keening call at prayer time. Some American missionaries have a small post in town, but there's no Christian churches. It's like anywhere else in the Orient."

Leighton only smiled. He was writing a dispatch to Grey. He told Morrison it was a letter to one of the scholars at the British Library about his progress on the translation. Under the pretext of posting the letter, Leighton rode into Adana the next day. He went, however, to the British consul, a scholar who had elected to end his days in what remained for him the Hellenistic world of St. Paul. The old man would send the dispatch in a diplomatic pouch when the steamer called at Mersin. The embassy in Constantinople would cable it to London.

Leighton wrote Grey about the survey brigade they had met in the mountains. He also recorded some rumors floating around the caravan camps outside Adana. One of Abdul Latif's men had heard talk of a large camp, miles off the caravan route. The scholar in Leighton did not like passing on such hazy information, but Grey had drummed it into him that any intelligence, even wrong intelligence, could help them.

"But won't it lead you astray?" Leighton had objected.

"Intelligence doesn't lead us anywhere," Grey countered. "It just gives us a picture. Vague information gives us a blurry picture, good information gives us a clearer picture. But," he added, "a blurry picture is better than no picture."

A disturbing incident took place in the camp while Leighton was in Adana. Broome returned to their tent after attending to some laundry and found a Bedouin rifling through Leighton's trunk. Broome, who was unarmed, accosted the intruder. The man, cloaked and hooded, lunged at the valet, whacking him on the head with the hilt of a long curved dagger. Broome's attempt to grab hold of the interloper failed as he crumpled to the ground. He was unconscious only a moment, but when he recovered and charged out of the tent, the Bedouin had disappeared.

Broome was certain the man did not belong to the caravan. They were camped in a large plain outside the city, surrounded by other caravans from east and west and open to any passerby.

"He could just as well have ripped open my gut," Broome told Leighton later as he described the dagger.

Leighton missed nothing from his trunk. Perhaps it was a thief disappointed in not finding anything of value, he thought. But why invade his tent, when those of Ali and the other merchants were likelier to have money or precious objects?

Morrison returned at dusk. He said he had ridden along the river and stopped to fish, though he caught nothing. He quickly determined that his own meager possessions were intact.

Leighton went with Broome to report the incident to Abdul Latif. The caravan leader questioned Broome closely about the stranger's dress and the valet gave what details he could. Abdul Latif said nothing, but Leighton was sure he would not let the matter rest. Bedouins detested thieves and dealt with them severely. Leighton expected Abdul Latif would question his own men and also speak to the caravan leaders camped near them.

Morrison waited until dinner to bring up the matter.

"I'm beginning to think you're a dangerous traveling companion," he said to Leighton in his half-playful, half-serious way. "Guns in the mountains, daggers on the plain..."

"Abdul Latif will find out if there are other reports of thieves at work," Leighton said.

Morrison rolled his eyes to express his skepticism. "More thieves who don't steal anything."

Leighton held his tongue. He was tempted to tell Morrison about his mission, but decided to wait. He felt he could trust the American, and it seemed unlikely he could keep the secret from him much longer. But he would wait for the right moment to confide in him.

~

The caravan departed from Adana without any further word of the mysterious thief. The windy cold of the mountains discouraged conversation during the long days of tramping through ravines that forced them again to proceed single file and steep inclines that the camels could climb only in slow, plodding steps.

At night, though, sitting at the fire in front of their tent, Leighton and Morrison deepened their acquaintance. Leighton told the American about his lost father and his grandfather's role as surrogate. Morrison said his father was an insurance broker in Hartford, so that he had benefited from a serene childhood, growing up in a large house with a white picket fence. It was his reading – the Leatherstocking Tales of James Fenimore Cooper and Melville's stories of the sea – that had fired his desire for adventure. Leighton wondered as Morrison spoke how a short stint with the Rough Riders could have slaked that desire. Even though the engineer tried to inject some drama into his work at Niagara Falls, Leighton suspected that someone who rode up San Juan Hill had a hankering for action that building power plants was not likely to satisfy.

Morrison was discreet about his personal life. Aside from saying he had not yet contemplated marriage, the American offered no details of romance or women he had known. Leighton himself had no truck with the bawdy humor and randy tales of the barracks, and was circumspect about his own social life. He welcomed Morrison's reserve and did not probe.

Morrison did, however, bring up Elena once, referring to her as Leighton's "lady friend from the German party."

"She is truly a beautiful lady," Morrison said. "She appeared to have real stature," a quality that Leighton surmised ranked high in Morrison's estimation.

Leighton had shared the details of his love affair with no one. He simply nodded in agreement.

"Stature she has," Leighton said. "How else attract a husband of Talaat's caliber?"

Morrison did not push the matter further.

~

Evenings, Leighton and Morrison used the waning sunshine for fencing lessons. Morrison had had only rudimentary instruction in the use of a saber during the Rough Rider training in San Antonio. Leighton was a practiced swordsman. His grandfather had trained him and the two had sparred almost daily when Leighton was at home. His skill became deadly serious in South Africa, where his saber had saved his life in two battles.

In their evening skirmishes, Leighton used his service saber and Morrison borrowed a scimitar from Abdul Latif. It was a fine piece of steel that the Bedouin kept sharp.

The two of them clanged away in front of their tent, sometimes drawing an audience of camel boys who sniggered at their antics.

"Die, infidel!" Morrison cried as he thrust the curved blade at Leighton during one of their sessions. Leighton easily parried the blow, catching the scimitar in an envelopment and disarming his attacker.

"Careful who you call an infidel," he said, breathing hard.

Morrison just slumped to the ground. "Your faith is stronger, effendi," he said, with only a hint of a smile.

Leighton grinned. "I think the occasion calls for some whiskey," he said. "Don't think that bloody tea will do it."

Morrison gave him a thumbs up. The coarse caravan tea was the only beverage in plentiful supply on the trip.

Leighton fetched the bottle from his tent, and poured them a couple of jiggers in small, round teacups.

"Cheers," Leighton said, raising his glass.

They sipped the Scotch in a companionable silence.

"Bill," Leighton said at length. Morrison raised his eyebrows at the unaccustomed use of his nickname. "I think it's only fair to make a clean breast of my situation with you. I know you have questions and I haven't been completely frank."

Leighton paused. Morrison sipped his whiskey.

"The Foreign Office has asked me to do some...scouting for them," Leighton said. "I am truly working on some Koran translations, but that is not the real purpose of my journey."

Morrison nodded, his lips pursed.

"I'm mentioning it now because I've observed your great sense of discretion," Leighton continued. "And it's obvious that my real mission has placed us all in some added jeopardy. I apologize for that, though there is really nothing I can do to better the situation for now."

He stopped, and sipped his drink.

Morrison spoke after some time.

"Well, partner, I have to confess that I haven't been totally honest with you, either." He smiled. "I really am an engineer, but I'm here on assignment from the United States government."

Leighton met his eyes. He broke into a grin. "Ha, we're both spies!"

"Be careful who you're calling a spy," Morrison said, looking around him to make sure that no one was in earshot. "The Turks hang spies." His grin belied his caution, however.

"The railway?" Morrison asked. He didn't wait for Leighton to reply. "I know it's a thorny issue in Europe. All you imperialists jockeying for the best positions in world commerce."

Leighton shrugged. "It is unfortunate that history pushes us to such rivalries," he said.

"History, yes," Morrison said. "And ambition. And greed." He stopped to think. "I'm not saying our own government is free of those motives. And I believe destiny plays as big a role as history. My country has grown too big to ignore what's happening in the rest of the world."

"I can't argue with that," Leighton said. "My hope is that our common heritage will keep us allies."

"A-men to that, brother," said Morrison, his grin returning. He reached up his cup in a mock toast. "So who is after you?"

"The Germans, probably. The Turks, maybe. Who knows?"

"And what is their objective?"

Leighton shrugged, and looked away, a troubled expression on his face. "Unfortunately, they seem determined to block my mission by whatever means necessary."

"And you think the Germans – or the Turks for that matter – would risk openly attacking a British lord?"

"Well, it's not exactly openly."

"Yes. Still, it seems awfully risky." Morrison rubbed his chin. "Don't you have the impression there's some other parties involved?" he asked.

"My rescuers? Yes, that's puzzling. I'm certain it isn't any government protection. But it's hard to know who's on my side without knowing for sure who's attacking me."

"Well, what about the railway? Don't you think it's a good thing for this part of the world? Help lift them out of this poverty?"

Leighton pondered the question for a moment. "If it were that simple, the answer would be obvious. But there's the position of the Ottoman Empire, its role in Great Power politics, even its treatment of its own subjects, to consider."

"Great Power politics. Whose interests do they serve?"

"For better or worse, it's the time we live in, my friend. Your U.S. government is not so immune to it or you wouldn't be here. Or are you going to tell me that you're here because Roosevelt is worried about poverty in Anatolia?"

"Teddy might surprise you. But, no, he worries about the balance of power as well." Morrison laughed. "We're a pair! Sitting here in the Taurus mountains, two helpless white men, deciding the fate of the world and the balance of power." He knocked back the last of his whiskey. "Bedtime, for me at least. Your secret is safe with me, though I'm not so sure that Abdul Latif doesn't have some suspicions of his own about your real role."

"Abdul Latif is a clever man and I presume that he presumes that all Europeans are spies," Leighton said, laughing.

~

The desert stretched in front of them, not sand, but hard red earth with outcroppings of flint along its low ridges. The line of the horizon blurred in the afternoon sun. It seemed to separate, a parallel line wavering in the sun's haze. This upper line slowly formed small bubbles. As their own mounts plodded steadily toward the horizon, camels and riders took shape in the shimmering line and another caravan, much larger than theirs, emerged from the desert. The camel lines were more than two dozen abreast.

The two caravans passed each other at some distance. Abdul Latif sent one of his drivers to confer about conditions along the route. He instructed his driver to warn the other caravan of the band they had encountered in the mountains.

Leighton watched the other caravan come and go. It disappeared, as it had appeared, in the shimmering horizon, a mirage in the desert heat. Leighton looked across the steppe, bounded on all sides by blurs that could obscure other caravans, other mirages – marauding Bedouin tribes, or armies from the Kaiser and the sultan. The entire region was like a grand mirage in the eyes of the West, colored more by its own ambition and fears than by a clear view of this arid land – a land between two continents, empty but for sand and palms, a hardy people, and now, it seemed, a petroleum bounty prized by modern technology. What would happen as the West – with its iron rails, oil-fired engines, and Maxim guns – reached out to grasp this grand mirage?

~

Now they traveled at night, the length of their trek determined by the distance to the next caravansary or oasis. The desert sun made days a blazing hell that prevented travel and made them seek shelter to rest. The nights came as a velvet cloak of relief from the light and the heat of the day. Men and beasts alike revived in the silver darkness of a desert night, lit by the stars and the waning moon.

At dawn after the first night on the desert they approached a caravansary, a mud-brick structure with shelter for sleeping and a large enclosure formed by shoulder-high walls. A dry wind from the expanse of desert to the south sprang up, carrying gritty sand that stung exposed skin. The wind gathered force, bringing clouds of sand and dust that obscured the rising sun.

They moved the camel trains quickly into the enclosure and the men retreated into the hostel to wait out the storm. The camels sat in the enclosure, legs tucked underneath, bleating occasionally as the wind flogged them with sand and dirt. The low walls impeded the storm's assault but did not block it from the open area. The keening of the wind discouraged conversation in the hostel.

The storm blew itself out after half an hour, a wave of the lashing wind that rolls over the desert, scourging it, keeping it pure. Leighton and Morrison unrolled their sleeping mats after Broome unloaded their mule. After devouring a bowl of the grain mush cooked for their meal, saying little, they lay down to sleep through the heat of the day.

Leighton awoke in the late afternoon. He rose quietly, donned his boots, and walked slowly through the rows of camels to the open gate. He went to a grove of tamarinds at the edge of the wall. The trees rose in sinewy columns, like so many ropes turned to stone. Their blossoms wafted a peppery fragrance through the hot, dry air.

"You love it, don't you?" said Morrison. The American had come up behind him.

Leighton smiled without turning. "It mesmerizes me, I'll admit," he said. "Love? No, I don't think so."

Morrison just grunted. Lovers sometimes were the last to know, he reflected.

"And you?" Leighton asked.

"Remember me, the hydraulic engineer?" Morrison laughed. "The desert is a nice place to visit – in some respects – but I wouldn't want to live here."

The two men stood in the shade of the grove. The sun still blazed above the horizon.

Live here? Leighton thought to himself. A life where shade is the greatest creature comfort? Perhaps, if one was born to it.

"Abdul Latif wants to leave at sunset," Morrison said.

Leighton turned his back to the sun, looking at the vast empty stretch to the east. "The journey seems endless," he said.

"Yes," Morrison agreed. "It's an act of faith that we're actually going somewhere."

Somewhere, yes, Leighton thought. Away from this nowhere in the middle of the desert. To Baghdad. The railway would reduce this wasteland to a curiosity, a passing phenomenon, as the iron horse pulled its passengers and freight to the muddy lands of Mesopotamia, the land between two rivers, the cradle of civilization. Perhaps nature had shielded that land with a desert for a reason, Leighton mused. Man should hesitate before removing that defense.

Leighton and Morrison turned again toward the sun, which now was descending rapidly below the horizon, disappearing in a parting gash of red.

The two men walked slowly back through the gate. As they entered, a band of half a dozen strange Bedouin mounted on camels swept by into the desert to begin their trek in the night. They headed south.

Abdul Latif nodded to the two Westerners.

"Those men had an interesting tale," he said. "They said they have seen a camp of ghosts in the desert."

"A camp of ghosts?" Leighton asked, wondering what had conjured up such fanciful imagery. "A mirage?"

"No, they saw it by moonlight. A large camp, many tents, filled with the dead."

Leighton became more alert.

"A European camp?" he asked.

"No, Turks, Kurds perhaps," said Abdul Latif.

"Dead?"

"Butchered."

"Where was this?"

Abdul Latif gestured east northeast.

Leighton looked at Morrison. The American shrugged.

"This camp, were they building something?" Leighton asked Abdul Latif.

It was the Arab's turn to shrug. "It is in the desert," he said. "There was, however, much wood, the Bedouin said, though the camp was days from any forest."

Leighton was now certain that the camp was a construction site for the railway. What had happened? he wondered. Who had butchered the workers? Were the Germans involved?

Abdul Latif left them to organize the caravan's departure.

"You're thinking it has to do with the Baghdad Railway," Morrison said.

Leighton nodded.

"You want to go look for it, right?"

Leighton nodded. Morrison laughed.

"And I'm betting you don't want to set out into the desert all by yourself."

Leighton shook his head, a wan smile on his lips.

"Doesn't take a mind reader to figure out your plan, but you have to ask."

"I have no right...," Leighton began.

Morrison attempted a glare.

"Would you be willing to accompany me, and Broome, to look for this ghost camp?" Leighton asked.

Morrison laughed again. "Wouldn't miss it," he said, and slapped Leighton on the back.

~

At the wadi a day behind the caravan, another group mounted their horses to continue along the caravan route. Ernst and his men rode in silence. The German had learned patience. He had learned to wait in the wastelands of Namibia, and to track through the peaks of the Atlas. He was a hunter who enjoyed the stalk as much as the kill, because the kill would come if the stalk was successful.

In Leighton's case, though, the interrogation would precede the kill. The Englishman had thwarted his stalker with the dispatch from Adana. Ernst had weighed an attempt to intercept the dispatch. But Hoffenberg had been precise about avoiding any overt action.

No matter, Ernst thought. He had time before the caravan reached Baghdad. The Englishman had seen little. What could his dispatch contain? Ernst smiled to himself. Ah well, I'll know soon enough.

~

It was late when he came home, nearly midnight. Lamps were left burning for him – the house, a surprisingly modest wooden structure on a quiet street, had no electricity. An old servant greeted him at the door, taking his fez and overcoat. Talaat Bey waved away offers of food. Work made him forget hunger. He walked briskly through the dark house, climbing the polished staircase quickly. The raki had curbed his appetite as well and made him feel buoyant as he ascended the steps. He paused at the top of the stairs. A sudden lust seized him and instead of turning to his own room he went directly to Elena's door. There he paused again. She was certainly asleep. It was not his habit to ravish his own wife. Yet, he reflected, she was his wife and he had seen too little of her in recent days.

He rapped on the door but did not wait for a response. The musky odor of her scent wafted over him as he entered the room. Elena stirred under the eiderdown comforter. He knew she slept in the nude and it aroused him further.

"Sire?" Elena asked.

Talaat grunted.

Elena sat up in bed, holding the comforter to her.

"Is there a problem?" she asked.

"No problem," he said. "I am weary, yet aroused. I need some respite from the demands of desire."

Elena gazed at him in the dimness of a small lamp she kept alight during the night.

"I am your servant," she said, with only the slightest irony in her tone, letting the comforter fall, baring her breasts. She began to caress her nipples.

Talaat grunted again and smiled. Ah, this Christian bitch, he sighed. What wonders she commands when she plays the temptress. He disrobed quickly as she threw aside her covering and stretched out on the bed, spreading her legs.

"Wider, spread your legs wider," he demanded as he thrust himself into her without a single caress. She obeyed and shut her eyes.

~

"This Englishman," Talaat said as they shared a cigarette afterwards.

Elena said nothing. Talaat was too clever for her to pretend she did not know which Englishman he meant.

"You know him well?"

"He was a friend of my father, a scholar who knows our languages, our literature."

Talaat looked at her, an eyebrow arched in question.

"I read him my poetry once. He acted as though it pleased him."

"So it was your poetry you shared," Talaat said, making it neither a statement nor a question.

Elena remained silent.

"I've heard so little of your poetry lately," he said.

"It's true, the muse has not smiled on me recently," she said, that hint of irony creeping into her voice again.

She reached under the comforter for his penis, which swelled at her touch, growing stiff. Talaat rolled over on top of her, sliding into her as she enveloped him in her fragrant arms.

~

Talaat had a report on the Englishman. The sultan's spies had kept records on all foreigners. Detailed records, it turned out, with names and dates. Hotel clerks served well as spies and Leighton's trysts with Elena at the Hotel Istanbul had been duly reported and filed away in the vast archives of the palace.

It did not bother him that Elena had been Leighton's lover. It did not bother him that she did not acknowledge it – even a Christian has some modesty. The meeting at the café did not bother him either, because he knew about it. What bothered him was wondering if there was something that he did not know about.

Elena now lived a carefully circumscribed life. She attended her church, visited her father, shopped in the European boutiques. She worked to make herself beautiful and desirable for him – and how she succeeded!

Talaat was not a believer. He belonged to a dervish sect, the Bektashi, but only as a political expediency. His religion was power, and the Bektashi were the largest sect in the Young Turkey movement, giving Talaat a solid base within the C.U.P. For the same reason, Talaat was a Freemason. He prized secrecy and was an early organizer for the movement, building an organization in Salonika that would help form the core of the C.U.P. when it came to power. Above all, Talaat was Turkish, more so in his mind because his patrimony was clouded. Family gossip had it that his mother's father, a mysterious person who died before she was born, was in fact a gypsy. Talaat had always closed his ears to this talk.

His political goal was for Turks to regain the strength and prominence they had enjoyed in earlier centuries. The pitiful Ottoman Empire embraced too many non-Turks – Jews, Armenians, Arabs, Kurds. And far too many Turks lived under the yoke of the Tsar in Central Asia. The Young Turks envisaged a revitalized Turkish empire stretching across the steppes. Enver and Djemal, who with him made up the central leadership of the C.U.P., had convinced him for that reason they were better off siding with the Triple Alliance powers in Europe – Germany, Austria-Hungary, and Italy – and against the Triple Entente powers – Britain, France and Russia. Victory in the coming European war would enable them to carve out a new Turkic domain from the Russian empire.

So for Talaat it was irrelevant that Elena was Armenian – it was sufficient that she was beautiful and desirable. The Armenian people were not Turkish, not even Muslim, and they had no place in the new empire he and his companions were building. But there was room enough for this Armenian beauty in his bed and on his arm. As for her father, he was an old man and was unlikely to survive the coming turbulence. The beautiful Elena would never see her lover again. Her future lay within the small world of her new life.

Talaat closed the dossier on Leighton. Hoffenberg had promised action against the Englishman and the Germans kept their word.

Chapter Sixteen

The three of them set out at dusk. The sky was clear and a half-moon loomed above the horizon. Leighton got his bearings from the stars that emerged dimly from the deepening blue of the sky. They struck a northeasterly route.

There was little conversation. All three of them were daunted by the risk of this expedition. Leighton, especially, worried that he was putting Broome and Morrison in harm's way in addition to risking his own life. And yet he could hardly forgo investigating the strange report from the Arabs. Nor could he make such a foray on his own.

Abdul Latif had generously procured a faster horse for Broome, in case speed became an urgent matter. But the three men knew there was little hope of outrunning danger the length of the plain. The terrain, midway between steppe and desert, offered no shelter or refuge. They would be at the mercy of any large band of assailants. All this hazard to chase down a mirage, a mere wisp of rumor.

"Why would the Germans start building a railroad in the middle of nowhere?" Morrison asked Leighton as they set out from the caravansary.

"What better way to remain unobserved?" countered Leighton. "It would remain only to connect the secluded track to more populous areas and the railroad would be a fait accompli before any Power could intervene."

"What a project!" Morrison exclaimed. "Building the pyramids may have been easier. There at least you could transport your materials by river barge."

"It must have been much the same building your transcontinental railroad in the United States," Leighton said.

"True enough," Morrison said. "The golden spike itself was driven in somewhere in the Utah desert, I believe."

"Golden spike," Leighton repeated. "You Americans, always putting on a show."

The moon was luminous now. The air, neither cool nor moist at night, nonetheless was sweet to the travelers after the sting of the hot daytime sky. Even so, they kept their horses to a comfortable walk. The stubbles of vegetation clinging to the rock, a sage color in the sunlight, appeared as dark gray blotches in the moon's glow. The flat terrain stretching in front of them was shades of gray – dark shadows showing what little contour there was, a whitish gray where stone reflected the feeble light.

Some time later, however, Leighton saw some shadows on the ground. The moon was sinking but shed enough light to reveal dark lumps ahead of them. By the time they reached the figures, Leighton knew what he expected to see. The partially decomposed bodies of three Europeans and their mounts lay there. Three human corpses were stretched out, arms and legs akimbo, in a shelter furnished by a circle of the three horses.

The horse cadavers had been stripped of all equipment. Their necks were slit. The men had delayed death by drinking the blood of the horses. There were no signs of foul play. Leighton and Morrison, covering their lower faces with kerchiefs, knelt over the corpses. Morrison held a flashlight while Leighton used his riding crop to lift up the front of one dead man's jacket. The label of a Berlin haberdasher was sewn into the lining.

Broome brought over a cylindrical leather case, which turned out to be empty.

"Clearly a map case," Leighton said, fighting an urge to whisper in the presence of the corpses.

"Were they lost, in spite of the maps?" Morrison asked. Desert routes, known to countless generations of travelers, bridged enough springs that a well-equipped traveler would not risk dying of thirst.

"Perhaps they strayed off the route purposely," Leighton said. "They may have feared an encounter."

The band they had met at the caravansary or other passersby had taken anything of value – compass, weapons, blankets. Leighton wondered that the jacket was still on its owner but realized that the thought of wearing Western clothes from a cadaver would not appeal to a desert Arab.

Further search produced no documents or any form of identification. Nonetheless, Leighton concluded from the clothing and the build of the men that they probably were German engineers.

The first glimmer of dawn appeared in the east. Leighton looked at Morrison and without a word they remounted to continue their trek in that direction. Leighton checked his own canteen. He kept consumption to a minimum. Abdul Latif had sketched a primitive map of springs and oases along the route they had planned.

In the early light, they found the tracks of the men and horses. The three men set out across the steppe, falling into a silence that they were somehow loath to break. The tracks ran true, due east. A compass had surely guided the Germans. They reached a well and put up a primitive fly tent against the sun, stretching a square tarp over high supports on two opposite corners and low on the other two.

After a fitful nap, the men set out again at dusk. The tracks had disappeared and they could only keep to the course due east. It was midnight when they reached the camp. They already knew what they would find there. The air was curiously pure. The desert air had removed all traces of putrefaction and the corpses were already badly decomposed.

Leighton went from tent to tent without a word, counting the corpses. The shapes hardly resembled anything human – black, twisted in their nightshirts and robes. Yet, they had been living, breathing, sweating human beings, with lives and families and homes somewhere. Casualties in a shadow war, they lay in uncomprehending silence as they quietly returned to dust.

Leighton's mind ground to a halt. He could not grasp the sense of this slaughter. Madness seized men in tribal or ethnic warfare – the Turks and the Armenians, the Boers and the Hottentots. But this – this was calculated murder, for a political end; cold-blooded, dispassionate, measured. Leighton bent over after he made his rounds, resting his hands on his knees as he took long breaths, calming the rush of blood in his ears, quelling the nausea rising in his gut. He straightened, wiped his mouth, and looked around him.

The rail ties were still neatly stacked along the roadbed. The animal pen, a crude structure of poles and chicken wire, held further cadavers – poultry and a few sheep. The camel tethers were empty. The beasts had chewed through the rawhide and taken their own chances in the arid landscape.

Morrison and Broome had retreated from the camp when they saw the butchery, leaving the inspection to Leighton. After a time, as the other two waited outside the camp, Leighton shook off his black mood and went to look at the tent the Germans had used. He brought several rolls back with him.

"Survey maps," he said. "This was certainly a construction camp for the railroad."

Morrison savored some of the cool water they had

pumped from the camp's well. Broome busied himself with building a fire.

"Who did this?" Morrison said.

Leighton looked around at the camp. "Nothing was taken," he said. "The wind has removed whatever traces the attackers left."

Leighton and Morrison did not discuss the obvious question. How many men had been involved if they were able to slay so many with such efficiency, without raising an alarm?

"Bedouin," Morrison said.

Leighton shook his head slowly. "Nomads don't kill," he said. The massacre was a brutal act of war, not the work of shepherds. "Arabs, perhaps," because, he thought, it could not be Turks or Kurds or Germans. "Not a Bedouin tribe, however."

"Arabs?" Morrison asked. "Which Arabs?"

Arabs. A people defined by a language, a religion, a desert. Tribes. Mosques. Veils.

"A good question," Leighton responded. "There is talk of brotherhoods committed to restoring Arab independence."

"What can spears do against a Maxim gun?" asked Morrison.

"Well," said Leighton, "who would have said that daggers can stop a railroad?"

Morrison grunted. "You don't think a few Kurdish corpses will stop the Kaiser from building his railroad, do you? All great projects have human bones at their foundation."

Stop the Kaiser, no, thought Leighton. Slow him down, perhaps.

~

They spent the day at the camp, dozing in the Germans' tent, studying the survey maps. It was only the maps for this stretch of the railroad, a pencil line drawn straight across the desert.

Leighton found other papers and had sufficient German to decipher references to the quarry and the expected rail shipments.

Did the Germans even know of this disaster? Would the rail caravan arrive and return with the rails, or just return with the news that a new crew was needed? And new engineers? Who would work here once word spread of the slaughter?

Leighton followed the completed roadbed for a few miles before the heat forced him to return. Such slow, painful work in this hot and arid environment, Leighton mused, so far from any civilization.

The three men waited out the heat of the day in the shelter of the Germans' tent. At nightfall, they would set out south and try to intercept Abdul Latif and the caravan. They resolved to sleep until then. Broome volunteered to keep watch. However unlikely it was that anyone would approach them during the hottest part of the day, it would be foolish to tempt fate while staying in the camp of ghosts.

The attackers were upon them before they could react. Leighton had just dozed off when he heard a muffled shout from Broome. He had scarcely opened his eyes when a blur of cloth covered him, stifling his own yell. Strong hands pinned his arms and legs while he was quickly tied. The blanket or tarp suffocated Leighton as he felt several pairs of hands lift him and throw him like a sack of grain across a saddle. He heard some grunts and then two shots. He struggled against his bonds but they were too tight. He tried to wriggle off the horse but found he had been strapped onto the mount.

The horse began to gallop in company with a sizable group. The pain was excruciating and Leighton gasped for air. He listened for any familiar voice, hoping to hear a sign of life from Morrison or Broome. He attempted to call out their names, but only a raspy sound came out as he choked for air.

The horses thundered around him, moving fast. The cloth over his head prevented air from getting to him, and the jostling against his ribs knocked out what little air managed to reach his lungs. He realized it was futile to struggle and useless to worry about Broome and Morrison. Perhaps they were similarly bound and strapped to horses.

Who were his captors? The same attackers who had slaughtered the Kurdish workers in the camp? Or the same attackers from the pass in the Taurus mountains? Where were his rescuers? Would they rescue him again? At least his captors seemed to want him alive, though Leighton was uncertain how long he could survive the beating he was taking in his present state.

Leighton listened for any exchanges between his captors, but the pounding hooves of the horses – it must be more than a dozen, Leighton reckoned – drowned out any other sound. At some point, he must have lost consciousness; when he awoke he still could not make out the speech of his captors. It seemed a mixture of Turkish and Arabic, but in dialects he didn't know.

The covering over his head kept him from using his other senses. The air seemed cooler and Leighton suspected they had stopped at a wadi. He realized he was thirsty. Gradually he became aware of the full extent of his discomfort. He ached. The riding had bruised his rib cage. Every muscle ached from the relentless jouncing he had experienced strapped to the horse's back.

No one paid him any attention. Whether he slept or listened, ached or thirsted, seemed to interest no one. He made no attempt to call out. He preferred that they ignore him. They had not killed him; they were taking him somewhere for some reason. Leighton worried about Morrison and Broome. He had led them into the wilderness, away from the safety of the caravan. If anything had befallen them, he would be responsible. Their only mistake was to listen to him. For himself, he wasn't worried. He had agreed to his mission and was soldier enough to know what the consequences could be.

The respite was brief. Leighton heard the rustle of men mounting their horses, the clanking of stirrups and sabers, and clacking of rifle butts. Some armed band, for its own purposes or those of a paymaster, had tracked him down to the ghost camp and was now spiriting him away across the desert to an uncertain fate. It must have to do with the railroad. So it must be the Germans, or their allies, or their mercenaries. None of it boded well for his surviving the ordeal, Leighton acknowledged to himself.

His discoveries would be vital to Grey, Leighton knew. It made sense for his adversaries to intercept him. He realized with a sinking feeling that they would want to know what he had communicated to Grey – information he would not willingly give over. Leighton had never been captured in war, never interrogated, never tortured. He had borne discomfort, pain even, in the course of his military service and his travels. But he had never had to test his mettle against any effort to force information out of him.

The pounding and jouncing had resumed, as the silent band proceeded on their way. Leighton put his worries and his pain out of his mind, and soon slept again, bound and strapped onto the saddle of an unseen horse headed for an unknown destination.

Chapter Seventeen

Von Bohlen was worried. Von Gwinner had not responded to his last two letters regarding the railway. Deutsche Bank had too much already invested in the project for von Gwinner to ignore it. His silence could only mean that von Gwinner was dealing directly with the Porte, or through the ambassador.

The German stopped pacing in his office. He went in to the hallway, headed for the washroom. He saw no one. The embassy was quiet; it was nearly five o' clock. He actually had no use for the washroom, but paced in there for a few minutes, washed his hands and went back to the hallway. He heard voices in the stairwell, but the sound was too muffled for him to recognize them. Perhaps it was Bieberstein – the intonation sounded German.

Von Bohlen was in the east wing of the embassy, his office around the corner from the central staircase. He walked to the corner. If the voices were headed to Bieberstein's office, they would go in the other direction from the stairs. Von Bohlen felt slightly ridiculous as he paused at the corner, his hand resting on the wainscoting. What would he say if he encountered someone? Who should he encounter, though?

The voices were speaking German. Von Bohlen identified Bieberstein and Hoffenberg. A third voice spoke German with a Turkish accent. It sounded familiar to von Bohlen. He recognized the voice when it spoke of Baghdad:

It was Talaat. Von Bohlen usually spoke to Talaat in Turkish, though he knew the interior minister spoke German. What was Talaat doing in the embassy? Usually he expected supplicants to come to him in the ministry. From the snatches of conversation von Bohlen could hear, they were talking about the Baghdad Railway. Why wasn't he invited to this mysterious discussion, after office hours, in the embassy?

Von Bohlen risked peering around the corner. He saw the three men going down the hall, Talaat's burly form with its dark bullet-shaped head between the two Germans. The sight mesmerized von Bohlen and he barely pulled back in time before Bieberstein turned in his direction to gesture to Talaat to enter his office.

Agitated, von Bohlen returned to this office. He went to the window and saw the official carriage standing in the semicircular drive in front of the embassy. He resented his exclusion from the meeting, but he knew immediately why he had been left out. He understood now why von Gwinner had been slow to answer him. Von Bohlen recalled his last meeting with von Gwinner in Berlin, just three months earlier. It had been raining – it was always raining when von Bohlen visited Berlin – the skies outside von Gwinner's office were gray, and the buildings had glistened gray. Von Gwinner himself was gray, his neatly trimmed beard, waistcoat and suit all various shades of gray. The two had argued about the railway.

"My dear von Bohlen," von Gwinner said, "the railway remains first and foremost a commercial enterprise. We are businessmen. Our task is to pay dividends to our shareholders."

"But the Young Turks clearly see it as a military weapon," von Bohlen countered. "They talk incessantly about troop mobilization – not grain, not trade – just troops, troops, troops."

"Every railroad – every road – becomes part of military strategy in a war," said von Gwinner. "But we are at peace and much as the politicians love to rattle sabers, it's in everyone's interest to remain at peace."

"You can hardly blame the British for opposing the railway when you hear the Ottomans talk about their troops," von Bohlen said.

"The British aren't worried about Turkish troops," von Gwinner said with a slow smile. "They are worried – and no, I don't blame them for this – about our own able forces deploying quickly throughout the region. But I have another lure in mind for our British friends," von Gwinner smiled openly now.

Von Bohlen waited for the Deutsche Bank management board spokesman to continue.

"Oil," he said, with another flash of teeth. "Mesopotamia, like Persia, is swimming in oil. And we have the concessions." He clapped his hands. "Siemens, fox that he is, had it thrown in the original concessions. The British want fuel for their ships. We can dangle the Mosul concessions in front of them."

Von Bohlen grunted. Yes, as part of the railway agreement, the Reich had obtained concessions to look for oil in the fields around Mosul, thought to be particularly rich in the substance. In Berlin, it was all about Europe. He was warning them about the Turks and they were talking about the British. The hubris of the Great Powers knew no bounds, von Bohlen reflected. They couldn't see the ambitions of lesser powers because their own ambitions blinded them. The Ottomans had 200,000 men under arms in this time of peace and more than double that number immediately available in the event of mobilization.

"The Ottomans will use the railroad to suppress their people, not feed them," Bohlen tried again.

"Ours is not to worry about the sultan's domestic politics," von Gwinner said, with a slightly patronizing tone.

"But if the Turks commandeer our railroad for troops, our shareholders won't get their dividend," von Bohlen said.

"Oh, I'm confident the Turks will pay their loan installments," von Gwinner smiled again, "whether they make money transporting grain or decide to transport troops on the railroad."

Von Bohlen remained silent. Arthur von Gwinner, the most powerful banker in Germany, wasn't interested in whether Anatolian peasants had enough to eat.

And now Talaat was visiting the German embassy to talk about the Baghdad Railway, and he was not thinking of the peasants' welfare either. Von Bohlen pulled a dossier from the stack on his desk – applications for letters of credit from German companies operating in Constantinople. Von Bohlen was no Socialist, no idealist with visionary goals. He believed capital earned its profit. He wanted grain for the peasants, but he wanted it paid for, with interest. War was economically useless. It was like a jewel – a luxury the Ottoman Empire could ill afford. Or any empire, he thought grimly.

Von Bohlen passed an hour, an hour and a half at his tasks. He heard muffled voices again and went down the hall to his listening post. All three men were proceeding to the main staircase. Their voices receded again as they descended the stairs. Von Bohlen looked around the corner down the central hallway. Seeing the way clear, he walked quickly, past the main staircase, to the far end of the hall, and stood at the door to Bieberstein's office, looking around for any embassy staff. He saw no one, and entered the office. He saw several map rolls on the conference table and went to look at them. The maps were labeled in Turkish and were stamped "Secret." Von Bohlen was surprised to see secret Ottoman documents in the German embassy. The countries were not formally allies.

Von Bohlen studied the maps, a frown on his face. They were evidently military maps and seemed to be a blueprint for mobilization. The maps traced the route of the Baghdad Railway and showed links and distances to main roads. Legends showed what conscript strength could move along each road to the railroad, like tributaries carrying the spring rainfall to the river. A river of oppression – pogroms against Armenians, exile for Kurds, subjugation for Arabs. The Young Turks were just like the old ones. They had chased the sultan from office and installed a dictatorship instead. The region would remain as benighted as ever. Europe was making no serious effort to bring the salvation of Christianity to these lands, nor, it was all too evident from these maps, was the Reich genuinely interested in lifting these poor heathens out of their poverty.

Von Bohlen always knew the military potential of the railway – he had used it himself to push forward his cause. But his cause – the cause of commerce, prosperity, civilization – seemed lost. His means to an end had become the end. He stood in the deepening gloom of the office, not moving, breathing in and out with some labor as his mind accommodated this new reality. Then, in a single moment, he let go of a lifetime of duty and obligation. He felt it slipping from him like a heavy mantle, leaving him naked, exposed. He straightened his back, lifted his head, looked around the room. He walked deliberately around the table to the door. He turned to look back at the table, the maps, the lost hopes. Von Bohlen treaded slowly down the embassy hall, back to his office. He would bide his time, then he would do what he felt he had to do.

~

Broome's head was splitting in two. He licked his chapped lips with a dry tongue and opened his eyes. Jabs of sunlight blinded him and he shut his eyes tight until they hurt, too. He tried to prop himself up.

Leighton. Where was Leighton? He opened his eyes and blinked against the sunlight. He was sprawled in front of the Germans' tent. He saw no one. He moved his head as much as the pain in his arm would let him, looking around. No sign of Leighton. Nor of Morrison. No sign of the attackers. No sign of their horses. No sign of life.

Broome groaned. His mouth was dry. He rose in a couple of quick, jerky movements, wincing at the pain, and lurched toward the tent. The shade of the tent blocked the searing heat of the sun and the slicing pain in his head relented for a moment. As his eyes adjusted again, he saw a figure lying face down at the entrance to the tent.

"Milord?" Broome managed to croak, though he could hardly hear it himself.

He reached down to shake the shoulder of the man lying there. There was no response as Broome took in the fact that it was Morrison who lay in front of him. The body felt warm to the touch. There was no sign of injury, but little sign of life. Broome held two fingers to the neck of the prostrate man like a hospital nurse and felt a faint pulse.

Broome spotted the canteen on the table next to Morrison. He took a small sip then held the canteen over Morrison's neck and let some water slowly dribble onto it. Morrison stirred, let out a grunt and turned quickly on his side, grabbing Broome's wrist with his free hand.

"It's me, Broome," the valet said.

Morrison's eyes were open wide, his pupils dilating to take in the scene in the darkness of the tent. He recognized Broome and his face relaxed, though his grip remained tight on Broome's wrist.

"Broome," Morrison said. "Broome."

He let go of the valet's wrist and slumped back in the cot. "Leighton?"

"Gone."

"How far?" Morrison asked, shaking his head to clear it.

Broome didn't grasp the question. Perhaps, he thought, his master was lying just a few yards from the tent.

"I got clobbered on the head, I think," Morrison said. He had fired his pistol at a horseman approaching the tent. The man, who seemed unfazed by Morrison's shot, which must have missed him, swung his rifle butt around at Morrison's head. That's the last thing he remembered.

"Horses," Broome grunted more than spoke, as pain, from his head, everywhere, seized him again. "Gone."

Broome slumped over next to Morrison, who watched him with glazed eyes.

Chapter Eighteen

Leighton woke up thirsty. His tongue stuck to the top of his mouth. He felt a sudden panic, swallowing hard, trying to disengage his tongue. An unreasoning fear gripped him that he would swallow his tongue. He breathed deeply, willing his attention to his other senses. It was dark where he was, and cold. His wrists and ankles were bound. He was in a small, enclosed place; he sensed walls near him. He tried to extend his legs to probe the space and discovered that ankles and wrists were also bound closely together. He was trussed like a hog being taken to market.

His tongue again seemed to swell up, and again he fought down the panic. How long had he been unconscious? Where was he? Who had taken him prisoner? He was in a seated position, his back against a hard surface that felt like stone or adobe. There was no sound except his own breathing. It was as though he had been locked into a pen somewhere and abandoned.

Was it locked? Where was the entrance? Leighton tried to maneuver into a kneeling position but his bonds prevented him. He lay on his side and tried to move away from the wall he had been resting against. His head touched another wall. He rolled over and came up against a wall opposite his original resting place. Then he squirmed down and touched the fourth wall with his foot. The space seemed to be no more than four or five feet square, he determined.

He detected no opening in the walls. It was either higher on the walls or above him.

Leighton rested, mustering his strength. He ignored the dryness in his mouth. There was also a pain in his left arm that felt like a cut or slash of some sort. He sat up again, pulled his knees toward him and attempted to stand. Hobbled as he was, he could only raise himself to a crouching position. He sensed the ceiling to his enclosure was not far above his head. He craned his neck around to look but the darkness remained absolute and he saw nothing.

He sat down again with a thud. There was an earthy, moldy smell to his enclosure. He leaned back against the wall and tried to breathe more slowly. The place was damp and soon Leighton was seized with a fit of coughing.

~

Rough hands roused Leighton from his fitful sleep. He blinked as they half led him, half carried him through the door, up some worn stone stairs and into a dirt courtyard. He blinked in the sunlight, trying to gauge whether it was morning or afternoon. Before he could keep his eyes open, his escorts pushed him into a room, open to the courtyard, but shaded and cool. The floor was earthen here, and the guards pushed Leighton down on his knees. A man in Western riding gear sat propped on some pillows in front of the prisoner. Leighton raised his eyes and saw a blur of black hair and pointed chin. As he focused, he saw the scar on the cheek, the high cheekbones and swarthy complexion of his captor. A flash came to him of a European standing by the train in Konya.

"I'm showing myself to you," said Ernst, in his heavily accented English. "And speaking to you. And yet it would be disastrous if you could ever identify me to the outside world."

German, Leighton realized.

"You may draw your own conclusions from that," Ernst said.

A melodramatic German, Leighton concluded. Not an effective threat if he meant Leighton's death was inevitable.

The Englishman cleared his throat, coughing. "Richard Leighton at your service. With whom do I have the pleasure—"

Ernst said nothing. He rose to his feet and slashed the riding crop in his right hand across Leighton's cheek, opening a red welt. "Save your manners for the devil," Ernst said. "You'll need them soon enough. See if you can charm your way into a cozy corner of hell."

Ernst sat down. "All I want from you is to know what you have communicated to London."

Leighton looked at his interrogator. He was thirsty. "May I have some water?" he croaked.

Ernst motioned to one of the guards, who picked up a drinking gourd, dipped it in a bucket and stood over Leighton, slopping the water into his face. Leighton captured what he could in his mouth and swallowed. "Thank you," he said.

Leighton looked silently at Ernst. "What happened to my companions?" he asked.

"Answer my question!" the German barked. "Your companions are dead and you will join them soon enough."

Leighton's eyes closed. The riding crop struck his back, once, twice, three times.

"I have no way of communicating with anyone in London," Leighton said, gritting his teeth.

Ernst rose and this time lashed out with his foot, striking Leighton's ribs with the hard toe of his riding boot. "At Adana, you sent a dispatch to London in a diplomatic pouch. What did it say?" Leighton crumpled and a moan escaped him as he winced with pain from the kick.

"I'm afraid ... it was some tedious ... questions ... about a Koranic commentary," Leighton managed to say before the riding crop descended again on his neck and shoulder.

"Don't insult me. I know you're one of Grey's spies," Ernst said. Leighton remained curled to the side where Ernst had kicked him. He scarcely felt the new welt on his neck.

"I'm a scholar," Leighton croaked, waiting for the next blow. "My interests are scholarly."

Ernst nodded to the two men who had brought Leighton up. They began kicking him from both sides. Leighton fell to one side and curled as tightly as he could into a ball, seeking to protect his head and face from the blows. They struck his ribs, his kidneys, his buttocks, his thighs, his shins, his arms, his hands, the crown of his head.

"Enough," Ernst said. "Take him down. No food, no water."

Back in his cell, Leighton let the pain penetrate slowly into his consciousness, relishing it as a sign of life. The pain was monstrous. It seemed every square inch of his body hurt. He felt some of the blows for the first time, as though the heavy boots of his tormentors were in the darkness with him. He tried to remain conscious. Were Morrison and Broome really dead? How long could he hold out against this torment? Soon, though, he succumbed to the pain and passed out.

~

Once again, it was several hands tugging at him that awakened Leighton. He steeled himself for the coming interrogation. His cell was a kind of storage cellar, with the door set two feet off the floor. Two burly men reached through this opening and grabbed Leighton's arms, pulling him up into a standing position. Then one of the men lifted Leighton onto a strong shoulder to carry him.

This puzzled Leighton. Earlier, his captors had been content to let him scrape along on his weak legs as they dragged him to his interrogation. Perhaps there would be no more questions. Perhaps it was now the time for disposal of unwanted rubbish. They didn't cover his head this time. It didn't occur to Leighton to cry out. Cry out to whom?

Leighton noticed that his captors were remarkably silent, not speaking, moving quickly and quietly. They carried him through a passageway and up some stairs and out through a door that was opened and closed gently. Outside, Leighton realized it was night, a dark night with no moon. There seemed to be half a dozen men surrounding him. Too many for one feeble European, he thought.

Two of the men lifted him onto a horse, this time sitting, his legs astride an Arabic saddle, leaning him against the high post at the front. "Can you ride?" one of the men said in English to an astounded Leighton. Ride? Unfettered? Who were these men? He managed to nod his head in assent.

The others quickly mounted and Leighton grabbed the post of his saddle as his horse lurched forward into a gallop. They were taking him away, away from his prison, away from the German and his questions, his whip. They spoke English to him. They didn't bind his hands or blindfold him. Weak and sore, Leighton had difficulty staying in the saddle. He almost wished they would tie him to his mount as before, when his fate was out of his hands, but he clenched the polished knob of the saddle horn and held on.

Still only silence as they left the prison behind. Leighton had a vague impression of groves of trees. Some sort of plantation, he reckoned, growing figs or dates or oranges. Was he near the Euphrates? The Tigris? He had so little sense of how long he had ridden in his previous journey. Hours? Days? He had ceased to feel any hunger – the pain from his ill treatment eclipsed any other feelings. The horses pounded into the darkness, though the ride jarred Leighton less than before. The horses' hooves were hitting softer ground, Leighton thought, no longer the hard sun-baked surface of the steppe. This was ground where trees could take root and grow crops. Moist ground, fed by canals branching out from a river.

After what seemed like a long period of hard riding, they stopped. In the dark, Leighton could hardly make out the surroundings. They had followed a road, but had not encountered any habitations, or at least none he could see in the gloom.

A horseman approached him, holding out a leather flask. "Water," he said in English.

"Thank you," Leighton said, taking the flask and raising it quickly to his parched lips. He drank only two long draughts, and handed it back to the horseman. The man, cloaked and hooded, nodded, the whites of his eyes flashing, and secured the flask to his saddle. The band started up again, at a slower gait than before. There was no sign of pursuit.

Leighton wanted to know who his rescuers were but the pace was still too fast for anything like conversation. His companions didn't converse among themselves and he wasn't sure what language they spoke, though he felt fairly certain it wasn't German. The English he had heard was obviously quite primitive, merely a few basic words.

Were these the men who had rescued him twice before – in the alley in Constantinople and the ambush in the mountains? Why? The question thundered inside Leighton's head. Who were they? What did *they* want from him?

The horses proved to be quite hardy and they rode at a fast canter for many miles. Leighton thought he saw a lantern off to one side, but they passed no settlements. As the thrill of his escape ebbed, Leighton became aware again of his aches and hurt. Hunger, too, made itself felt. He had not eaten since his abduction from the camp, which must be days by now. Pain and anxiety had kept hunger at bay until now, but the security he felt among his rescuers let him become aware of his empty stomach.

They stopped again at a small stream. Leighton by now reckoned they were in the mud flats between the Tigris and the Euphrates. As the horses drank, the same horseman returned with his flask of water. This time, Leighton drank more. As he handed back the flask, he asked, "Food?" Unconsciously, he pointed to his mouth and rubbed his stomach. The cloaked figure reached into a small pouch hanging from his saddle and handed to Leighton what turned out to be a dried fig. The Englishman bit off a small piece of the fruit and chewed it slowly. It was fully macerated by the time he swallowed it. He knew he risked a colic if he ate too quickly after so long a fast.

Leighton risked further communication. "Friend?" he asked, pointing at the horseman as he bit off another small piece of fig.

The horseman yanked at his reins without answering and returned to his position at the head of the group. Still, there was no conversation among his rescuers. Leighton noticed there was the glimmer of dawn on the horizon. They had been riding, he could see now, toward the dawn, heading east from wherever it was they had rescued him.

As he swallowed the last of the fig, Leighton was hit by a wave of exhaustion. He slumped forward in his saddle, clutching at the horn to keep from falling off his horse. He must have uttered something, for one of the horsemen appeared at his side, grabbing him by his shirt and barking out a guttural signal. The lead horseman returned and put a gloved hand underneath Leighton's chin, raising it to look at Leighton's face. Leighton tried to hold his eyes open, but they had a will of their own and shut. More guttural commands.

Arabic, Leighton thought, though he couldn't decipher the words. He felt a rope being wrapped around his waist and tied to his saddle horn. His hands were not bound, but the reins were lashed around his wrists.

Leighton shivered, suddenly cold. He wore only the cotton shirt and wool pants he'd had on when abducted. A cloak was thrown roughly over his shoulders and two hands reached over to pull the drawstrings tight and tie it around his neck. Leighton felt much better and attempted a smile to show his appreciation.

"Ride," the lead horseman said. Not so much a command as a statement of fact. Leighton thought of nodding, but had no idea if he actually made any movement with his head. Two of the band were on either side of him as they set out again toward a sunrise in full glory.

Chapter Nineteen

Ernst counted briskly as his body rose and fell in a regular rhythm. Sixty, sixty-one, sixty-two – he usually did a hundred pushups as part of his morning routine. There was a knock at the door, which he ignored. Sixty-five, sixty-six, sixty-seven. The knock again.

"*Verdammt!* What is it?" he said as he paused his exercise. Sweat immediately poured down his skin, dripping off his nose.

"The prisoner, he is gone," said a timid voice from the doorway.

Ernst jerked his head up, rising swiftly and gracefully as part of the same motion. He looked at the Arab who brought him the news, a huge lug sneered at by his comrades for his weak mind. Only he had been stupid enough to deliver the bad news to the German captain.

Ernst grabbed his whip and lashed it in a savage motion across the Arab's face. A bloody welt appeared down the side of the man's face, as he stepped back several paces.

A dangerous grunt escaped Ernst's mouth as he reached for his pistol. The Arab broke into a run as Ernst, still barefoot and in his underwear, came out of his room and strode down the hall. He intended to shoot the guard dead who had let the prisoner escape. When he arrived outside at the entrance to the cellar, however, he saw the man lay in a pool of his own blood, a gash across his throat.

"When?" Ernst snapped at the small cluster of men standing a safe distance away.

"The wound is still fresh, perhaps an hour, half an hour," ventured one of them.

"Fetch the horses," Ernst said, as he turned and marched quickly back down the hallway. In five minutes, having donned his riding clothes and boots, he swung himself onto his horse and led the band from the house. The scout was already ahead of them, following the fresh tracks of Leighton's liberators.

"There were several men, perhaps half a dozen," the Arab leader told Ernst as he joined him. Ernst looked ahead without expression.

They were heading east, and the sun blinded them as it rose in the sky. Ernst's heart sank. Leighton and his liberators had perhaps an hour's head start, but their horses were not fresh. They, too, were heading into the heat of the day. The problem was the irrigation zone that lay ahead. There, fruit orchards provided cover and the marshy ground and irrigation channels would permit their quarry to literally muddy the ground and make their path difficult to follow.

Ernst whipped his own horse to spur the men on.

When they reached the orchards an hour later, though, Ernst began to lose hope. The scout followed the trail into the orange groves. The shade was welcome, but the ground was a hash of mud and animal droppings. Farm workers with donkeys were busy hauling bushels of fruit across the same paths taken by the fugitives. The scout came back to Ernst, perplexed. Perhaps the fugitives split up, or perhaps other mounts had crossed the path, his gestures – a wave of the arms, a shrug – said.

Ernst dismounted and slapped his whip against his boot as he paced in front of the men.

Leighton had escaped him. Perhaps, Ernst seized on the idea, he had fallen into the hands of other enemies. But who?

Not the Turks; they were kept apprised of the Germans' intentions. Were other British agents at work? Did Britain have allies among the Arab tribes that he was not aware of?

Leighton would head for Baghdad, if he was free to go where he pleased. Ernst would have to intercept him there before he could do any mischief.

Ernst had thought to bring his saddlebag with the gold. He told the men they would head east to the Tigris River and follow it into Baghdad. He was determined they would ride hard and arrive there before Leighton.

~

Leighton didn't know whether he was awake or asleep. He rode in what seemed to be a conscious state, but his dreams, too, were of riding – bouncing, jolting, weaving, leaning as the horse moved beneath him. He remained upright by some miracle. Rigor mortis, he though wryly and felt his cracked lips stretch into a smile. But there was too much pain for him to be dead. Training, he decided. All those long hours on horseback as a soldier for Her Majesty. That was the miracle.

The ground was flat and soggy. Isolated trees and bushes dotted the landscape. At the top of one slight mound, however, Leighton saw a camp in the distance, a large settlement covering several acres. His companions exchanged some quick, guttural remarks at the sight. Their destination, Leighton realized.

The tent of the Bedouin chieftain dominated the camp, rising above the other structures like a temple. Covered in thick black wool held taut by long ropes, it stretched the length of a rugby pitch. Leighton's captors led him to the entrance where armed men pulled aside two flaps for them to enter. Inside, as their eyes adjusted to the darkness, lanterns reflected the gleaming white khaffiyah of the chieftain and his retinue. A tall man, dressed in a black and yellow striped robe with wide sleeves, clearly was the leader. Leighton bowed slightly to him by way of obeisance. The name Ali Rashid floated out of the courtly Islamic greeting whispered by his guides.

Ali Rashid gestured with a long tapering hand for the newcomers to sit amid the carpets and cushions covering the floor. Ebony servants brought food on large brass trays, piles of rice and roasted meat with bowls of dried fruit. Leighton again ate with hesitation after so long without food. He nibbled at the mutton chops, and chewed slowly on raisins and nuts. Cardamom-flavored green coffee was served and the chieftain spoke rapidly in a low voice to the leader of Leighton's band.

Leighton's eyes had adjusted to the interior of the tent. It was a large structure; the reek of untreated wool permeated the enclosure. Rugs and hangings rendered the habitation comfortable, but they were not the sumptuous appointments of a prince.

Leighton tried to figure out where he was and who these people were. They had "rescued" him from the German, but to what end? Was he to be held for ransom? What had become of the German? His force was no match for the hundreds of men here. Who were these men? A tribe? An army? Whose side were they on? Not the Germans? Not the Turks? How had they found him?

Leighton greedily took the tea that followed the serving of coffee. The hot, sweet liquid restored him further. He watched the chieftain and the leader of the men who brought him here. Other conversations were going on in quiet tones.

"Englishman!" the peremptory call from the chieftain sounded like an order rather than an address. "Speak!"

All conversation ceased. Leighton straightened but did not rise. "My lord," he began in English. "I am most grateful for your hospitality..."

The chieftain turned again to Leighton's rescuer, speaking to him in Arabic, but now loud enough for Leighton to hear. He waited for the chieftain to finish. Before the other man could respond, however, Leighton intervened. "No, my lord," he said now in Arabic, "I was not searching for the railway. There was a report of dead Europeans and I was searching for them."

The chieftain studied Leighton. If he was surprised that an Englishman spoke Arabic, he masked it well. When he spoke to his companion, though, it was again in a whisper so that Leighton could not hear.

"You speak of Europeans," the chieftain said to Leighton. "Yet not all Europeans are your friends."

Leighton had no answer to that.

"You say you search for Europeans, but you continued to search after you found them," the chieftain said.

"I thought there may be more in the camp," Leighton lied.

The chieftain studied him. "You thank me for my hospitality," he began. As Leighton tried to voice his gratitude again, this time in Arabic, the chieftain cut him off with a wave of his hand. "You do not thank me for rescuing you from your enemies?"

"My gratitude is boundless for the many services my lord has performed for me," said Leighton, seeking refuge in a general effulgence of gratitude. He was too uncertain who his enemies and friends were.

The chieftain grunted, and spoke again to his companion, who shrugged his shoulders. "We have a saying," the chieftain said, addressing Leighton again. "The enemy of my enemy is my friend. I am the enemy of your enemy. Am I not your friend?"

"It is a wise saying," Leighton said, "and a true one. I welcome as friend any enemy of my enemies."

The chieftain gazed at Leighton as he interpreted the nuance of his response.

"Do you doubt that the Europeans who build the railway are your enemy?" he asked.

"I am a simple scholar," Leighton replied. "Builders of railways are not my enemy."

The chieftain smiled, his eyes hooded. He spoke at some length to the man next to him.

"You want to go to Baghdad?" the chieftain asked Leighton.

"Yes, it was my destination," Leighton said.

"This can be arranged," the chieftain said.

Leighton's relief must have shown on his face, for the chieftain smiled again.

"Rest here tonight," he said. "We will speak again in the morning."

~

Two women, covered from head to foot in robes and veils, escorted him to a small tent. They handed him a robe and motioned for him to remove his clothes. Sweat and blood caked his shirt, and his clothes bore the dust of desert and cell, the mud of the marshes. He gave them up gladly. A boy brought him yet another cup of tea, which he drank gratefully. The warm liquid soothed his nerves and the exhaustion of the past few days swept over him. He lay down on the pallet prepared for him and had barely pulled a woolen blanket over him before he fell fast asleep.

It seemed only moments later a voice awoke him. "English!" the voice repeated several times. Leighton opened his eyes and saw the chieftain squatting next to his pallet.

Leighton tried to rise, but the chieftain arrested his efforts with a small gesture.

"Rest, English," he said, "but I must speak with you. My name is Ibrahim Ali Rashid. I am chief of this vast tribe you see. I am friends with many other tribes." He paused. "You are Lord Leighton and you are on a mission from the British Foreign Office." Another gesture cut short Leighton's protest. "These things are true," Rashid said.

"The Turks and the Germans are building a railway. This railway will bring soldiers to our desert and to our marshes. We will lose any chance ever to be free of the Ottoman yoke."

"But the sultan is your caliph. It is your religion that makes you swear fealty to him," Leighton interjected.

Rashid spat to one side. "The sultan is a heathen, he is not godly. The Young Turks are even more godless, with no respect for Allah or his prophet. We Bedouin serve Allah, not the sultan, not these godless Rumi." He paused to spit again.

"But the sultan has guns and cannons. You have only spears and knives," Leighton said.

"We are not so toothless," Rashid said, flashing a big grin as if to demonstrate his point. "Our knives and spears can inflict great harm."

Leighton thought of the Kurds slaughtered in the German camp.

"But it is true, the sultan's soldiers have rifles and cannons, and the railway will bring them to chase us and kill us, and we will not be able to defend ourselves."

Rashid looked at Leighton. His dark eyes were set deep in a Semitic face, with a prominent hooked nose, a pointed chin covered by a neatly trimmed beard.

"The railway can carry the sultan's soldiers, and their allies, through the desert, to the sea," Rashid said. "They can threaten the British in India. Your enemy, as I have said, is my enemy, and we should be friends."

"What would you expect from our friendship?" asked Leighton, abandoning any pretense of being a simple scholar.

Rashid smiled to acknowledge Leighton's new willingness to reveal his true identity.

"Rifles," he said. "Ammunition."

Leighton raised an eyebrow.

"That's all," Rashid said.

That's all, reflected Leighton. War.

"The British cannot deliver rifles to the sultan's subjects so they can throw off his rule," Leighton said. "It would mean war with the sultan, and war with his allies."

"The sultan does not need to know that the British are delivering rifles to us," said Rashid. "It must be kept secret."

Easier said than done, thought Leighton, with spies in every corner of the Ottoman Empire.

"It is difficult to keep secrets," Leighton said. "My mission is a secret," Rashid flashed his grin again, "known to friend and foe alike."

"Ah, but the English are resourceful," Rashid said. "They, too, have friends who can help them."

A rustle behind the chieftain and a veiled woman gave him some neatly folded clothing. "Ah, your garments," said Rashid, laying them next to Leighton. Leighton could not imagine how they had been able to launder and dry his clothes. London's finest hotels, with all their machinery, would be unable to match that service.

"Your escort to Baghdad awaits you," said Rashid. "Tell London of our needs. We will be friends." With that, Rashid backed quickly out of the tent and disappeared.

~

An Arab revolt? Was such a thing possible? Could Muslims rise up against the caliph?

It was a religion based on surrender, not revolt. The very word Islam meant surrender. Surrender to Allah, surrender to the *ummah*, the community, the greater good, the source of salvation. The Muslim's daily prayer affirmed there was no God but Allah and Mohammed was his messenger. The caliph stood in place of the prophet. And now a devout Muslim was talking of a revolt against the caliph?

Leighton puzzled over these questions as he rode with his "escort." Food and sleep had made him a new man. He rode under his own steam, upright in his saddle, able to take in his surroundings. He wore his own clothes, clean and fresh, with a robe over them against the dust and sun. And bugs. Now in the marshes, the sun beat down with somewhat less force, but the insects buzzed in the moist air and bit where they could find exposed skin. He readily took some unguent as protection against the insects despite its harsh odor of animal stench. His guides still had little to say to him and kept deliberately apart when they stopped to rest the horses. Leighton felt they were riding parallel to the course of the Tigris, in a southeasterly direction. It was still more or less the route foreseen for the railway. Leighton wondered if the German officer was giving pursuit.

The Ottoman empire was Turkish, but it was also Muslim, and this seemed sufficient to command the loyalty of its Arab subjects – at least until now. The Young Turks certainly were more Turkish than Muslim – was that enough to change Arab attitudes? Leighton wondered what tribe this chieftain led. Perhaps it was only certain tribes who were willing to challenge the rule of the sultan. Or perhaps it followed the deep rifts in Islam, between Sunni and Shiite.

For Leighton, it was hard to accept this sheikh as an ally. The man was a cold-blooded murderer, not a warrior. The slaughter of the Kurdish workers was an outrage, a criminal act. Yet, there was truth in this Arab saying about friends and enemies. London wanted the Baghdad Railway stopped and would not be too particular about the methods any allies used.

Leighton knew there was no place for his qualms in London's master strategy. However dubious Rashid's methods, the tribe was fighting for its own land, its own independence. They were not mercenaries, but could serve as allies.

Chapter Twenty

Elena knew it must happen quickly. She had worn Western clothes and carried a bright yellow parasol to make herself easy to follow. But it all depended on the timing, on everything following the course they had planned.

It was a desperate measure, but Talaat was too clever to deceive any longer. He had intercepted one of her letters to the courier. He could not crack the code, but he could recognize it as code. He evidently preferred to let her continue her subterfuge, to see where it led, and crack down only when it suited him. Elena didn't want to wait until that moment. She would be lost and perhaps others with her. No human being could withstand the methods applied by Turkish interrogators to extract information.

Elena walked along the quay. Mustafa accompanied her, like a latter-day eunuch, guarding this harem of one. Mustafa would disappear, too, in the second act of their charade. The quay teemed with its usual activity – wagons hauling grain and bales of cotton, stevedores stacking crates as cranes transferred them from ships docked along the piers, passengers streaming to and from the ferries.

Elena's father had set sail for Italy last night. By the time Talaat learned of it, Elena would be gone. There might be other reprisals – against her cousins, her village – but Elena had to weigh that against the threat posed to the underground operation here. These decisions did not come easy to Elena;

she anguished over them. Sharing a bed with Talaat, whom she despised, also had not come easy. But life itself was not easy, and Elena did what she had to do to further the cause of her people. The world was on the brink of change, and the Society wanted that change to favor the Armenian nation.

She was at the pier near the end of the Golden Horn, where dhows and other small sailing vessels clustered. Elena measured her step, forcing herself not to increase her pace as the crucial moment approached. Mustafa lumbered at her side. Elena didn't dare look around for her watchers; she knew they were there.

As she reached the edge of the pier, a flock of pigeons suddenly escaped as a stack of three cages of birds fell over. There was a flurry of feathers and several men running around grasping in vain for the fleeing pigeons. Elena's yellow parasol continued to bob along the quay past the pier, and Mustafa's fez was also visible through the feathery storm. Only when the pigeons were gone was it clear that Mustafa himself was now carrying the parasol and Elena was nowhere to be seen.

It was a simple ruse, if a bold one. While the pigeons created a diversion, Elena handed the parasol to Mustafa as one of the men on the pier threw a dark hooded cloak over the young woman. Together, the two ran in a crouch down the pier, diving into the first dhow. They made their way through the densely packed boats. This is where Elena had decided on a twist. Rather than take flight in one of the dhows, she climbed back on to the quay at a spot shielded by stacked crates and stepped quickly into a closed carriage that waited there. At the same time, a dhow did set sail, wending its way down the Golden Horn to the Bosphorus.

Elena watched through the curtains of her carriage as two men in black suits raced along the quay, keeping the slowly moving dhow in sight. She knew they would mobilize the police and soon have a launch in pursuit of the dhow. The brave men sailing it would allow the police to search thoroughly, all the while protesting their ignorance of any woman in Western clothes, or any woman at all.

Mustafa, meanwhile, cast aside the parasol and turned into an alleyway leading into the maze of Stamboul. Elena had planned her flight overland, not trusting that any vessel would escape the narrow waters of the Bosphorus. The risk of discovery would be constant by land, but she had a head start and many directions to go in.

Elena shuddered as she thought of Talaat's rage. She had taken a big step past the point of no return. But it was just another step on the path she had chosen. She had willingly taken on this mission, as she had others, to gain some security for her people. Now, however, she could not rest easy as long as Talaat was in power. Ottoman territory had become mortally dangerous for her, and even Europe was not safe from Talaat's assassins. She had always known that this is how the mission would end. In fact, this was the favorable outcome.

The velour plush of the carriage seats seemed like the lining in a coffin. Her companion, an Armenian, reeked of sweat and sour clothes. The small carriage put her in too close a proximity to the man, who evidently had not bathed in weeks. This would be her lot in the coming days and weeks. She rapped against the front of the cabin, signaling the driver to proceed ahead. The single-horse carriage would go slowly anyway, but especially so in the congestion on the quay.

Elena's thoughts turned to Leighton. He was caught up in something bigger than he knew. She had done what she could to protect him. She worried it was not enough.

~

Leighton's group reached the river by dusk. Ali Ahmed, the leader, ordered the men to set up camp on a hillock where the ground was firm. Leighton had noticed the horses slowing down in a strange muck along the river. It wasn't just mud that slowed them. There was a curious, oily liquid that appeared to seep out of the ground. It made the mud particularly treacherous. When he dismounted, Leighton dipped his fingers in the viscous liquid and rubbed them together. It dawned on him at last that it was petroleum that was oozing out of the spongy earth. Leighton knew that Mesopotamia had been a famous source of bitumen throughout history. He wasn't familiar with petroleum, but knew that it was a hydrocarbon product like bitumen.

Leighton recalled Churchill's words about the importance of petroleum as a fuel. Automobiles, of course, ran on petrol, which was derived from petroleum. Churchill said the Royal Navy would be switching from coal to oil-fired engines. Well, Leighton thought, this petroleum would certainly be easier to obtain than the coal mined with such labor in the British Isles.

For Ali Ahmed and his men, the oily slime was only an unwelcome impediment, and had no value. Ali was a slight man, by far the smallest in the group. Yet he seemed to command obedience without question. The tents were quickly raised. The six of them made ready to share two tents, while they had set up a third tent for Leighton's exclusive use. He looked forward after the long day in the saddle to a restful night. His body still ached all over from the beating at the hands, and feet, of his captors.

Supper consisted of dates and a hard, unleavened bread. Leighton found the meal surprisingly satisfying. Without any conversation with his comrades, Leighton retired to his tent. There he lay awake some time, his thoughts dwelling on Elena. Her marriage to Talaat continued to perplex him, it seemed so unlike her. She had shown a good deal of feeling during their meeting, and it had rekindled something in him, a flickering passion he thought had been extinguished. Would he see her again?

They set out early the next morning, just when dawn had lightened the sky, but before the sun emerged over the horizon. Within a few miles, they came upon a village. There was a considerable amount of activity for such an early hour. The men from the village were finishing a trench several yards in length. Ali and his men paused to watch. With the trench finished, everyone in the village – men, boys, women, girls – began moving through the surrounding fields, sweeping before them with sticks and branches. The grass came to life, teeming with movement that at first bewildered Leighton. Then he discerned the black, hopping shapes of thousands of locusts. The creatures plagued the Mesopotamian steppes and marshes, devastating pastures and crops like a scourge.

The villagers drove the black insects toward the trench, converging on the ditch from all sides. The hole quickly filled with squirming masses of the creatures, who were trapped when a dense netting was pulled over the trench.

Ali smiled.

"They will feast for several days now," he said. He glanced sideways at Leighton, who maintained an indifferent composure with regard to the unusual hunting expedition.

The whirring of the trapped locusts filled the air, discouraging further conversation. Ali motioned to his men to move on. They would leave the villagers to the spoils of their hunt.

As dusk approached once again, the group reached a ferry station. Four men were drinking tea in front of the shabby wood shelter. One of them arose to talk to Ali and quickly negotiated the passage. The four men then helped Ali's group to push several large round baskets toward the edge of the riverbank.

The *gufas* were made of coiled ropes of tightly bound marsh grass. Saplings curved along the inside of the basket gave the ungainly vehicles some structure. The outside was sealed with bitumen to make it waterproof. The baskets varied in size – some only four feet in diameter and others reaching up to twelve feet. Leighton had heard of these basket boats, virtually as old as the Nile, but had never seen them actually used.

He boarded a smaller basket with one of Ali's men. His companion handed him a long pole with a short narrow paddle fastened to the end and explained with gestures that they both needed to paddle to keep their boat going straight. The horses were loaded into larger baskets and their reins lashed tight on the mooring loops on each side. They were skittish but apparently familiar with the mode of transport.

In the fading light, Leighton saw designs of marine shells embedded in the bitumen covering the baskets. Often these were in rosette shapes with blue beads at the center. Leighton reckoned these were not just adornment but served in the mind of the basket builder to ward off the evil eye.

With much splashing and groaning along the shallow embankment, the small fleet of *gufas* was pushed into the river. Planting his feet firmly on the hardened bitumen covering the floor of the basket, Leighton began paddling in rapid strokes, keeping an eye on his companion to match his rhythm. Once his foot slipped on the wet floor and he missed a stroke. The basket immediately began to rotate and started to drift downstream, prompting a burst of guttural reproach from his fellow rower. Leighton resumed his rowing and the basket got back on course.

The river was about a quarter of a mile wide at this point, its muddy yellow stream concealing surprising strength. Paddling required constant exertion to fight the current. Leighton was quickly soaked through from the river's spray.

The tall reeds of the opposite bank cast a faint silhouette in the dusk. The men labored in silence, with a muffled cry when another basket bearing three horses and four rowers briefly spun out of control. The crossing took less than half an hour, though Leighton's aching muscles made it seem much longer to him. Men and horses disembarked from the basket boats. The ferrymen roped the baskets together and immediately began their return trip across the river.

The group rode a distance after reaching the opposite shore, looking for a suitable camping place. Leighton was feeling his isolation more intensely now, but it was obvious the men were under instructions not to engage him in conversation. He wondered once again what had become of Morrison and Broome. He hoped that by some miracle they had avoided any harm in the German's attack and found a way to get out of the desert safely.

Leighton slept badly that night. He started twice when he heard a noise in the dark. Each time he recognized it, belatedly, as a noise that belonged in the camp, but his first reaction was fear. Asleep, his dreams kept him on edge. Once he awoke in a sweat. He had felt the cold, sharp blade of a dagger sliding across his throat with such intensity he lit the lamp to make sure his neck was slick with sweat and not with blood. He had no weapon. His escort appeared to keep a watch, but Leighton was not wholly certain that he had nothing to fear from his escort. Were these among the attackers who had slaughtered the Kurds at the construction site?

The next day brought them to desert again. It was a barren land of dust, rather than sandy, like the veldt in South Africa. Leighton knew they were nearing Baghdad, which sat in the middle of a plain. They had crossed to the eastern side of the Tigris in the *gufas* to enter the main part of the city by the northern gate. The British Residency, like most of the public buildings, lay in the larger part of the city on the eastern bank of the Tigris. Leighton was eager to reach the safety, and comfort, of the British mission. He could use the telegraph there to communicate with the embassy in Constantinople. He had much to tell them.

Chapter Twenty-One

Baghdad shimmered in a yellow haze, the sheen of mud-bricks under a bright sun. The colorful ceramic of mosque domes and minarets pierced the haze with unexpected brilliance, like gems in a setting of gold. The city seemed to rise out of a blanket of leafy fruit trees and date-palms, flat and vast as it sprawled across the Tigris. The swelling river cut through the plain, traced by a border of lacy willows. Dark patches of beetroot outlined a network of irrigation ditches branching out from the river.

Leighton knew from his previous visit that this shimmering first view masked the grime and poverty of a city removed by centuries from its glorious days as the capital of the Abbasid caliphate. The decay had shocked him on that first visit. Garbage littered the streets and sewage flowed down the central gutter in each main road on its way to the river. Meager fires burned glumly in open spaces, attended by women bent and furtive. Disease flourished in the twisted lanes of the city as the canals, drying up under Turkish negligence, had vanished, so that the inhabitants were forced to draw their drinking water directly from the polluted river.

In the eighth century, Baghdad had ruled the world, the leading court of the leading civilization. The reign of Harun al-Rashid as caliph had conjured up the Arabian Nights and other myths that had sustained Islam for centuries. That Baghdad of legend was gone, its bricks long returned to dust. The glory of Baghdad lay in history and myth, not in the present.

Still, Leighton's pulse raced as they made their slow way to the city in the distance. He would be able to telegraph Constantinople and relay his observations to the Foreign Office. Then he would return to Constantinople by sea – a much quicker and more comfortable way to make the trip.

He surveyed his escort. What were their plans? Their orders? Would they merely deposit him at the city gate, wait tactfully for a gratuity, bow, scrape and ride away? And what about the German officer? Had he given pursuit? Was he even now lurking in the distance, waiting to reclaim his lost prey?

Leighton looked up at the horizon to the west. Orchard groves blurred the line of sight across the river. A glint of light stabbed through the brownish green landscape – reflection off a gun, a field telescope? He gazed into the distance for a time before turning and spurring his horse to catch up with his escort.

~

Ernst lowered his binoculars. The double-barreled telescope, a new product from the Leitz optical works, provided a far superior view of the distance than the collapsible field telescope he had used in the past. He had seen the Englishman turn in his direction. Perhaps the sun had spotted his stalker for him. Ernst shrugged in the shade of the orange grove. So what? Let the Englishman grow anxious. He would not be allowed to reach the safety of the British Residency.

It was by chance that Ernst had actually located his quarry before reaching Baghdad. He had spotted the small camp in the dawn and followed the Bedouin band as they made their progress on the other side of the river. Ernst was not anxious. He had never visited Baghdad but had a map of the city. A pontoon bridge connected the western side of the city to the eastern, very nearly at the location of the British Residency along the river. Ernst and his men would be in place before the Englishman arrived.

~

Morrison picked his way carefully through the narrow lane. He ignored the glances of the Arabs, who were not accustomed to seeing a European in this part of town and had probably never seen a white man as dirty as he was. He stepped into a doorway to let a donkey laden with wicker baskets pass by him.

The American leaned against the doorframe, grateful for the rest. He had not slept in a bed for weeks, and the past few days had been particularly grueling.

Broome had stayed in the camp with the caravan. The two men continued to hope that Leighton would be able to make it to Baghdad. Who were his abductors? Were they the assassins who tried to shoot Leighton in the mountains? Were they his mysterious rescuers?

If Leighton made it to Baghdad, he might seek Morrison and Broome at Ali's camp. The two men had been able to rejoin Ali after yet another band of Bedouin had found them in the desert and agreed, for a handsome bakshish, to return them to the caravan.

During the final days of the trek to Baghdad, Morrison had marshaled his arguments for finding Leighton alive. He told himself that Leighton was as likely to survive as he and Broome, and the two of them had made it safely to their destination.

Rested, Morrison began walking again, turning through the maze of streets, guided by an internal compass. The dinginess of the city surprised him. People had a sallow, unhealthy look and dust was everywhere. The lanes were narrow, with lattice-work balconies crowding into the space overhead, casting the pathway in shadow. Odors of cooking grease from the dwellings could not mask the smell of sewage. As Morrison approached a larger street, he heard the hoof beats of several horses. More by instinct than any reasoning, Morrison ducked under an awning near the corner. In the shadow, he watched half a dozen men on horseback parade past. Bringing up the rear was a European with a scar on his cheek – marking him as a German – and eyes that darted in every direction.

Just before he passed out of sight, the German looked directly at Morrison. The American was in the shadow of the awning, but perhaps his white face shone like a luminous moon even in the darkness. Morrison half expected to see the German returning around the corner, whip in hand, to search him out. Morrison remained still. He heard a horse snort. He realized he was holding his breath and forced himself to slowly exhale and inhale. If the German was here, perhaps it meant Leighton was on his way to Baghdad. Morrison started from his place, stepping carefully into the stream of humanity and matched his step to those under way. He must find his way to the British Residency and figure out a way to head off Leighton and keep him from falling into the hands of the German and his band.

There was a flash of light on steel in front of him and Morrison caught a quick glimpse of the German's white face as he threw himself against the wall so that the dagger thrust by him, missing by a couple of inches. He pushed a man next to him across the outthrust arm of his attacker, parrying a second jab with the long curved blade. Morrison turned to run, jostling the people in his way, hearing a shout and some curses behind him. He dodged around a corner, ran down a narrow street, pushing aside a man carrying a round tray of dates and bananas on his head. He turned right into an alley, but he felt that his pursuers were right behind him. He plunged into a doorway, open except for strings of beads hanging across it. The room, a kitchen with a hearth, was empty. Morrison bounded up a stairway where light poured into the room. He found himself on a narrow terrace at the top. Still no one in sight. Morrison ran down the terrace toward the back of the house. There was a wall, which Morrison quickly clambered over, landing on another terrace, where there was a short staircase leading up to a flat roof. He ran up the stairs and across the roof. He leapt over the narrow gap to a neighboring roof, ran to a chimney and crouched down behind it. He listened for sounds of pursuit. Hearing only the hubbub of the street below him, he peered around the corner. A woman in a scarf was hanging up laundry two houses over, but otherwise there was no sign of anyone.

So the German had seen him! And now he knew that Morrison was alive and in Baghdad. Morrison sat still until his pulse rate returned to normal. He looked around his hiding place. He was in a corner of the roof hidden by the chimney, bigger than most, emitting a thin white smoke. The abutting buildings were lower so Morrison was out of sight of the neighbors. He decided to settle in and wait some time before going back down to the street. The German and his men could not wait so long if they were searching for their real quarry. Morrison was unarmed, but he anticipated no trouble from the occupants of the house. He knew the Muslim religion disposed people to be kind to strangers.

Morrison waited until the sun passed its zenith. The streets below grew quiet. His position behind the chimney, in the shade until now, became hot as the sun moved across the sky and the chimney no longer blocked its light. Morrison moved around the chimney to the far side of the roof, where a square opening revealed a steep staircase, almost a ladder. Morrison backed down the stairs. There was a large room with a table. A girl was setting the table for the midday meal. She started when she caught sight of Morrison. The American smiled at her, gave her a mock salute with two fingers and went down a broader staircase to the ground floor and through an open door to the street. The girl made no sound or movement as he disappeared out of sight.

Morrison had regained his orientation on the roof, which gave him a view of the eastern bank of the Tigris. He knew he must get there to warn Leighton.

Chapter Twenty-Two

Leighton often wondered about the fate of Broome and Morrison. Had they been killed or hurt in the ambush? It seemed unlikely they had also been abducted. The German clearly had targeted Leighton. Had his companions languished in the desert, their mounts gone or dead? If alive, had they given up hope for him?

Baghdad loomed ahead. The walls had been torn down and a park of sorts fashioned along its traces. Whatever the original plan, the result was a hodgepodge of ditches and mounds, with occasional flat spaces hinting at an esplanade. As with the rest of the city, this project suffered from the neglect of the Turkish overlords, who had little interest in aiding the Arab population, let alone maintaining the glory of Arab history.

The old northern gate, built in the 13th century, had been shut for hundreds of years, ever since Sultan Murad IV had recaptured the city for the Ottomans. The road into the city bypassed the crumbling gate and plunged into the maze of city streets at some distance from the old wall.

Leighton watched his escort closely, looking for some indication of what was to happen. Ali Ahmed halted his men and rode over to Leighton.

"We have arrived at Baghdad," he said without ceremony. "We leave you now."

Leighton nodded in acknowledgment, wondering how to formulate his thanks.

"Sheikh Rashid awaits your response to his offer of alliance," Ahmed Ali continued, in a speech that obviously had been rehearsed. "He will find you in Constantinople." Leighton decided that the last sentence probably sounded more ominous than intended in Ali's fractured English.

Ali made a motion for Leighton to dismount. Apparently Sheikh Rashid counted his horses. Leighton made a motion as if to take off his robe and give it back, which Ali rejected with a quick shake of his head.

Before Leighton could make any further response, Ali turned his horse back to the road and motioned his men with a raised whip-hand to follow him. With Ali leading Leighton's horse, the band pounded off on the dusty road north.

Leighton watched them ride away and turned to look at the sun. It was past its zenith, starting a slow descent toward the west. Leighton started into the city on foot. It took him a few moments to regain his "land" legs on the rough terrain of the road. He had been on horseback for weeks and was not accustomed to walking. He felt suddenly vulnerable, and wondered at the nonchalance of his rescuers with regard to their future ally. If his German pursuer had followed Leighton here, he was now free to snatch his prey again. Leighton looked around him. Donkeys, horses and the occasional ox jostled down the main thoroughfare with crowds of men and women on their various errands. Leighton wondered if other minions of Rashid had taken over safeguarding him. He regarded the horsemen he saw closely, looking for any sign of attention from them. He did receive the occasional glance from passersby on foot, though it was not unusual for Europeans to affect Arab dress. There were no other Europeans in view.

Leighton followed the mass of people heading into the city. The British Residency was in the center of town, on the river, he knew. He had stayed there several days on his previous visit. He wondered if his caravan had made it to Baghdad, where it was camped, and about Broome and Morrison's fate. His main concern, though, was keeping a watch for his German nemesis.

Leighton felt uncomfortable on the main road. But he ran the risk of getting lost if he went into the labyrinth of side streets. The sun was rarely visible from the narrow lanes. He might be able to orient himself by the river, however. He stopped in a square and looked around. Dingy stalls fronted on two sides of the square. A withered old man in a grimy robe sat under a nebk tree with several children clustered around him for a lesson of some sort. A woman shrouded in black tended a brazier that emitted a thick dark smoke. Off to the right was a street that should lead down towards the river. He could continue to make his way southwards, alternating in a westward direction toward the river.

He had resolved on this course of action and turned toward the street when a hand clamped on to his arm at the elbow. Leighton whirled to fend off his assailant, pulling back his free arm to throw a punch.

"Whoa, hold on there, tiger," said his attacker, raising his hand to ward off Leighton's threatened blow and releasing his grip on Leighton's arm. "Didn't mean to set you off."

Leighton stepped back and put together the robed man in front of him with the voice of his friend. "Morrison!" he exclaimed, reaching forward to embrace his friend. "Good show!"

Morrison had a big grin. "I took a chance you'd be coming into town this way," he said. "There's a nasty-looking German on your trail."

Leighton still felt an ache in his ribs where his captors had pummeled him with their feet. "Yes, I know. He's the one who kidnapped me in the desert." Leighton was also grinning, but stopped. "Broome – how is Broome? Why's he not here?"

"He's fine. A little worse for wear after a nasty blow to his head, but all right." Morrison was poised to tell the story of their rescue from the camp, but a glint of sun off a brass plate at one of the bazaar stalls around the square stopped him. "Let's find a less exposed place to talk," Morrison said. "I'm sure the German and his men are waiting for you at the Residency, but this square just feels too open."

Leighton led the way to the side street, explaining his plan.

"But what about the German and his men? How will you evade them to get into the Residency?" Morrison asked.

"An excellent question," said Leighton, stopping as they stepped into the shade of the small street. "Perhaps we should go to the Turkish constable and request an escort. After all, a British subject still gets some respect from official quarters."

Morrison shrugged.

"The Customs House is along the river just before the Residency," said Leighton. "I believe there's a constabulary there."

The side streets were dark in the shade, but not empty, which suited the two men. They stopped to flatten themselves against the wall as a mule lumbered by loaded with panniers of what appeared to be garbage, forcing both men to clap their hands over their nose and mouth. When they could resume their path, Leighton told Morrison about his adventures.

"Does this mean there is an Arab revolt?" Morrison asked after Leighton recounted his conversations with Rashid.

"Hard to say how much of that is going on and how much of it is just talk," Leighton said. "However, the attack on the German camp was certainly a bold action."

"Will Whitehall support these tribes, do you think?"

Leighton stopped in his tracks. "Yes," he said after a pause, "I think they will. But they must be crafty about it."

They could now see the river through the openings afforded by cross streets.

They came to a square that fronted on the river. Clusters of people crowded around bazaar stalls. The low-slung arcades of the Customs House were on the far side of the square. Leighton and Morrison remained in the shadow of the side street and surveyed the square carefully. Morrison nudged Leighton and pointed to the southeast corner of the square.

"That fellow looks like one of the horsemen with the German," he said. "They wore black cloaks like that, with hoods, over white robes."

The man Morrison pointed to was standing near the Customs House, making no pretense at doing anything other than roaming the square with his eyes, watching, waiting. At that moment, his eyes fixed on the street where Leighton and Morrison were standing. He turned to one side and whistled in such a piercing fashion that it was audible across the square. Then he started across the square in the direction of Leighton and Morrison.

Leighton looked around the square and then, to Morrison's surprise, began walking toward their stalker. Morrison followed, not sure of Leighton's intentions. With a sudden change of course, the Englishman plunged into a crowd around a stall selling brass pots and pans.

"Thief!" he shouted, in English. "You are nothing more than a common thief." He pushed through the crowd and in a single movement threw the merchant's table of pots and pans over, creating a huge clamor as the metal utensils scattered over the ground. "Junk! All junk!" Leighton continued to shout like someone deranged. The merchant began shouting at Leighton in Arabic. Leighton turned toward the crowd.

"This man is a thief. His pots and pans are junk." He picked up one and rapped his knuckles on the bottom of it. "Leak. They all leak. They don't hold water."

The merchant moved to grab the pot out of Leighton's hands. But Leighton turned and threw the pot down into the others. The merchant grabbed his arm, shouting at people in the crowd to help him restrain this madman. Morrison watched their stalker. He was holding back, outside the crowd. Morrison went to his friend's aid, pushing aside the merchant. The crowd began shouting and several men stepped forward to help the merchant and restrain the two Europeans. As a melee developed, there was a sharp whistle and several men in brown uniforms with fezzes parted the crowd, using thick batons to push people aside. By then, several men had hold of Leighton and Morrison. Leighton continued to complain in English about the faulty wares of the store. The constables reached the stall and pushed aside the men holding Leighton and Morrison, with constables taking their place on either side of the two men.

"I'm a British subject," Leighton began shouting. "English. English."

Leighton muttered something to the sergeant in Turkish. The man blew his whistle and directed the half dozen constables into a formation around Leighton and Morrison. He called double time for his troop and led them out of the square down the street along the Customs House, toward the British Residency. As they marched quickly along inside their escort, Morrison asked Leighton: "What did you say to him?"

"Only the truth," Leighton said. "I told him I am a British envoy and assassins were about to attack me."

"And he believed that?"

"It's much easier to believe that than it is that an Englishman is upset about shoddy goods in the bazaar," Leighton said with a smile.

Morrison saw two of the black-robed men who belonged with the German, but caught no sight of the German himself as they were jostled along to the Residency.

As they approached the British bastion, an imposing edifice with colonnades and arches, the sergeant blew his whistle, and the large wooden door of the Residency swung open, so that the constables could enter with their charges without breaking stride. The wooden door closed after them.

They were in a large courtyard paved in stone. Graceful arcades lined the courtyard and a large exterior staircase led up to the first floor offices. The Turkish sergeant whistled again, as a uniformed British soldier approached him from the gatehouse. Leighton came forward.

"Leighton, on special mission for the Foreign Office," he said. "The sergeant here has handily extracted me from a sticky situation in the city and kindly escorted me here." The British soldier, a non-commissioned officer nodded with deference to Leighton, and looked at Morrison. "An American comrade," Leighton explained.

Leighton spoke rapidly in Turkish to the sergeant, expressing his gratitude. He had no money for bakshish but implied in his gratitude that the sergeant's unhesitating decision to convey Leighton to safety would not go unrewarded.

Morrison was shaking his head. He had not imagined his friend capable of such decisiveness. It was only minutes since an armed and dangerous enemy had been bearing down on them. Leighton had decided on his ruse, been right in calculating the response of the Turkish constabulary, and said just the right words to get them to safety.

The sergeant whistled his troop into formation, while the British soldier gestured for the door to be opened again. The constables marched out in normal step. A clerk emerged from an upstairs office, and made his way down the staircase. He wore a tropical suit, a starched shirt, and a look of confusion on his face.

Chapter Twenty-Three

"Leighton, is it you?" A man with a cane, his left sleeve pinned together where his arm was missing, stood at the banister of the first floor balcony, peering around the clerk.

Leighton looked up at the man. "Farnsworth!" he exclaimed. "What on earth are you doing here?"

The man, whose face, with iron-gray mustache and eyebrows, seemed chiseled from granite, broke into a wide grin. "I'm the British Consul in Baghdad. Did no one tell you?"

Leighton bounded up the steps and clasped both shoulders of the older man. "No, it must be one of Whitehall's biggest secrets."

Farnsworth laughed. "Curious, because I know all about your mission."

"At least someone does," Leighton bantered back. "I'm still groping in the dark."

"I wasn't sure when you would make it here," Farnsworth said.

"I wasn't sure I would make it at all," Leighton said. "I've got some hostile forces on my tail."

"Come, let's sit in my office," Farnsworth said, turning awkwardly as he lifted his left leg stiffly and swung it around, pivoting on the cane and his right leg. Farnsworth, a colonel in the 18th Hussars, had lost his left arm and left leg at Ladysmith. Leighton had not served under his command, but became acquainted with him in the officers' mess. He had visited the older man often in the field hospital as he recovered from his wounds – injuries other men could well have succumbed to.

Leighton motioned for Morrison to come up the stairs and join him, the two followed Farnsworth into a spacious office with windows giving out onto the river. A paddle-boat glided near the opposite bank, belching smoke from its chimney.

"My comrade, Morrison, an American," Leighton said.

"Pleasure," said Farnsworth, motioning to the two visitors to take a seat at a mahogany table with massive carved legs. The room was filled with mahogany furniture, punctuated by brass tables and decorative objects.

"You're very much at home here, it seems," said Leighton, taking it all in.

"My predecessor had excellent taste," Farnsworth said. "I've only arrived six months ago."

He sat at the table, holding his artificial leg in front of him. "So who are these hostile forces chasing you?"

"There is a German, probably military. He has hired some ruffians and has been chasing me since Constantinople, I believe." After much thought, Leighton had connected the European getting off the train in Konya with his abductor in the desert.

"The Germans would be so bold as to show their hand in this way?" Farnsworth said in surprise.

"They did not expect me to live to tell the tale," Leighton said. He told Farnsworth about his rescue by the Arab tribesmen and his stay at Rashid's camp.

"An Arab revolt?" Farnsworth said, shaking his head. "Seems unlikely. Muslims turning against their caliph?"

"Nationalism seems to be trumping religion in this case," Leighton said with a shrug.

Unbidden, the clerk who had first faced Leighton from the balcony brought in a tray with tea service. He set it on the table.

"Thank you, Clarkson. We'll serve ourselves," Farnsworth said, inviting Leighton and Morrison with a gesture to help themselves.

Leighton related his findings about the railway – the camp in the desert and the slaughter of the workmen, the engineering team in the Taurus mountains.

"I must cable Constantinople so they can inform Grey," Leighton said.

"Yes, momentarily," Farnsworth said. "What are your plans?"

"To return to Constantinople as quickly as possible," Leighton said. "Assuming I can elude my pursuers."

"I'm sure we can help you with that," Farnsworth said. "We'll spirit you down to Basra by paddle-boat, and you can board a cargo ship there." He paused, mentally reviewing a timetable. "In fact, you're in luck. The paddle-boat leaves early tomorrow and will take you to a steamer that leaves the next day."

Leighton looked at Morrison, who nodded. "My man is camped outside the city," Leighton said. "Would it be possible to have a couple of your soldiers go fetch him?"

Farnsworth didn't reply. He picked up a bell sitting on the table and shook it vigorously, making a loud clanging noise. The clerk appeared at the door. Morrison described where the caravan was camped and Leighton gave a description of Broome.

"You've been most kind, Farnsworth," Leighton said. "Now, perhaps, if I can send my cable."

"Of course. Clarkson will take care of you." He rang the bell again. When Clarkson appeared, Farnsworth asked him to take Leighton to the cable room and escort Morrison to one of the guest rooms. "No doubt both of you will welcome a bath – or a shower. Both are available here and we have hot water all the time, so please take advantage of our facilities."

"We're very grateful for your hospitality," Leighton said. "And perhaps we'll have a chance to catch up on things at dinner."

"Of course," Farnsworth said. "We don't dress for dinner, but perhaps we can find some fresh khaki for you to wear."

~

As Leighton composed his cable, he worried what to tell Grey about his encounter with Rashid. The code employed even for sensitive diplomatic cables was rather simple. Also, the embassy in Constantinople would be relaying the cable, so there was a chance of a leak there. He decided to suppress Rashid's name and to describe his proposal in general terms. He focused his narrative on the evidence of railway construction that he had seen. He would have to supply details of Rashid's offer in person. If Rashid did contact him in Constantinople, he would have to use his own discretion regarding his response. The thought troubled him, though he was certain what Grey would want to do.

Leighton kept the cable short, only 250 words. He handed it to the cable officer for coding. He glanced out the window, which faced onto the square outside. He looked for any sign of his pursuers, but in his limited view saw only typical denizens of the bazaar milling around the square.

The stakes were high for Britain. A secret alliance with Arabs ready to revolt against Ottoman rule – a treacherous bargain. An alliance with a butcher and murderer. However, Leighton had no illusions about the injustices perpetrated by the sultan, not only against the Armenians, but also against the Kurds, and, yes, against the Arabs. If Britain must take sides – and, with the risk of a European war running high, it must – then the sultan had no greater moral claim than Rashid's Arabs.

Grey had said to stop the railway. Rashid's men would do that. Armed with rifles supplied by Britain, they could swoop out of the desert and play havoc with any construction site.

How would they find them? The route was clear enough, but it covered hundreds of miles. How would they know where exactly work was being done?

Leighton walked around the balcony to Farnsworth's office. He was no longer there, but Clarkson came bustling out of the anteroom, and led Leighton up another staircase to a guestroom. Leighton saw the bed – a simple iron frame with a thin wool mattress – and flung himself onto it. He was desperate to bathe, but the bed was paradise to him after weeks on the march. His misgivings vanished as he fell asleep instantly.

~

Leighton awoke from a heavy, dreamless sleep. Someone was standing over him, reaching toward him. He lurched upward, raising his arm to parry the blow.

The figure drew back. "It is only I, milord," said Broome's familiar voice. As Leighton's eyes focused, he recognized the balding, stooped figure of his valet.

"Broome!" he said, leaping off the bed. Before either of them grasped what was happening, he had his arms around Broome in a bear hug, thumping him on the back. "Good show, good show," Leighton repeated.

Leighton stepped back. Broome had evidently bathed and shaved, his skin giving off a ruddy, scrubbed look.

Morrison had mentioned a blow to the head, but no wound was evident.

"I'm relieved to see milord in good health," Broome said, breathing hard after Leighton's embrace. "We were really quite worried," he said with his gift for understatement. Now, he smiled, but kept his arms at his side. "I've drawn a bath."

Leighton looked for his watch. "Dinner is in half an hour, but the colonel said they would wait for you," Broome said. Leighton, who had fallen asleep in his clothes, allowed Broome to undress him. Even after their laundering at Rashid's camp, his clothes were stiff with grime and perspiration.

"Morrison said you had taken a blow to the head," Leighton said as Broome scrubbed his back with a brush. The bathtub was a large, cast iron vessel. Leighton wondered that it had found its way to this far corner of the globe.

"It was nothing, milord," Broome responded. "It is all healed now. I understand milord suffered some rough treatment at the hands of those bandits."

Leighton, basking in the effect the warm water and soap was having on his tired body, nodded. "It was, indeed, rough. But now I feel very good."

Having exchanged the essentials, the two men continued in silence. Broome left the room briefly to allow Leighton to finish his bathing. When he returned, he fetched the towel he had hung across the hot water pipes and draped it over Leighton's shoulders as he emerged from the bath. In moments, Leighton was shaved and dressed, the two falling into the routine as though several weeks had not intervened to interrupt the pattern.

The meal itself was splendid. It was, of course, lamb, the only meat readily available. But Farnsworth served one of his few bottles of claret to celebrate the occasion, and it was a joy to Leighton and Morrison simply to eat off bone china. Two other senior staff joined them in Farnsworth's private dining room, which, with the candles, china and claret transported them back to England for a brief couple of hours. Morrison entertained the group with some of his Rough Rider tales.

Farnsworth had arranged for the paddle-boat to stop at the dock of the Residency. Two of his soldiers would board first to make sure that no hostile agents had slipped aboard.

"I doubt that my mad German will continue to pursue me now that I've had a chance to cable my findings home," Leighton said.

Farnsworth shook his head. "If he is truly mad – and his behavior indicates he is – such logic may not stop him."

So it was that the five men stood the next morning at the postern gate giving out to the small wooden pier that served the Residency. Broome had brought their luggage from the caravan, though now they had packed the bare essentials into light portmanteaus that they could easily carry. It was still dark with faint whorls of mist hovering over the water of the Tigris. One of Farnsworth's men held a lantern. They heard the paddle-boat before they saw it, its wheel churning the water in its wake as it glided at a fair speed toward the dock.

The pier was approachable only by water. Nonetheless, Leighton kept a watchful eye. Despite his reassurances to Farnsworth, Leighton felt he had not shaken his nemesis. As harmful as a cable might be, it could not convey the same information that a live Leighton could. His enemy would find reason enough to do away with him if the opportunity presented itself.

When the paddle-boat docked, the two soldiers boarded and went through the vessel. It was a simple affair – a single passenger cabin sat in front of the bridge, with crates stacked on the deck in front of it. There was more storage space behind the bridge, for the paddle-boat service handled far more freight than passenger traffic. The wooden benches in the passenger cabin were mostly empty. A group of people that appeared to be an extended family with women and children clustered in a back corner.

The soldiers motioned for Leighton, Morrison and Broome to come aboard. They sat in the front. Crates blocked their view through the front window and a lifeboat obscured their view on the right side. The two British soldiers stepped back onto the pier and waved the captain on his way. Leighton had retrieved his service pistol and Farnsworth had provided all three men with rifles for the voyage. The Tigris remained wide and navigable through to Basra. The passengers might be vulnerable to a sniper attack from the shore, but it would be difficult for a boat to approach and board the paddle-boat unobserved. Farnsworth had seen to it that the captain was fully briefed and Leighton observed one of the crew with a rifle strapped to his back.

Leighton pointed out the crew member to Morrison. "It seems we're in good hands," he said.

Morrison nodded. The German had surprised him once and he didn't want to be surprised again.

Broome busied himself with the luggage. He didn't like the fact that Leighton had carried his own portmanteau on board and now secured all three pieces of luggage under the seats. He carried another small bag with provisions for the voyage. The men settled onto the benches as the paddle-boat churned its way to the middle of the river and set its course southward.

Chapter Twenty-Four

The paddle-boat could reach a speed of 15 knots an hour, but loaded as it was, it cruised at 12 knots. The boat stopped at cities on both side of the river to take on and discharge cargo and sometimes passengers. It would make a longer stop at Kut to take on coal and water. In all, the trip was scheduled to last at least 24 hours, arriving at Basra the following morning.

Broome procured some blankets from the ship's steward, a Bengali who doubled as the cargo master. The three of them made themselves as comfortable as possible on the wooden benches. It was dawn as they boarded and the sun broke the horizon as they cleared Baghdad.

Leighton and Morrison fell into the practiced sleep of travelers, while Broome kept the first watch. The paddle created a comfortable thumping sound as it churned through the water. The pistons driving the paddle could be felt in rhythmic vibration rather than heard. Broome faced east, their exposed side, as the swaying lifeboat blocked the view to the west. The family in the back likewise nestled in for a long trip.

The river, sluggish and muddy, shone a tawny lion color in the sun. Marine smells of water and plants mingled with a fetid odor of rot. The movement of the boat created a pleasant flow of fresh air through an open window in the front of the cabin.

The stops were brief – a quick rope over the pylon, and a passenger or two boarding, or small baskets and crates loaded onto the boat. Broome scanned the docks whenever they approached the shore, looking for any suspicious figure waiting to board. He also surveyed the coast, watching for groups of horsemen or the telltale glint of a rifle barrel or telescopic lens. The first few hours passed without incident. Morrison awoke and stared silently out the window as they sailed downstream. Fruit trees and palms gave way to flat fields of grain as they rode the Tigris to its confluence with the Euphrates.

At midday, Broome unpacked some of the provisions – the usual figs and dates, but also some ripe goat's cheese, flatbread and fresh oranges. He spread a small cloth on the bench and set out the food, laying his field knife next to the sparse meal. As if on cue, Leighton awoke and eagerly ate his share, chewing everything at length to derive the maximum satisfaction.

"Splendid!" he pronounced, as he washed it down with drinking water from a canteen.

Morrison volunteered for the next watch, so Broome drifted off to sleep and Leighton stared idly out the window.

"What will you do about Rashid's request?" Morrison asked.

"We must find a way to deliver the rifles so that they cannot be connected to the British government," Leighton said. "Europe is a tinderbox and revelation of this kind of perfidy could be the match to set it off."

Morrison remained silent for a while. "Maybe we could help," he said at last.

Leighton, who had been looking out the window, turned to face his companion. "We?"

"The United States."

Leighton pondered his friend's ability to speak for the nation on this point.

"A three-way deal," Morrison continued. "Britain orders rifles from an American supplier. American ships deliver them not to Britain but to Constantinople or Aleppo. Rashid or his allies take delivery and disappear into the desert."

"Why would the Americans do this? The country would surely remain neutral in a European war."

"Neutral, yes," said Morrison. "But that wouldn't keep us from taking sides." He laughed.

Leighton laughed, too. "A country of many contradictions." Leighton knew that Teddy Roosevelt often spoke of his country carrying a big stick. How reliable was Roosevelt? How reliable could he be out of office? In any democracy, a return to power remained uncertain no matter how popular a politician was. Disraeli and Gladstone had learned that lesson in bitter defeats.

"Springfield. Best rifles in the world," Morrison resumed. "We've been outfitting our army with them. Teddy personally suggested some improvements. It now has a knife-style bayonet. It uses pointed bullets and has a shorter barrel – particularly useful at short range for riders on horseback." Morrison mimicked a rider lifting the rifle to his shoulder and firing. "It's called the weapon of silent death – your enemy will be hit before he hears the shot that killed him."

"It's very risky for Britain," Leighton said. "Even with this subterfuge, the arms could be traced back to Whitehall."

"Not in this century," Morrison said confidently. "The paperwork would disappear in a top secret file. The Springfield Armory is owned by the government."

"The newspapers, your legislators?"

"A few Bedouin skirmishes in the Syrian desert won't attract the attention of our yellow press, or our Congressmen," Morrison said. "They have enough local scandals to keep them busy."

"Not even when it's reported that the murderous Arab tribesmen were using American rifles?"

"Springfield rifles have found their way to various parts of the world. Who's to say where these originated?"

"Yes, it would be a hard trail to follow," Leighton mused aloud. "Much harder than if our Enfield rifles were found."

"There would be no suspicion of British involvement."

Leighton nodded, looking at Morrison's proposal in his mind, turning it over to see any flaws. Any flaws? One leak along the chain would result in scandal, scandal that could bring Britain closer to war. Still, the American angle would confuse the issue, make it difficult to pin anything on Whitehall.

Broome woke up and all three men spent some time readying their rifles. The crew members, however, put their arms aside. They had work to do at Kut. A boy moved through the passenger cabin lighting lanterns, and Leighton signaled to him not to light the lanterns in the front part of the cabin where they were making their camp. The boy, a lad of fourteen, needed no further encouragement to avoid the Europeans and their guns.

As the steamboat approached the pier, Leighton and his companions could see the stevedores preparing the hand-operated cranes to load cargo. Lamps lit the harbor and cranes, but the surrounding buildings and terrain remained dark. Leighton, Morrison, and Broome hunched in the passenger cabin. The chances of even an expert marksman spotting them and hitting them were very small, Leighton realized. Yet he had enough evidence of his foe's tenacity that he preferred not to take any chances.

The boat remained docked for an hour at Kut. At one point, several men on the pier started shouting, and then a loud thud shook the boat. Leighton and Morrison reached for their weapons, but Broome, who was keeping watch at the door to the passenger cabin, reported that a crane operator had simply misjudged the distance in lowering a large palette of grain sacks. The boat departed, somewhat lower in the water after taking on cargo and coal, with several new passengers. Broome had examined the passengers as they boarded and saw nothing to arouse his suspicions. The three companions sat up in their seats again but refrained from lighting a lantern in their end of the cabin. Broome parceled out more dates and bread. It was Leighton's watch and Morrison stretched out on a bench between two blankets, emitting a soft snore as soon as his head settled onto a third blanket folded into a pillow. Broome remained awake, his eyes fixed on the blank, dark window.

"Looks like we may have lost our pursuer," Leighton said.

Broome looked around to him. "This boat is very vulnerable," he said, "especially in the dark."

Broome was right, of course. Easy enough now for a boat to come right alongside the steamer.

"The government is going to help the Arabs?" Broome asked quietly.

"It may be the way to stop the railway," Leighton said.

Broome pondered the situation for some moments. "Would it bring down the Ottoman government?"

Leighton frowned. "Not likely, not by itself. Whitehall does not want the Porte to fall. It would create chaos."

"And yet, in arming its enemies, it would speed that fall, it seems to me," Broome persisted. "It would involve Britain in this region."

Leighton had no answer to that. Britain had enough to do with minding Egypt and certainly didn't need to take on great areas of Asia Minor as well. And it would open up a whole new terrain for Great Power rivalry. Or war.

"I'm sure Grey does not want to be involved in this region," Leighton said. "He just wants to keep down the risk for India." Yet, Churchill's words about the petroleum in Mesopotamia, the fuel for a new generation of Navy destroyers, nagged at Leighton in the back of his mind. Stopping the railway, blocking Germany's interest in the region, did embroil Britain in a way the empire had not been involved before. Where would it stop? What if the Ottoman Empire did collapse? Who would step into the vacuum? Russia? Germany? France? Britain could not allow any of those Powers to gain an edge in the Orient. "Would it be such a bad thing for Britain to be involved?"

Broome shrugged. "These are people with history, with their own religion. They have lived under the rule of their religion. Perhaps they would not like to live under European rule," he said.

Leighton bit his tongue. Perhaps the Indians, the Egyptians, the Hottentots, felt the same way. And yet the British Empire imposed its rule on them – bringing them improved conditions and the chance at Christian salvation. Would that be the result in Mesopotamia? Would it become another colony in the empire?

"It depends, I guess, whether it serves British interests to mind things here," Leighton said finally.

Broome nodded. Of course. It was the answer that counted. Broome was quiet then, and soon his head had slumped forward and he slept. Leighton pondered their conversation in the dark. All but one lantern had been extinguished in the cabin. The other passengers were asleep, or quiet. The paddle continued its rhythmic thumping in the dark as the boat turned to meet the Euphrates.

~

It was shortly before Qrnah, just above the confluence, that the attack came. The first warning Leighton had was not anything from the water, but a scraping sound on the roof of the passenger cabin. Leighton immediately raised his rifle to his shoulder. When he heard a second scraping sound above, he fired into the ceiling. The shot woke Broome and Morrison, and unleashed pandemonium among the other passengers. Leighton turned to see a black-robed Arab entering the front door of the cabin and he aimed his rifle. Before he could shoot, the figure was blocked by several of the passengers pushing to get out of the cabin. Leighton heard glass breaking behind him, then the roar of a rifle shot as Broome fired at an arm holding a pistol through the broken window. Blood sprayed the window as someone cried out in pain. The pistol fell to the floor as the bloody arm was withdrawn. More glass shattered and Leighton felt rather than heard the whistle of bullet tearing past his head into a post. He pointed his rifle at the source of the shot and fired. The other passengers were torn, not sure whether huddling under the benches was safer or getting out of the cabin and its gunfire. Fleeing passengers blocked both exits, providing an unintentional defense for the three targets of the attack. The darkness and close quarters further disadvantaged the attackers.

A trapdoor opened in the ceiling and a rifle barrel poked through. Morrison wheeled and reached out his arm, grabbing the barrel and pushing it up as it fired. The bullet crashed into a beam. Morrison released the scorched barrel and thrust his own rifle up through the trapdoor, pulling the trigger as he did so. There was a muffled explosion and more blood sprayed the cabin. One of the passengers, an old man, fell back from the door with a curse, a dark stain coloring his robe, as another robed figure pushed through the door. Leighton saw the gleam of a curved dagger flashing in an arc toward Broome. Leighton parried the dagger with his rifle, knocking the hand back as he yelled a warning to Broome, who dodged to one side. The hand kept its grip on the dagger and now slashed toward Leighton. Leighton caught the wrist of his attacker and managed to deflect the blow enough so that it only caught his shirt. He saw a second dagger coming at him and ducked into it, colliding into a solid wall of taut muscle. He felt a searing pain on his hip as the blade continued on its path. Morrison swung the butt of his rifle over Leighton's head, making a loud thwack as the wood connected with a skull. Another shot rang out, throwing one of the passengers into Broome, who fell as a second shot slapped into the bench behind him. By now, the other passengers had lost all reason and rushed in a frenzy to the doors and shattered windows, desperate to find any way out of the death trap. Leighton heard several splashes as they plunged into the river.

There was another shot outside the cabin and more screaming. The body in the trapdoor fell to the floor and another rifle barrel appeared at the opening. Leighton fired his rifle blindly through the trapdoor and heard a groan and thud as another body slumped to the roof.

Suddenly it was still. No one was pushing toward them. The floor was slick with blood. Splintered wood and broken glass were everywhere. A few passengers whimpered in the far corner. Leighton whirled around twice, his rifle at his shoulder. The hot stream on his hip had grown cold and wet. Morrison stepped over two bodies to the front cabin door, leading with his rifle to see if he would draw fire. Broome extricated himself from underneath the woman who had stopped the bullet meant for him. She was alive, but bleeding heavily from a wound in her shoulder.

A crewman entered the back door of the cabin and found three rifles pointing at him. He threw up his hands and yelled in English, "Don't shoot." It was the Bengali steward, who kept muttering "Mother of God" over and over. Leighton put aside his rifle and put his hand on his

wounded hip. He held it up, covered with blood. "Broome,"
he called. "I'm hit." The dagger had creased his skin but not
hit the bone. Broome came with the canteen and a towel,
cleaning the wound as quickly as he could. The cut was not
as deep as he feared. He folded the towel into a compress
and told Leighton to hold it tight on the wound.

Three of the passengers were down. The Bengali steward
was attending to the bleeding woman. Morrison checked the
pulse of the old man who was stabbed and found none. He
turned over the body of the attacker who had been in the
trapdoor. He had been killed by a shot through the heart. He
was Arab, not German. Morrison went outside and circled
around the passenger cabin. No sign of any other attackers.
The rest of them had escaped.

"They must have had a boat," Morrison said as he
returned to the cabin. The steamer now had turned toward
shore, heading for Qrnah. Leighton looked at Morrison. They
could not afford to be held up in Qrnah for official inquiries.
Qrnah was at the head of the Shatt al Arab, the waterway
formed by the confluence of the Tigris and Euphrates. It
was 20 miles from Basra. "We'll need horses," Leighton
said. He was still breathing hard from the battle. Morrison
nodded. He took the Bengali steward aside – Broome was
bandaging the wounded woman – and Leighton saw him slip
the crewman several folded bills.

The wound on Leighton's hip had stopped bleeding.
Broome tore two strips from the towel and made a bandage
of sorts for the cut. The crew began cranking the cranes
holding the lifeboat, positioning the boat over the water
and lowering it. Morrison gestured to Broome to fetch his
portmanteau as he picked up his own and Leighton's. The
three men stepped out onto the narrow deck. Morrison
climbed down a short rope ladder into the lifeboat. Broome
handed him the luggage and the rifles. Then the two men

assisted Leighton, who winced involuntarily as his hip bumped against the steamer railing. Broome clambered down the ladder into the boat. One of the crewmen, an Arab, was sitting aft in the boat. He had already inserted two oars into their locks and motioned to Broome to mount the two oars in the fore of the boat.

The steamer, which had slowed during this operation, turned toward the shore, picking up speed. Broome and the Arab crewman began rowing, heading toward the dark shore. Morrison held his rifle ready in case their attackers were still lurking on the river. The crewman steered the lifeboat toward the shore south of the dock. Leighton fired a quick question to him in Arabic, and received a sharp guttural response.

"He says we will be able to obtain horses on the shore," Leighton said. Arabs loved their horses, and any market town would have at least one stable with mounts. The moist air at the river's surface chilled Leighton and Morrison, sitting still without any jackets. Broome, however, perspired with the effort of rowing, his forehead glistening in the light of a half moon.

They reached the shore quickly. It was dark where they landed. The dock, a half-mile up the river from them was beginning to stir, ablaze with lanterns. The stop in Qrnah was a scheduled one, but the carnage on board would require them to fetch the Turkish commandant.

"'You were never here'– that's what the steward told me when he went to ready the lifeboat," Morrison said.

"Smart. But what about the missing lifeboat?" Leighton asked.

"The attackers took it."

"And why did they attack? What if they question the passengers?" Leighton worried aloud. "Why should they?" he asked rhetorically, answering his own question. "Besides, they will be reluctant to volunteer information to the Turks."

"In any event, we need to put as much distance as possible between us and this town," said Morrison.

Leighton nodded. The Ottoman administration worked with a remarkable degree of inefficiency, but there was no need to put it to the test.

The crewman led them up the embankment along a shoreline with wooden sheds. He stopped at one and thumped loudly on a double door that was barred and padlocked. A horse whinnied inside the building. A figure emerged from a smaller door to one side, dressed only in a shirt that reached down to his knees. He carried a rifle and was cursing in Arabic. There was a rapid exchange between the two Arabs. Leighton produced a roll of cash and handed it to the crewman, who peeled off one of the bills and passed it on to the stable guard. The man went back in his side door and returned quickly with a ring of keys, selecting one to open the padlock. He pulled aside the bar and swung open the double door, motioning the group to follow him. Without lighting a lantern, he gathered harnesses and saddles from hooks lining one wall. Stalls lined the other side of the stable. Most of them appeared to have occupants. The stable guard moved quickly from stall to stall, saddling three horses with practiced movements. Broome found some rope and quickly secured the portmanteaus behind each saddle.

Leighton spoke directly to the stable owner in Arabic. The man shrugged. The crewman gave him some more bills from Leighton's roll. The man went around to his side entrance, and some minutes later returned with a boy in tow. The youth, not more than fourteen or fifteen, was still tying his breeches shut. He went into the far recess of the stable and came back with a smaller horse.

"Our guide," Leighton explained.

Without any further conversation, the group mounted, and, with the youth in the lead, followed the path along the shore. They turned inland after a couple of hundred yards and came to a narrow road. The boy never looked back, but broke into a gallop on the road. The three men followed him.

Chapter Twenty-Five

The sun had risen by the time they reached Basra. Their guide led them through the town to the docks.

Basra itself was a grimy collection of narrow streets and flat-topped mud houses, with the occasional flourish of a cornice carved in wood. The docks were piled with wooden crates and bales of cotton and hay. Few ships were moored at the moment and activity was minimal, though one group of coolies was busy loading a riverboat at the far wharf. Low sheds and tents covered the ground between the dock and palm groves that stretched out in the distance. A string of small donkeys sporting gaily decorated saddles was making its way toward one of those sheds.

Leighton took this all in as their horses picked their way through the crowded piers. They made for a small ship flying the Union Jack. It sat low in the water, already loaded. Leighton and Morrison kept their rifles at the ready, surveying the harbor area for enemies.

A seaman appeared on the deck of the British ship. Farnsworth's telegram had evidently arrived, for he motioned them forward. A second uniformed figure wearing an officer's cap came to the railing. The ramp was down and the men dismounted. Leighton muttered a quick Arabic blessing to the guide, who strung the horses together and started his journey back to Qrnah.

The officer didn't speak to the men as they climbed

aboard, only nodded and gestured for them to move quickly down a staircase. The visitors paused for their eyes to adjust to the gloom below.

"Lord Leighton?" said a man wearing a captain's hat, extending his hand as he emerged from what looked like an officers' mess. Leighton took his hand with a quick bow. "Captain Ferguson, at your service," the man said.

"Morrison," said Leighton, stepping aside with a gesture toward his companion. "My man, Broome. Thank you, captain, for waiting for us. I hope we have eluded our pursuers and will not cause you or your men any trouble."

Ferguson only nodded at this and turned to his first officer with a quick command. The officer disappeared into the mess and moments later the ship began to move, backing away from the dock.

"You'll have to share a cabin, but it has two bunks," Ferguson said to Leighton and Morrison, taking them down the gangway. "Your man can bunk with the crew." Leighton and Morrison said nothing. The displaced officers were likely to be bunking with the crew as well.

"There are uniforms from the company for you to wear," Ferguson continued. He opened a door on the starboard side of the ship.

As Morrison stepped through into the tiny cabin, he slapped at a sand fly on his neck. "Cream is in the drawer there," Ferguson said, pointing a small dresser bolted to the floor. The thick unguent used by the Arabs had worn off, exposing them to small insects. The word in the merchant marine was that only armor plate could actually keep the pests out – there was no mesh fine enough to resist their advances.

The door closed and the two men smiled at each other. The cabin was scarcely large enough for them both to stand in the space. "I'll take the top bunk," volunteered Leighton, half a head shorter than his companion. He quickly unbuckled and removed his boots and clambered into the top bunk, using the short ladder bolted to the bunks. Morrison located the cream and smeared some of the clear jelly onto his face, neck and hands. "Glory be," he sighed as he slipped into the lower bunk, flexing his knees to fit his entire frame into the recessed bed.

The two men were exhausted from the battle and the whole anxious trip from Baghdad. While the cramped quarters and the flies left them anything but comfortable, they quickly fell asleep as the ship turned its prow downstream and picked up speed.

The three guests stayed below as the ship plowed its way down the Shatt al Arab toward the Gulf. The waterway was wide enough and deep enough for ocean shipping, but a sniper on the shore would have no trouble hitting a target on the ship's deck. Once the ship attained the Gulf itself, Leighton and his companions would be able to spend time on deck.

The ship, ironically named the *Basra*, was a small cargo ship with a single funnel that plied between Basra and Constantinople. It was part of the British shipping operation that was threatened by the building of the Baghdad Railway. Captain Ferguson clearly had a notion that Leighton's mission was related to the railway, and dropped hints to see if he could pry some information out of his visitor.

"We have to keep the Union Jack flying on the Shatt," Ferguson said, concluding a long peroration on his part about the importance of British influence in the Orient. Leighton continued to listen. "I mean," Ferguson added, "it wouldn't do to have our shipping pitched out by a railroad from some foreign power."

Leighton refused to rise to the bait, not even to observe that Britain itself was a foreign power in these waters.

At one point, early the next morning, the captain brought Leighton up to the bridge, moving quickly along the deck to keep his exposure to a minimum. "See, over there," he said, pointing to two dredging vessels on the eastern shore. "They're building a new terminal – for petroleum." They were now near the mouth of the Shatt, where it poured into the Persian Gulf. The eastern coast here was Persian territory. "Anglo-Persian," Ferguson confirmed. "They'll be shipping oil from here for our navy ships." He looked again at Leighton. "The Gulf has to remain a British lake, I'd say."

Leighton nodded absently in assent, as though trying to absorb the geopolitical wisdom the captain had bestowed on him. Leighton did look with interest at the dredging work. It was in this hinterland that Anglo-Persian had struck oil two years earlier. The plan, as Leighton understood it, was to build a pipeline to carry the oil to the terminal here, to load it into specially built tankers. The discovery of petroleum was creating a whole new industry, Leighton reflected.

"I see what you're saying, Captain," Leighton said. "My own interests in this region are scholarly, but I know my colleagues in Westminster are putting a high value on the oil discoveries here."

Leighton knew the captain was right. The discovery of oil made it imperative for Britain to keep control of the Gulf. An alliance with Arab leaders could help further that goal. The Arabs would throw off Ottoman rule sooner or later, and Britain could establish itself as a reliable friend by helping their cause at this juncture. His mission had taken on new importance with Rashid's overtures. London could achieve its goal of stopping the Baghdad Railway while assuring its future in the region. Leighton knew he needed to suppress whatever qualms he had about the justice of this alliance in order to achieve this dual objective.

By the time they were on the relatively open sea of the

Gulf, Morrison came up to the deck and Leighton joined him there.

"It looks like we shook them," Morrison said.

"Yes, it does," Leighton agreed. "I have to say that my German nemesis, for all the menace that he displays, has been singularly ineffective in obtaining his objective."

The two men made themselves comfortable on the deck, using some collapsible wicker chairs provided by Ferguson. Broome brought them tea, and Leighton made notes in a small journal he had included in his "flight" baggage. His Koranic commentaries and his Scheherazade remained with the rest of his luggage, which Farnsworth would forward to London. The *Basra* would take somewhere between eight and ten days to reach its destination, depending on prevailing winds and the passage at Suez.

The sea air was a tonic after the long trek across the desert. The Gulf's surface showed only the faintest ripple, so the ship skimmed along smoothly. The water here, more gray than blue, still was more like the sea than the muddy waterways behind them.

At midday, it blew its horn in greeting to the large mail steamer under way from Karachi. They were giving the ship a wide berth to avoid rocking in its wake, but still Leighton could make out a number of figures on the passenger deck, many of them waving with exaggerated gestures. Leighton made a huge waving motion back to acknowledge the greeting. The British Empire lived by its mail, and the mail steamer was a symbol of the benevolent rule Britain had bestowed on much of the world. Steamers carried instructions and information between the imperial headquarters and its colonial outposts. They kept the lines open for military and commercial operations in every corner of the globe. Leighton wondered how much mail was waiting for him in London after so many weeks away.

Chapter Twenty-Six

Fitzmaurice read Leighton's cable slowly. He had ordered the encrypted text decoded before he would allow it to be forwarded to London, and now was perusing it in his chambers. The surveyors in the Taurus mountains did not surprise him. The planning for the Baghdad Railway would continue even as the Porte tried to end the political impasse on its construction.

A building camp in the Syrian desert was another matter altogether. This was in clear defiance of the understanding between the Porte and His Majesty's Government. This worried Fitzmaurice, though it in some measure vindicated his distrust of the Young Turks. It bothered him that his sources in the German embassy had failed to keep him informed. Leighton's report of the attack on the camp, however, was even more unsettling for Fitzmaurice. An Arab revolt was a preposterous idea, and a dangerous one. And yet, here was clear evidence that resistance had erupted in violence. Was it an isolated incident? This type of attack was unprecedented under Ottoman rule.

Fitzmaurice sipped his Irish whiskey. He brought a small supply back with him from each visit home and nursed it carefully through the months. He remained convinced that the Young Turks were a passing phenomenon. Their rule would crumble as a result of their own ineptitude, and the sultan would be able to reassert his control. Europe needed the Ottoman Empire. The balance of power was precarious enough without throwing the entire Orient into the equation. The C.U.P. was a band of hoodlums with no clear set of goals. They would stumble and fall and the beys would switch their fealty back to the sultan.

An Arab revolt, however, could destroy the whole fragile structure. Coming after the losses of Bulgaria and Bosnia in Europe, an Arab revolt could fatally weaken the empire in its eastern territories – the empire of the fearsome Turk, built up through centuries of conquests, would sink into history and Europe would have to go to war to apportion the remnants.

Fitzmaurice drained his glass and savored the smoky aftertaste of the whiskey. He put the decoded copy and the original encrypted cable into a folder that he set on top of his bureau. He had to admire Leighton's pluck in surviving his caravan to Baghdad. The Germans seemed to have him marked for elimination, however, and everyone knew how efficient the Germans were. Fitzmaurice wished no ill to Leighton, but the game was too important for an amateur to spoil the delicate balance that professional diplomats were maintaining in this region. No, there was no room for an Arab revolt in the world of 1910. Far better that the Germans and Turks build their railroad so that the sultan's troops could put down any unrest in these desert lands. It seemed unlikely that Leighton would leave Baghdad alive. Should he return to Constantinople, the Germans, or perhaps the Turks, would make sure he did not deliver his message to London.

Fitzmaurice picked up another typewritten sheet. One of their spies in the Interior Ministry reported that Talaat's wife had gone missing, evading those watching her through a ruse. Was her disappearance related to her dalliance with Leighton? Fitzmaurice wondered. Even if not, Elena's flight would hardly dispose Talaat kindly to the Englishman. Had Talaat really believed an Armenian would remain faithful to him? Hubris or naïveté. Perhaps the woman had fled to join the Armenian underground, or to meet Leighton in London. If the latter, she was probably destined for disappointment.

The dragoman paced his room. It bothered him to suppress the cable. Nor did he like the notion that he might be complicit somehow in the murder of a British subject, particularly such a high-ranking subject, by keeping silent about his suspicions. The cable was addressed specifically to Sir Edward Grey. A decoding error? Hardly. Nor was it sufficient that Leighton not show up to ask about his cable. There were the cable clerks and the coding officers both in Baghdad and here who witnessed the cable and knew its contents. He could argue that the risk of interception by the Turks, even of a coded message, was too high to relay the explosive contents of the cable. But then he would be obliged to put the cable in the next pouch to London, in two days' time. Perhaps he could delay a week with the argument that the embassy needed to verify or at least interpret this information. In the end, though, he would have to send it. Leighton had been wary about putting names in his dispatch. Without Leighton to fill in the gaps, especially the name of the Arab leader who was willing to forcibly oppose Ottoman rule, there would be little London could do to follow Leighton's lead. Bad enough that the notion of an Arab revolt would be planted in London's mind, but Fitzmaurice could do much to dampen any expectations on that score, starting with his own commentary on Leighton's cable.

Yes, that was it. Happy with his chosen course of action, Fitzmaurice poured himself another Irish whiskey.

~

Von Bohlen's nerves could not take much more of this. He was waiting and watching for an opportunity to meet with the British visitor from London, the one he had briefly met at the Bosphorus reception. But some remarks yesterday had unsettled him.

He was at a meeting with Bieberstein and other embassy officials to discuss some tariff issues. Construction materials for the railway had a special exemption from import tax and this was mentioned in relation to a Krupp shipment due to arrive in the coming week.

"We must see that the railway project proceeds in a timely fashion," Bieberstein said.

"Yes, we must keep our Ottoman hosts happy," Hoffenberg said with a quiet chuckle. Bieberstein shot him quick glance of warning. "And of course our friends from Deutsche Bank," Hoffenberg added with a smile and a nod toward von Bohlen.

"What of the British objections?" von Bohlen asked.

Bieberstein looked at the banker. "Do you know of any new objections?"

"New? No, not new. But I gathered their envoy was here to reiterate the British opposition to the project."

"Which envoy was that?" Bieberstein asked.

"The Orientalist, the one who attended our reception. Leighton I believe was the name."

Bieberstein smiled broadly. "My dear Bohlen, the distinguished Lord Leighton is a scholar. His interests are scholarly. However did you get the idea he had any message regarding the railway."

Von Bohlen's eyes narrowed. He had no official knowledge of Leighton's mission. His own alertness, and a passing friendship with one of Bieberstein's attaches, had brought that information to him.

Before he could formulate a reply, Hoffenberg piped up again. "Lord Leighton departed Constantinople weeks ago. He is in no position to object to anything," Hoffenberg said with some irritation. Bieberstein shot him another glance. "I mean to say, he has no official standing and he is pursuing his research in Baghdad. It's not likely he will return to Constantinople," Hoffenberg, a new smile playing on his lips, "or so my sources in the British embassy tell me."

Von Bohlen shrugged. "As you well know, the Deutsche Bank is very much interested in a rapid completion of this project." He looked at Hoffenberg, who pointedly ignored his glance. What took Leighton to Baghdad – did he go by sea or by land? And what made Hoffenberg so sure he was not returning to Constantinople?

These questions tormented von Bohlen. He needed information and dare not approach the German embassy officials. He had resolved to attend a French reception this evening in the hopes of encountering someone from the British embassy who might know more about Leighton.

The reception was at the Pera Palace, hosted by the Compagnie Universelle de Suez, which operated the Suez canal. While Britain and France controlled the company, and the canal, the group paid lip service to the titular ruler of Egypt with such small events. Only one director had made the trip from Paris, so attendance was likely to be at sub-ambassador rank. All the better for von Bohlen's purposes – lower-ranking personnel were usually easier to pump for information, he found.

The company had made sure to have plenty of champagne on hand and the party was well under way when von Bohlen entered the banquet hall. Waiters in white ties and jackets with gold braid circulated with caviar and canapés. Von Bohlen waved them all away. His stomach was too unsettled for such delicacies. He shook hands briefly with the Frenchmen at the door, and looked around the room for any acquaintances from the British embassy. He had guessed correctly – attendance was at the subaltern level.

He spotted a flash of red hair and headed for the British dragoman, Fitzmaurice. The Irishman was a fixture at any official event in Constantinople and von Bohlen had often spoken with him.

"Good evening," von Bohlen said with a slight bow as Fitzmaurice turned toward him, a canapé in one hand and a champagne saucer in another. Fitzmaurice nodded, waving both arms to indicate why he was not free to shake hands. "My dear von Bohlen," he said by way of greeting.

The two men surveyed the party together. "Even less distinguished than last year," von Bohlen commented.

"Present company excepted," Fitzmaurice flashed a grin.

"Oh, indeed," von Bohlen responded, not quite mustering a smile. "And how is the distinguished dragoman these days?"

Fitzmaurice hesitated, a bland response on his lips. He thought it curious that von Bohlen – Mr. Baghdad Railway himself – should seek him out amid his own preoccupation with Leighton and his mission. "Well enough," he said finally, "all things considered."

Von Bohlen looked askance at him. "And you?" Fitzmaurice asked him before he could reply. "Is all well with the great Deutsche Bank?"

"The bank prospers," von Bohlen said with no hesitation. "It is a golden age for Germany."

"And your railway?"

Von Bohlen looked at him. "That, as you well know, sir, is a sensitive subject."

"Sensitive, no doubt. Yet one wonders what the fuss is about," said Fitzmaurice.

"You are much closer to the answer to that question than I, as it is your government which is making the 'fuss,'" von Bohlen said.

"London of course sees everything from a European perspective, a political perspective," Fitzmaurice said. "Here, we are better placed to see the practical side of your project."

"Are you saying the embassy has been supporting the railway?" von Bohlen asked.

"Support would be too strong a word," Fitzmaurice said. "But I have often noted the merits of the plan, both officially and unofficially." He smiled. "I believe it could help stabilize the situation here in the empire," he said vaguely, "though of course I fully understand my government's concerns about our trade concession in Basra."

"And what of your visitor? Was he not here to affirm London's opposition to the railway?" von Bohlen asked.

"My dear Bohlen, you surprise me! If you're referring to the distinguished Lord Leighton, he is a scholar, an Orientalist – not a politician. Certainly not a diplomat. If London wants to affirm its opposition to the railway, it would do so through its appointed ambassador."

"And yet I've heard talk that he was here in connection with the railway," von Bohlen persisted.

"Talk. So much talk here in Constantinople. You know better than I how little credence one can give all this talk."

"And this Leighton, is he still here, pursuing his scholarly research?"

Fitzmaurice laughed. "No, his scholarship has taken him to Baghdad – by caravan. Hopefully his sense of adventure has not put him in harm's way. The overland route always entails some element of peril, I fear."

Von Bohlen was trying to absorb the new information as he responded. A caravan! The caravans often followed or closely paralleled the planned route for the railway. Leighton had artlessly put himself in a position to observe some surveying for the route.

"Strange that he would subject himself needlessly to the risk," von Bohlen said.

"Ah, you know the English, nothing if not eccentric," Fitzmaurice said, letting a little of his Irish brogue show as if to place some distance between himself and the English. "Think of our great lady explorer, Gertrude Bell, who constantly puts herself in danger in her archeological pursuits." Miss Bell had passed through Constantinople in the previous year, and was feted at several embassies.

"Ah, yes, Miss Bell," von Bohlen said. Harmless, eccentric. Was that the description of Leighton? "And Leighton, is he seeking lost ruins in the desert?" Or something else?

"My friend," Fitzmaurice said, grasping von Bohlen's arm and leaning toward him confidentially. "Forget Leighton. If you have any concerns about the railway, come to me. I am the one who can help you."

Von Bohlen listened to the dragoman. There was no question the Irishman had influence in the embassy. The question was how he would use that influence. "Thank you, my friend," he said. "I'll be mindful of that should the occasion arise."

Fitzmaurice released his arm. He smiled at von Bohlen, made a gesture to show that his glass was empty, and walked away without a further word.

~

The *Basra* docked at Port Said for half a day as the ship took on cargo and coal. Leighton and Morrison watched the work on the pier as they leaned on the deck rail.

"I can't believe how much easier the Suez Canal was to build," said Morrison. "The Panama Canal is having a lot more trouble." In fact, a French team under Ferdinand de

Lesseps, the builder of Suez, had given up the effort and now an American-backed company was building the canal.

"Suez has the advantage that the isthmus is flat and connects two bodies of water at the same level," Leighton said. This trip was his third through the canal.

"Damn straight it has the advantage. It's the locks that make Panama such a challenge," he said. "And yet, you see it at work and you know it's worth it," he added, shaking his head.

Leighton only nodded. The wonders of modern travel – steam engines, trains, the canals – made it possible for an empire such as Britain's to flourish. Flourish too much, he thought, in the case of the Baghdad Railway.

The trip had gone quickly. They had reached the canal yesterday evening and now were docked at the gateway to the Mediterranean. Deprived of his reading materials, Leighton had passed the time with his journal. He called it a journal, but it was not a diary of their trip, or even this mission. It was rather an interior journal. He realized that even during his travels he rarely took the time to explore his memories, his thoughts. He had read about Sigmund Freud, a Viennese neurologist who had some revolutionary ideas about what one could learn by delving into one's own memories.

Leighton's own reflections were not systematic, nor did he intend to share them with any medical practitioner. He was intrigued, though, about the absence of his father from his life and the succession of figures – his grandfather, his teachers – who stood in for that role. He felt it somehow explained his enormous devotion to duty. He was at a loss to understand how. He knew many men equally devoted to duty who, as far as he knew, had grown up normally with their fathers in their lives. Yet it was duty that controlled Leighton's life. It drove him to succeed in these scholarly researches, but it also drove him to serve the Crown, as a soldier and now as a...whatever role he was playing now.

Only once did Leighton confide his musings to Morrison. Leighton awoke in the night soaked in his own perspiration. In his dream, he had again felt a sharp blade sliding across his throat, severing his life from his body in the way those knives had killed the Kurdish workers at the railway camp. Evidently, Leighton had cried out, for Morrison inquired if he was all right. Leighton assured his companion that he was. Morrison resumed his regular breathing – thankfully the American did not snore loudly – but Leighton remained awake the rest of the night.

"The camp bothers me," Leighton explained to Morrison the next day. "I can't get the image of those slain workers out of my mind."

Morrison waited before replying. "Is it so different from battle? The slaughter there?"

Leighton did not answer directly. "When I was in South Africa, I saw some auxiliaries flog a Hottentot to death. The man could not have committed a crime to deserve that death."

"It seems," Morrison said, "you put a great store by justice. It's the injustice of these deeds that bothers you."

Leighton smiled. "Yes, that's my conclusion as well. What causes me confusion still, is that justice often is absent from the affairs of men – even those affairs otherwise deemed righteous."

"Ah, my friend," said Morrison. "Philosophers have tried for centuries to understand human nature. It is flawed, as we know from our scriptures."

"Yes, human nature is undoubtedly flawed," Leighton said. "But does that excuse an individual's actions? Patently not, or our jails would be empty. Can some actions in war be just and others not? The lawyers tell us they can be. And yet the victor rarely is called to account for misdeeds. And what of the individual who is the agent of these misdeeds. Can he be called to account?"

Leighton knew he would finish his mission regardless of his misgivings about the actions of the Arab tribes. He knew it was his duty and his duty trumped his sense of morality. He had stopped the flogging, but too late to save the victim. He would aid Rashid and his men in committing further murders to promote British objectives. How much more sleep would he lose over that?

What were the British objectives? Protect India? Find petroleum? Win a European war, if it came to that? Leighton could only support these objectives. And if it meant supporting an Arab revolt with unforeseeable consequences? Or putting rifles into the hands of murderers? That was harder for Leighton to go along with.

Other thoughts had accompanied Leighton on the trip, thoughts he was not willing to trust to his journal. He thought of Elena, of their passion, their intimacy. He missed her. Their two encounters in Constantinople had revived this terrible yearning it had taken him months to suppress.

He worried for her as well. He had concluded that her marriage to Talaat was a sham and her purpose was political. It was a dangerous game. His lovely Elena had become a secret agent, too. Would she recognize her peril in time?

Chapter Twenty-Seven

Hoffenberg turned red. "*Verdammt, verdammt nochmals,*" he cursed, tearing the cable into shreds and throwing it into the wastebasket. Bungler! More than a thousand miles of barren terrain and this prima donna of an assassin could not fell a single effete aristocrat? Incomprehensible! The cable spoke of Arab intruders, the Bengali guard in Baghdad, an American mercenary – a litany of failure. He would return Ernst to the infantry.

Talaat would need to know. The prospect of admitting to their failure galled Hoffenberg. But he had an ace up his sleeve, he recalled with a grin. He rang for his coach. Relations were such that Talaat always had time for the military chargé d'affaires from the German embassy.

"Hoffenberg," Talaat said when the German was ushered into his office. Talaat dispensed with oriental courtesies when dealing with Europeans. Nor did he adopt European courtesies – he remained seated and did not offer his hand.

"Distinguished pasha," rejoined Hoffenberg, more polite. "I've received a dispatch from our IIIb intelligence bureau – "

"I know what IIIb is," Talaat interrupted.

"Regarding the whereabouts of your, uh, wife," Hoffenberg finished. Had he divorced her? Ex-wife? Traitorous whore? What was the best term for her.

"Elena?" Now Talaat stood, hand outstretched.

Hoffenberg handed him a single, typewritten sheet with the decryption of a German dispatch from Sofia.

"In Varna?" he said, reading through the contents quickly. Varna was the main Black Sea port in Bulgaria.

"Yes, pasha Talaat," Hoffenberg said.

"She taunts me!" he said, his face flushed. The Turks were bitter about the loss of Bulgaria, proclaimed an independent kingdom two years earlier.

Hoffenberg smiled inwardly. Talaat would not be able to gloat over his failure to suppress Leighton. "Perhaps she is going to the Armenian homeland across the Black Sea," Hoffenberg said.

"More likely joining the anti-Turk underground in Macedonia," he said.

Talaat's eyes smoldered, but he did not face the German. Whatever plans he had for Elena, he was not sharing them.

"I have some other news," Hoffenberg took a deep breath. "The British spy, Leighton, escaped my man in Baghdad."

Now Talaat looked at Hoffenberg, turning a darker shade, his eyes blazing. His look made any comment unnecessary.

Hoffenberg did not offer the excuses Ernst had made to him. "He will be reprimanded," Hoffenberg said.

"Now the man is dangerous," Talaat raged. "Word of the Syrian massacre is spreading. He is sure to have heard of it. Perhaps his caravan stumbled upon the camp in its passage."

Before Hoffenberg could grovel and admit that the task exceeded his resources, Talaat volunteered. "It appears I must take care of the bastard myself. Is he returning to Constantinople?"

"According to my information, he boarded the

freighter *Basra*, which is due in Constantinople in two days," Hoffenberg said.

Talaat grunted, as if to say at least Hoffenberg could provide useful information. "Tell me," Talaat said. "Is he so clever or is your man so inept?"

"It seems he has had help," Hoffenberg said. "My man spoke of 'Arab intruders.'"

"What kind of 'Arab intruders'?" asked Talaat, his interest piqued. "What kind of Arab allies might our British friend have?"

"Certainly only brigands, pasha Talaat," Hoffenberg hurried to add. "They are for hire. My man had his Arab band."

"Yes, you're no doubt right. A little gold in the right hands...." he trailed off. Leighton did not seem the type to hire thieves to do his dirty work. And yet, how else could he muster Arabs in the desert? "Could it be the same cutthroats who massacred the Syrian construction camp?" he voiced his thought.

A chill ran through Hoffenberg. The enemy of my enemy.... He did not like the prospect of Arabs uniting with the British to sabotage the railroad.

"You see," said Talaat. "I tell you, he is a dangerous man. I must take care of it." The last was spoken more to himself, and yet Hoffenberg sensed it as a dismissal.

"At your service, esteemed pasha," Hoffenberg said, backing toward the door. Talaat had sat down again and paid him no attention.

~

It was dusk as the *Basra* steamed across the Sea of Marmara toward the Bosphorus and the Golden Horn. It followed the path traced by the lighthouses along the shore, slowing its engines as it drifted northeast toward the Bosphorus.

Finally, the ship slowed to a stop as the engines reversed. A dinghy swung free from its post and was slowly lowered into the water. The cables were detached and the men in the boat mounted the oars and began rowing toward the shore.

Leighton, Morrison and Broome sat in the boat with their portmanteaus. They were heading to Bakirkoy, a fashionable suburb located just to the south and west of the city on the coast. Leighton had decided to avoid any trouble with his return to Constantinople. It was possible, perhaps even likely, that his enemies knew of his embarkation on the *Basra* and had prepared a reception for him.

They saw a ferry pull away from the small dock, chugging toward the Asian side of the Bosphorus. As they neared the shore, Leighton saw the stone embankment looming before them as the boat turned toward the wooden pier the ferry had used. It seemed deserted after the ferry's departure.

The three passengers clambered onto the pier, waving a silent goodbye to the crew members. There was little traffic along the road leading past the pier. A couple of cafés were lit and the sound of dice could be heard. Cypress trees lined the road, giving off a warm scent of pine in the night air. More by instinct than any overt indication, Leighton led his two companions toward some streetlights where he hoped to find the train station and a connection to the city's main station, Musir Hamdi Pasha.

It was the station, and – a good sign – some people were waiting there. After only a quarter of an hour, the small suburban train pulled into the station and the men boarded it. Their white skin and European dress drew stares from the other passengers, who appeared to be largely domestic workers from the middle class homes in Bakirkoy. The train proceeded slowly along tracks also used by the Orient Express. The track actually wound around the peninsula through the Topkapi palace and gardens, though it was too dark to see any of the surroundings.

At the station, Leighton remained wary, though he did not think his adversaries would expect him to arrive by rail. It was late to chance the embassy and it could be watched. Instead, Leighton led Morrison and Broome through the narrow streets, teeming with patrons of the restaurants and cafés, to the Hotel Stamboul, the scene of his trysts with Elena. There was a suite available and Leighton promptly took it. If the clerk at the front desk thought it strange for three Europeans to arrive with only overnight bags, he kept his observations to himself. The suite was perfect, two rooms with a small servant's alcove.

"I won't be able to sleep if I can stretch out to my full length," said Morrison with a laugh as he viewed the spaciousness of their quarters.

Broome made a move to turn down Leighton's bed. "Broome, please don't bother. I won't be needing your services this evening." His man smiled in gratitude. He had not slept well in the hammocks of the crew's quarters aboard the *Basra*. Moreover, his sense of privacy had not permitted him to take his usual dose of laudanum, for he was never alone in the cramped quarters. He thankfully withdrew to the comforts of a bed and his medication.

Leighton and Morrison sat on the hotel's small veranda. There was no whiskey but the night clerk brought them a bottle of *raki* and a pitcher of water. He also brought a small plate of feta cheese and olives and a basket of bread. The veranda faced out to the Sea of Marmara. The silky, moist air of the city was comforting.

"This is an unexpected pleasure, after all our adventures," the American said.

Leighton delicately spit an olive pit into the cradle formed by his thumb and finger and placed it on a separate plate. He sipped the milky raki from his glass. "Yes, it is," he agreed. But his mind was already facing the challenge of tomorrow — getting to the embassy.

Morrison knew this. After their weeks together, the two men lived in an easy symbiosis. He also knew that Leighton's fears were not unfounded. Aside from the *Basra*, the embassy was the only sure lead his hunters had. In the balmy evening air, the two men planned a strategy for the next day.

~

The sky was overcast and a faint drizzle moistened the air. Leighton felt the weather aided their plan. Broome set out ahead of them, walking to the Galata Bridge and up the hill toward the embassy. Leighton and Morrison followed a few minutes later. As expected, they encountered no difficulties in Stamboul. When they crossed the bridge, they approached the embassy slowly from a side lane. They watched from under a hotel umbrella as Broome walked up to the entrance unmolested, presented the guard with a note, and followed a steward into the building. In another quarter of an hour, the gate opened and the embassy motor-car emerged, its top up against the rain. The car went down toward the bridge, but only moments later it returned. At that moment, two mounted constables spurred their horses to close off the road in front of the embassy. Three men in long black coats came out of a café and motioned to the driver to turn off the engine.

"What is the problem?" said an irritated Maitland, leaning out the window. The military attaché was dressed in civilian clothes.

"Routine inquiries, sir," one of the men in black coats responded politely.

"But I'm from the British embassy and I'm on embassy

business," said Maitland, gesturing at the small Union Jack attached to the front fender of the car.

"Are you alone, sir?" asked the official, peering into the gloom inside the car, where the curtains were drawn.

"Alone? Of course I'm not alone. Who do you think is driving this machine?"

"Are there other passengers, sir?"

"I've told you this is an embassy car. It is British property," Maitland said in an irritable voice.

"Of course, sir, but it is on Turkish soil and does not have diplomatic privileges," the official said in a sterner tone.

"Well, look for yourself then, if you must know," Maitland said.

As this debate was taking place, Leighton and Morrison came out of the side lane and walked toward the entrance. They traversed the twenty yards quickly, masked by the umbrella. The gate swung open as they approached and before the Turkish officials even saw them, they were safe in the embassy premises. Maitland quickly satisfied the officials that he had no other passengers, and his car was allowed to enter the embassy drive as well.

"Well done, old boy, you have a future on the stage," Leighton greeted Maitland as he stepped out of the car.

"Insolent Turk," Maitland said, taking the hand Leighton held out to him. "The Young Turks are setting up a bloody police state."

Leighton kept silent. The police state had always been there, but kept out of sight of foreigners.

"Leighton, old boy, how have you weathered your trip?" Maitland asked. It was not an idle question. Leighton's return surprised him. He thought Leighton's mission not only a fool's errand but suicidal.

"Well enough, thank you," said Leighton.

"You're as dark as a coolie," Maitland said with a laugh.

The time in the desert and at sea had left Leighton bronzed by the sun.

"Nothing that time can't fix," he said. Leighton, who had often acquired a tan during his expeditions, actually fancied the outdoor look.

Maitland looked at Morrison. He was not going to mention the Baghdad Railway in front of a stranger.

"Maitland, Morrison," Leighton said, introducing them to each other. "Morrison was my companion on the trip. He served with Teddy Roosevelt in the Rough Riders."

Maitland shook hands with the American. He took him for a spy.

"Well, let's get inside," Maitland said. They had remained in the courtyard of the embassy, near the garage.

Once inside, Maitland turned to Leighton. "Your note said you may be pursued. Was that what this fracas outside was about?"

"I fear so," said Leighton. "I wasn't sure what form the harassment would take, but it appears to take an official Turkish form."

Leighton briefly related the attacks en route and his suspicion the Germans were involved.

"Nasty business," said Maitland. He clapped Leighton on the shoulder. "Good show evading all that. It might be best if we put you up here at the embassy until this sorts itself out."

Leighton agreed, though he wondered how "this" would "sort itself out."

As the men came up to the front parlor, Morrison held Leighton back. "Now that you're safely delivered here, I'll be off," he said. "I'll return to the Pera if you need me."

Leighton nodded and shook his friend's hand. "Right. We'll talk once I know more." Know more about Grey's reaction to his cable, know more about Rashid's network.

Without a further word, Morrison excused himself with a bow from Maitland and headed back downstairs to the entrance.

Maitland raised an eyebrow. "A useful man in a tight situation," Leighton said. He knew Maitland wanted confirmation that Morrison was an American agent, but he decided to withhold that information for the time being.

Chapter Twenty-Eight

Von Bohlen decided he was not a very good spy. For several days, he had spent his mornings at the café across from the British embassy. He brought a newspaper, a Turkish paper, which he pretended to read. He pretended because he had found that if he actually read the newspaper, he quickly became too engrossed in it to mind what was happening in front of the embassy. He had chosen to sacrifice his mornings. This meant if he was truly to meet Leighton in this fashion, the Englishman must oblige him by coming or going in the morning and not exclusively in the afternoon.

Von Bohlen distrusted Fitzmaurice profoundly. His intuition was so strong against the dragoman that he felt whatever the Irishman said, the opposite must be true. If Fitzmaurice said that Leighton had nothing to do with the Baghdad Railway, then he must be intimately involved with it. If Fitzmaurice said Leighton was unlikely to return to Constantinople, then it was likely he would, and probably soon, or Fitzmaurice would not have been so adamant about it.

It was not much to go on, von Bohlen admitted to himself ruefully. And he had little to show for his conviction. What if Leighton had left Constantinople for scholarly pursuits?

There was a commotion in front of the embassy. Police stopped a car. Two mounted constables blocked the car's path to the embassy and several plainclothes officers – or were they secret service – closed in on the car. Soon, the horses retreated, leaving the way free for the car to enter the embassy. Von Bohlen, who remained oblivious to the surreptitious entry of Leighton and Morrison, was left wondering what this commotion was about. He was not the only one keeping an eye on the embassy. Would he even have a chance, then, of speaking to Leighton? What if the police seized him before he had a chance to speak to him? What good, in fact, was his whole plan if the police were after Leighton?

Von Bohlen ordered another coffee, his third. He continued to watch the entrance, his newspaper folded on the table in front of him, forgotten. Shortly after the car entered the embassy, a tall man dressed curiously and carrying a folded umbrella came out. Von Bohlen recognized the man! He had observed him talking to Leighton during the reception. An American, someone had mentioned.

Before he had time to think, von Bohlen was on his feet, moving to intercept the tall man. Just as it seemed the two would collide, von Bohlen stopped, tipped his hat, and said, "Excuse me, please."

The tall man stepped back, he seemed wary.

"My name is von Bohlen, from the Deutsche Bank. I thought I recognized you from our reception earlier this year."

The tall man did not seem reassured by the reference to Deutsche Bank.

"At the German residence on the Bosphorus," von Bohlen prompted.

"I remember the reception. I don't believe we've met," said Morrison.

American, yes. "No, I don't believe we had the pleasure," von Bohlen acknowledged. "However, I did meet someone you may know, a British subject, Lord Leighton," von Bohlen said, smiling with what he hoped was encouragement.

Morrison's eyes narrowed with suspicion. "I'm not British, I'm not a subject, and I'm not lord of anything," he said.

"But you know Lord Leighton," von Bohlen insisted, ignoring this small tirade. It was a trait he had developed in his years as a banker. You must insist if you are to close a transaction.

"Do you have business with Lord Leighton?" Morrison asked.

"No, no, we met at the reception and chatted," von Bohlen improvised. He had not actually exchanged words with Leighton. "You see, I'm intimately involved in the Baghdad Railway."

Morrison glanced back at the embassy, a gesture which elated the banker. It confirmed both that Leighton was here and that he was involved in the Baghdad Railway.

Before Morrison could tell him again of Leighton's scholarly credentials, von Bohlen barreled on. "I understand Lord Leighton is interested in the project and I may have some information he would value." There, he had done it. Treason.

Morrison looked around. The constables had quietly moved closer to where the two men stood. There was no sign of the black coats, but they were almost certainly watching.

"Can I buy you a coffee, a tea?" Morrison said, gesturing to the café von Bohlen had just left.

"Perhaps we could simply take a short walk together," von Bohlen smiled encouragingly again.

Morrison sized up von Bohlen, and nodded. They walked past the café and turned down a side street toward the Grande Rue de Pera.

Having made his declaration, von Bohlen now found himself loath to continue. "You said you had information," Morrison prompted him.

"Yes," said von Bohlen, taking a deep breath. "Very sensitive information."

"You are willing to share this information with Lord Leighton?"

Von Bohlen hesitated. Did he need to explain anything to this man? What did he care for his motives, a mixture of feelings he scarcely understood himself.

"Yes," he said, finally.

It was Morrison's turn to think. They turned on to the Grande Rue, with its European-style boutiques, its grand embassy facades. Was this a trap? Leighton believed the Germans were trying to assassinate him.

"It's unusual that a German would want to share information about the railway with the British," Morrison said.

"Yes, it is," von Bohlen agreed. "I find myself in an unusual situation."

Morrison realized von Bohlen would not confide in him. This was Leighton's matter, he would turn it over to him.

"I can talk to Lord Leighton on your behalf, if you like," Morrison said.

"That would be helpful indeed," von Bohlen said. He needed time to think. "Where can I reach you?"

"I'll be returning to the Pera Palace this afternoon," Morrison said.

"Perfect," said von Bohlen. "I will contact you there. Tomorrow." He stopped, bowed slightly to Morrison, and hesitated. "However, I must see Lord Leighton myself to deliver this information to him, that is understood." Morrison nodded his assent. Von Bohlen bowed again, and said, "Thank you, sir. My name is von Bohlen. And you?"

"Morrison. William Morrison," Morrison said. He didn't anticipate that von Bohlen would ever be calling him Bill.

"Thank you. Good day." Von Bohlen turned and walked back up the Grande Rue toward the German embassy.

Morrison continued down the street toward the Galata bridge. Why would Deutsche Bank have information for a British agent? What kind of information? What would Leighton make of this?

~

"What's going on, Leighton?" Maitland said when the two of them reached the front parlor.

"What happened out there? Who was it who stopped you?" Leighton asked.

"They were a bit vague, and my Turkish is not that good."

"They were Turkish?"

"Yes, that much I can attest to."

"Why did they stop you?"

"Security, they said. They have reports that foreign embassies may be under threat."

"From whom?"

"Our discussion didn't get that far. I told them I was the security officer for the embassy, and of course they let me pass."

"It seems a pretext to get a look inside the car, to see if I was in there," Leighton said. "Apparently the Germans have handed over the matter to the Turks, since they were unable to achieve their objective."

"What is 'the matter' you are referring to?"

"The 'matter' appears to be your humble servant. A German officer was chasing me across the desert to Baghdad and made at least three attempts on my life."

"How do you know he was German?"

Leighton told Maitland about his capture and interrogation at Ernst's hands.

"He showed himself to you because he thought you would never live to tell the tale," Maitland said.

"That's my presumption."

"Well, good show," Maitland said. His own skepticism about Leighton's mission had been vindicated. He had thought it to be dangerous and considered it a tribute to Leighton's courage – and luck – that he had returned unharmed. "We forwarded your report from Adana," Maitland added.

"And the cable from Baghdad?" Leighton asked.

"Cable?" said Maitland. "I've seen no cable."

Leighton shifted in his chair. "About ten days ago, before I embarked on the voyage home." Leighton made it sound like a family holiday.

Maitland rang for a butler and asked him to fetch Fitzmaurice.

"Do you know of a cable from Leighton?" Maitland asked when the Irishman entered the room.

Fitzmaurice took in the situation. He went over to Leighton and grabbed his hand. "Good show! So glad you made it back safely." Leighton half rose to return Fitzmaurice's greeting with a tight smile. Turning to Maitland, Fitzmaurice said, "Yes, the encrypted cable. It went in the pouch this week."

Maitland shot Leighton a glance. Leighton's eyes flashed but he said nothing. "Why wasn't the cable forwarded?"

"It was deemed too sensitive, even in code," Fitzmaurice said immediately. "We have numerous indications that our codes are no match for the sultan's codebreakers."

"Deemed by whom?" Maitland said.

"Well, in the ambassador's absence, it was I who took the decision," the Irishman said. "I read the decrypted version and realized it was too dangerous to risk interception."

Maitland flushed. "In the ambassador's absence, you should have consulted with me before taking such a decision."

Fitzmaurice flushed as well. "It seemed an obvious precaution to send it by pouch."

"Why only this week?" Leighton said.

Fitzmaurice turned to him. "It seemed wise to verify some of the information. To suggest to Whitehall that an Arab revolt is brewing is not a step to be taken lightly."

The two men stared at each other. Leighton saw that Fitzmaurice was confident of his hand and had played it boldly.

"No matter," Leighton said. "Grey will have the information shortly. He can do little until I make a full report. The cable was a precaution in case I was prevented from making a report in person."

"Arab revolt?" asked Maitland.

Fitzmaurice started to answer, but frowned and turned to Leighton.

"I've encountered some Arab tribes who want to resist Ottoman rule and have made the Baghdad Railway a target for sabotage," Leighton said.

He related to Maitland and Fitzmaurice the scene at the construction camp, including details he had omitted from the cable.

"My God!" said Maitland.

"Yes, the devil's allies," said Leighton.

Fitzmaurice ran his finger around the inside of his collar and cleared his throat.

"Brigands," he said. "That's all they are. Brigands."

Leighton regarded the dragoman. "Perhaps," he said. "But it is a massive force, not a band of thieves."

Leighton would not discuss Rashid's request for rifles with the embassy personnel. Fitzmaurice seemed hostile to the notion that there was really a challenge to the sultan's power.

"If the Turks are using police to track you, what will happen next?"

"Well, I will accept your kind offer to reside in the embassy. Obviously, they cannot seize me here." But neither would Rashid's agents be able to contact him here, Leighton thought. He needed to make himself available to them.

"Yes, of course," said Maitland. He didn't voice the obvious question: For how long?

"I need to return to London quickly," Leighton said. He wanted to contact Elena, but if Talaat was after him, that would be far too dangerous. He had asked Morrison to return to the embassy at the end of the day. He needed some way to get outside the embassy without giving Talaat's men a chance to seize him or do him harm.

Chapter Twenty-Nine

Leighton and Morrison took tea in the library. In fact, it was whiskey, served with an assortment of finger sandwiches. The library itself, with plush red leather chairs and dark wood paneling, looked more like a club on Pall Mall than anything in Ottoman Turkey.

"Certainly better than what Captain Ferguson served on the *Basra*," Morrison said.

"So von Bohlen has some information of value to me, about the Baghdad Railway?" Leighton asked after Morrison had related his encounter with the German banker.

"Yes, that's what he said. He was acting a bit peculiar."

"Perhaps treason doesn't come easily to him," said Leighton. He knew little about von Bohlen. All he knew about Deutsche Bank was that it had emerged as a financial powerhouse on the continent and had its fingers in German operations worldwide. It certainly had the capital to fuel Kaiser Wilhelm's ambitions to make Germany a colonial power on a par with France and Britain. It was Deutsche Bank's involvement in the railway that made it such a threat. Left to themselves, the Ottomans would be floundering around for decades trying to fund the project. "Deutsche Bank is hand-in-glove with the Kaiser, of course. Both are ruthless enough in promoting Germany's goals." Financiers in London's City were equally ferocious in backing Britannia's rule as well. It was all part of the Great Power rivalry.

"Well, that's what I thought," said Morrison. "You can imagine my surprise when this stout German in a black suit approached me."

Leighton smiled, but his brow remained furrowed.

"What could he have?" he asked aloud. "And how can I get it from him?"

"I'm happy to serve as a go-between, to arrange a meeting," said Morrison. "He made it fairly clear, though, that he had to deliver this information directly into your hands."

"How am I to get out the embassy?"

"Well," said Morrison, "do they actually know you're *in* the embassy?"

"Of course," said Leighton, "they were searching vehicles entering the compound and are still unaware that I've reached my sanctuary." He paused. "Still, I don't think it's wise simply to stroll out in broad daylight. The watchers may have a description, or even a photograph. And once out, how will I get back in?"

"It seems to me any embassy will do the trick – keeping you out of the hands of the Turks. Why don't I get you into the American embassy? The Turks won't be watching it."

"A British peer seeks asylum in the American embassy?"

"It won't be in the newspapers," Morrison said with a smile. "No one will know."

"It's close enough, just on the other side of the Pera Palace," said Leighton.

"It's not as grand as your embassy, but there's some construction going on there now, which should make it easy to enter without being observed," Morrison said. "The ambassador, Oscar Straus, is thick with Teddy – Teddy appointed him to his Cabinet, the first Hebrew to have that distinction. I'll have a word with him."

The Palazzo Corpi had been built by a Genoese merchant family and used as the U.S. residence for nearly three decades.

While splendid enough as a private home, it was more modest than the Great Power embassies in Pera.

"Let's arrange this meeting with von Bohlen, then," Leighton said. "There is also the matter of Sheikh Rashid. His men are supposed to contact me."

"They have proven resourceful enough in the past," said Morrison, his face deadpan.

"So you think they will find me even if I remain hiding in embassies or flitting about Constantinople in disguise?"

Morrison shrugged. "They found you before you knew they were looking for you."

Leighton looked skeptical. He needed to get back to London quickly and fill in Grey on the details of his mission. He had resolved to make the pact with Rashid because he was certain this was what Grey wanted. Morrison's plan to ship American rifles seemed a good one.

"All right, let's decide what to tell von Bohlen," Leighton said. The two men sat in the library for an hour, making their plans, before Morrison returned to the hotel.

~

Leighton went to see Broome in their quarters. The embassy guest room, while less grand than the Pera Palace, was quite comfortable. It was in fact a small suite, with a sitting room and an alcove for Broome as well as the bedroom. It was in the same wing as the ambassador's residence, so that his servants were at Leighton's disposal.

Broome was propped up in his bed, a narrow steel-frame affair, with a book in his lap and a bottle of beer on the stand next to him. His reading glasses were perched on his nose.

"Don't get up," Leighton said as he entered the alcove.

"Will you be wanting supper, milord?" asked Broome.

He squirmed on the bed, uncomfortable at addressing his master from a sitting position.

"No, don't bother. I'll ring the servants for a cold plate momentarily," Leighton said. "We have a plan, and I need you to run an errand for me in the morning."

Broome listened to Leighton's instructions and nodded that he understood. Leighton once again was grateful for Broome's quiet competence. As a veteran infantryman, he was more resourceful than the typical domestic servant. Leighton had taken Broome aside on their voyage from Basra and expressed his appreciation for Broome's valor during the battle on the boat – and during the whole trip.

"It's more than is asked of most valets," said Leighton, "or indeed of most infantrymen."

"I'm at milord's disposal," Broome responded.

"I'm sure it's more than you expected when you signed on with an idle aristocrat who dabbles in Oriental scholarship," Leighton said.

Broome clearly debated with himself whether to make any response to this. "Milord is hardly what anyone would call idle," he finally said.

Leighton laughed. "In any event, I want you to know there is a tidy bonus in all this for you."

Broome smiled and nodded in appreciation. "Milord is most generous."

"I'm afraid this trip is not quite over yet," Leighton said. "There may be more trouble before we get back to London."

Broome rubbed his head where he had received the blow in the desert. "My head's still in one piece," he said.

That was a good thing, thought Leighton now, for he definitely needed Broome's head in one piece.

~

As instructed by Leighton, Morrison would set the rendezvous with von Bohlen at the German fountain at the Hippodrome. Constantinople had had one of the biggest racing courses in the ancient world, the pride of Emperor Constantine's city. History had dismembered the structure. Four magnificent bronze horses were spirited away in the attack on the city during the Fourth Crusade to grace St. Mark's cathedral in Venice. The sack of Constantinople by the Turks in the 15th century finished the job. Today it was a large square with paving stones tracing the original race course. A couple of obelisks and columns from the original Hippodrome were preserved for display. When Kaiser Wilhelm visited Constantinople in 1898, he decided the square needed more decoration and donated a carved marble fountain, now known as the Kaiser Wilhelm fountain or the German fountain.

Leighton thought it appropriate for a meeting with the German banker. Moreover, it was in the open, in case this was a ruse by the Germans to lure Leighton out of hiding. In daylight, there would be many passersby to protect against mischief, yet not so many as to create opportunities for a stealthy assassination in a crowd. Leighton did not think it a trick, because it was too obvious. Also, why would the Germans devise a plan to lure him and then have the Turks chasing him to make it difficult.

Von Bohlen was waiting for Morrison in the hotel lobby when he returned from his meeting with Leighton. The German stood to draw Morrison's attention to him. In the artificial light of the lobby, von Bohlen looked pale, the pouches under his eyes were dark. His head, uncovered in the hotel, was bald on top, except for a few strands of gray hair. He appeared less nervous than this morning in the street, but Morrison could not determine whether it was calm or resignation.

"I hope you haven't been waiting long," said Morrison.

Von Bohlen shrugged, as if to say, What does it matter?

"I've talked to Lord Leighton," Morrison continued. This brought a wan smile to von Bohlen's face, a late confirmation that his surmises had been correct. "He will meet you," Morrison said, "tomorrow, at 3 p.m., at the German fountain in Sultanahmet Square."

Von Bohlen closed his eyes for reflection, then nodded. "It will be difficult tomorrow, but I will be there."

Morrison waited. Was there more? Did he want to be paid? Von Bohlen's eyes had a distant look. Morrison thought he detected a gleam in the unfocused eyes. Tears from a banker or a trick of the light, Morrison could not tell.

Von Bohlen straightened; the men were still standing. The German picked up his homburg from the coffee table and put it on his head. A quail feather poked out of the band, giving the banker a jaunty air belied by his countenance.

"Please convey my thanks to Lord Leighton. I look forward to seeing him at the appointed time," von Bohlen said.

The banker turned and walked stiffly across the lobby and out the front door, without any further word. Morrison watched the door after it swung shut, pondering what was going on inside of von Bohlen. Where had those distant eyes been staring?

~

Von Bohlen walked through the mist, now dense enough to moisten the cobblestones of the street and pavement. His own flat was not far. He walked slowly, in no hurry to return to his empty quarters. His housekeeper would have banked a fire in the coal fireplace before leaving, and set out a plate of sausage for his dinner. Despite his decades abroad, von

Bohlen had not lost his taste for the minced meats of his homeland.

Tomorrow at 3 p.m. at the German fountain. This British aristocrat was not without a sense of humor, von Bohlen thought. The gift of the Kaiser. The Kaiser gives, and von Bohlen takes away. The fountain would remain, but the iron track that the Kaiser and Deutsche Bank wanted to plant across Asia Minor – that would be taken away. By me, von Bohlen shook his head ruefully, the most loyal servant of the Kaiser and the bank.

There would be a war. How could it be avoided? Everyone wanted it. Or rather, everyone wanted everything, and that would result in conflict. Perhaps some day, after that war, the Baghdad Railway would be built, and would bring enrichment to the territories it passed through. Not now, however.

Von Bohlen had counted on more time to lay his plans. He must improvise. The ambassador was in town. Would he be in his office tomorrow? Would he leave it empty long enough for von Bohlen to acquire the objects he wanted to deliver to Leighton? Von Bohlen shrugged as he walked. He had assented to the appointment as if he had control of his actions. Perhaps he would be able to keep his rendezvous with the British agent, or maybe not.

If not tomorrow, then perhaps the day after. The British could wait. They knew when patience was required. He admired that about the British. The Kaiser could never wait, because he lacked the confidence that things would come to him. The British had that confidence. If he must betray his fatherland, then it was good to betray it to such a competent rival, von Bohlen thought. The British would honor his betrayal. They would stop the railway.

Chapter Thirty

Broome left the embassy at 10 in the morning to run his errand. He just missed Morrison, who entered the gate shortly afterwards.

Leighton was filling in Maitland and Fitzmaurice on his plan when Morrison was brought to him in the front parlor. Leighton introduced his American friend to Fitzmaurice.

"I'm fortunate to have found a comrade," Leighton said. "If it weren't for Morrison, and Broome, I wouldn't be alive to tell the tale, I don't think."

Maitland smiled faintly at Morrison; Fitzmaurice's scowl didn't change.

"See here, Leighton," Fitzmaurice said. "We can't risk having an incident here at the embassy, especially with the ambassador absent."

"But I think the risk of an incident is much higher without my subterfuge," Leighton said. "You wouldn't want a visiting subject of His Majesty taken into custody either publicly or surreptitiously right in front of the embassy."

Fitzmaurice muttered something under his breath. Leighton only caught the word "devil."

"The devil may well take me in the end," he improvised, "but in the meantime, I am trying to spare you the embarrassment of my disappearance."

Morrison remained deadpan during this exchange.

"You haven't told us why you need to go out," said

Maitland.

Leighton looked at the two of them, silent for a moment. "Let me just say," he began, "that I have a lead that may be important to my mission." Leighton felt in no way obliged to share all the details of his mission with the embassy staff. "It may be nothing, and in any case, something you are probably better off not knowing."

Fitzmaurice flushed and Maitland frowned. Leighton reported directly to Grey. He was not in the Foreign Office's chain of command. That was the way Grey had set it up. There was nothing really that either of them could say.

"Very well, I will instruct the guard at the gate," said Maitland. "Leighton, you realize there is little the embassy will be able to do if you 'disappear.'"

Leighton nodded. He had formed his opinion of the embassy and found Maitland's appraisal optimistic. He expected nothing from the embassy at this point. Maitland and Fitzmaurice departed, leaving Leighton alone with Morrison.

"You wouldn't know these guys are supposed to be diplomats," was Morrison's first comment.

Leighton smiled. "No, they're not very diplomatic. You see, though, that we are on our own in this venture."

"I did speak to Ambassador Straus this morning," said Morrison. "He said a British lord is always a welcome guest in the embassy."

"Nice to know I'm welcome somewhere in Constantinople," said Leighton, shaking his head and looking at the door through which his countrymen had just exited.

The two men conferred for half an hour before Morrison left. They would meet again at the Hippodrome in a few hours.

~

At 1 p.m., a sedan chair approached the British Embassy. The conveyance was decorated in gold leaf, tracing a tree-branch pattern on black lacquer paint. Two massive Nubians dressed in white robes carried the chair. Curtains were drawn across the windows in the front and on each side, so that the occupant of the chair could not be seen.

Sedan chairs had grown rare in Constantinople, as carriages and then motor-cars became more common. However, parts of the old city remained inaccessible to these modern vehicles, and some old-fashioned grandees continued to use the sedan chair for their personal transport.

The mounted policeman outside the embassy watched the progress of the sedan chair as it came down the narrow street from the Grand Rue. The policeman looked over to the café, where the black-coated men from the Interior Ministry sat. One of the men shook his head. They would not risk insulting a bey with business at the embassy.

The red-coated Grenadier Guard at the entrance to the embassy swung open the gate as the chairmen approached with their burden. They carried the chair to the front door of the embassy building and set it down slowly, descending to one knee to lower the chair to the ground. Watching from outside the gate, the policeman saw a rotund figure in a black cloak and fez come out of the small cabin and mount the short flight of stairs into the embassy. A merchant eager to export his wares to Great Britain, he decided.

Inside the embassy, Broome removed the cloak and unstrapped the pillow he had used to pad his figure. Leighton gave him a quick pat on the back. "Good show. You can have a career on the stage if you ever tire of my employ," he said with a laugh.

"Do you think a famous actor could go about London in a contraption like that?" Broome rejoined. "It's not a bad ride. No jolts."

"I'll see for myself soon enough," Leighton said. He had sent Broome to Mehmet Ali's shop in the old town near the bazaar. In one of their many conversations around the campfire during the caravan, the merchant had spoken of his custom of riding a sedan chair. He had done so with an engaging air of self-mockery, making fun of his girth and weight and the hardship it imposed on his chairmen. Ali was still traveling on the caravan on the way back, but Leighton had sent a short note to his oldest son, who readily put the chair at Broome's disposal, along with an appropriate disguise.

After an hour, deemed a suitable amount of time for the visiting bey to have conducted his business at a slow Oriental pace, Leighton put on Broome's disguise – pillow, cloak and fez – in case curious eyes were still watching the building entrance. Leighton, taller than Broome, hunched over as he prepared to take the few steps to the waiting sedan chair. He descended the stairs and stepped into the conveyance. The chairman closed the door and took his place in the front of the chair, so that the two men could lift it smoothly. The gate once again swung open to let the chair exit. The constable on horseback was not visible and the black-coated men in the café showed no interest in the sedan chair's departure.

The quarters were a bit cramped and while there were no jolts, Leighton felt every step taken by the powerful chairmen. They carried the chair across the Galata Bridge and up the hill toward the Hagia Sophia. At the mosque, Leighton rapped the window for them to halt. He unstrapped the pillow, took off the cloak and fez and left them all inside as he emerged from the small carriage. He tipped the two bearers generously and told them to return the chair to Ali's warehouse.

Leighton crossed the square, keeping an eye out for constables, assassins or any other suspicious characters. It was a time of day when tourists took over the square. Two groups clustered in the center of the square, listening to their guides explain the wonders of the Hagia Sophia. A photographer crouched under his hood, ready to capture the mosque in full sunlight. Unless von Bohlen had betrayed him, Leighton didn't expect any trouble this far away from the embassy.

Clouds interrupted the sunshine from time to time, but it was a typical Bosphorus day. Leighton relished the fresh air after two days cooped up in the embassy. He came to the edge of the Hippodrome area and headed down the right lane toward the German fountain. He did not look in the direction where Morrison was to have stationed himself, where the mosque's wall abutted the Hippodrome area.

Leighton continued down the tree-lined lane. He saw the obelisk off to his left, and bore to his right. The fountain came into sight, but there was no one there. As he approached, though, a European in a dark wool suit and black homburg came around from the other side. He was carrying a satchel and a tubular contrivance of some kind. Leighton recognized von Bohlen from the reception.

Von Bohlen stopped to wait for Leighton at the fountain. His hands full, the German did not doff his hat when Leighton arrived. Leighton merely nodded in greeting.

"Leighton, at your service," he said.

Von Bohlen said nothing. His face was pasty white in the sun, his eyes sunken. He stared at Leighton for a few moments. Finally, he lifted the hand holding the tube – a leather map case by the look of it.

"I have something that will interest you," von Bohlen said. "A map. A map of the railway."

Leighton nodded, not smiling. A German map showing the exact route of the railway would be very helpful, though the Foreign Office had been able to plot out a fairly accurate map from various documents that had come into its possession.

"This map is different than others you have seen," von Bohlen said, as though reading Leighton's thoughts. "It shows the plans for branch lines leading off the main railway."

Leighton knew of no plans for further development of the railway. The effort of simply getting the main line under way had kept everyone's focus on that task.

"Military plans," von Bohlen said.

Ottoman intentions had been secondary in British thinking. The notion that the Porte could use the railway to keep its subjects in line had not escaped Whitehall, but was less important than the threat posed to India. Still, the information could be vital if Britain was to ally itself with an Arab resistance.

"It also shows the extension to Basra and Koweit," von Bohlen continued.

This was far more interesting, Leighton thought. Britain had sought a compromise on the railway by claiming the right to build the stretch that actually connected Baghdad to the Gulf, but had failed to gain the concession.

Von Bohlen handed the map case to Leighton. A Turkish couple in European dress strolled past the fountain, but paid no attention to the two Europeans.

Von Bohlen held the satchel in both hands. "This will interest you even more," he said. He paused, put the satchel under one arm and held it there while he pulled out a handkerchief from his suit pocket and blew his nose. "This is the latest version of the concession agreement," he said, as he put the handkerchief away. "It contains a new codicil."

Von Bohlen gripped the satchel again in both hands. "This could start a war," he said gravely. "It *will* start a war."

Leighton remained mute. It was von Bohlen's moment. Treachery, even for noble motives, defined a life. Leighton waited for further explanation, but von Bohlen was silent as he handed the satchel to Leighton.

Without a further word or gesture, von Bohlen strode off, leaving Leighton with the map case and satchel in his hands. The German headed toward Hagia Sophia. Leighton stayed at the fountain, looking around for any sign of trouble, then followed in von Bohlen's steps back the way he had come toward Hagia Sophia. As he approached the mosque's wall, Morrison stepped out of a shadow to show himself. Leighton walked toward him. Without a word, Leighton handed off the two cases to Morrison and continued walking across Hagia Sophia Square toward the Topkapi Palace. Morrison stepped back into the shadow and walked in the opposite direction, along the wall toward the Marmara embankment.

Leighton passed several of the wooden houses typical of the old town, with the second level jutting out into the street. He turned a corner to head in the direction of the bridge when a strong hand roughly grabbed his arm.

"Come with me," said a voice in Arabic.

A thin young man in Arab robes released his arm and went back around the corner toward Hagia Sophia Square. He did not stop to see if Leighton followed his command.

After a brief moment of hesitation, Leighton followed the Arab. He saw two Turks that he had passed on the street interrupt their conversation and begin walking behind him. Was he walking into a trap? Leighton wondered.

The Arab ahead of him quickened his pace and Leighton followed suit. A fruit-seller on the far side of the square took off his apron and set out to intercept Leighton. He realized that they intended to take him prisoner. The Arab leading Leighton dashed down a narrow side street. Leighton followed him at a run. As he turned into the dark, narrow street, he saw the Arab holding open a wooden postern gate along the wall on the left. Leighton didn't stop to think but

ducked into the open door. The darkness forced Leighton to
arrest his descent down the stairs. The Arab, closing the door
behind them, lit a lantern and brushed past him and led the
way down the steps. Leighton listened for sounds of pursuit,
but they had managed to disappear down the steps before the
pursuers rounded the corner.

At the bottom of the stairs, they came into a large open
space and the Arab followed a stone path that appeared
to have pools of water on either side. As he came into the
open space, Leighton saw that it was filled with huge pillars,
reaching three stories high. The massive carved bases of the
columns sat in tepid water.

Leighton figured it had to be one of the cisterns dating
back to Byzantine times, when aqueducts had supplied fresh
water to the city and it was stored in these large underground
pools.

Leighton felt sure that his Arab guide came from
Rashid. He was more puzzled by his Turkish pursuers. Had
they followed him from the Hippodrome? Had von Bohlen
betrayed him and handed off worthless papers so that the
Turks could arrest Leighton for treason?

Moss covered the stone path and Leighton took care not
to slip as he kept up with the Arab. The lantern cast their
shadows against the pillars, creating a ghostly effect.

They came to another flight of stairs leading up to a
wooden trap door. The Arab removed a bar across the door,
and slowly pushed it open. He stuck his head out and looked
around before waving Leighton to join him. Leighton came
out into a narrow lane shaded by a stone wall that ran along
the opposite side.

"Sheikh Rashid," the Arab said, "says you are to ship his
gift to the House of Nathaniel in Aleppo."

Leighton nodded. Nothing in writing. A Jewish merchant.
Clever. A gift, yes – rifles for a revolution.

"You go now," the Arab said. "Go home, to London. Use the sea route of the Orient Express."

The Arab backed down the stairs and closed the trapdoor behind him, leaving Leighton alone in the lane. The blank side of the cistern in front of him reached two stories high, while the stone wall just a few feet behind him was a good 10 feet high. Leighton set out down the lane in what he hoped was the direction of the Golden Horn.

Why would Rashid specify that he take the sea route of the Orient Express, by ship up the Bosphorus and into the Black Sea to Constanta? The Romanian port city was the terminus of a branch of the Orient Express that split from the main line in Belgrade. Because it completed the connection to Constantinople by ship, it was known as the sea route.

Leighton was nearly to the end of the lane when a mounted constable appeared at the entrance. He sat quietly in his khaki uniform, both hands on the horn of his saddle as he waited for Leighton to approach. Leighton knew that flight was useless against the horseman, so, not breaking his stride, he continued in the direction of the waiting constable, facing his fate.

Chapter Thirty-One

Von Bohlen walked ahead without looking back. He had done what he resolved to do. Leighton would see soon enough how deep von Bohlen's treachery went. What a gift! But a well-deserved one. The English really were much better at empire than the Germans. As for the Young Turks – shallow, calculating men – they had squandered their right to inherit Osman's empire.

The banker walked at a fast pace. He walked a half hour each morning before going to his office in the embassy. Faint odors of jasmine and bougainvillea wafted above the smell of wood smoke and humanity that permeated the city. A cloud passed across the sun, casting the street into shade. Von Bohlen remembered the weeks of overcast skies in western Germany, the damp, the chill. His body preferred the warm climate of his new home, but in a stroke, he had betrayed his old home and his new home.

Von Bohlen tried to imagine Leighton's reaction as he read the secret codicil to the Baghdad Railway agreement. The map would show the spurs to Kars, to Damascus, to Koweit. In exchange for building these additional branches, the Germans were guaranteed passage for their troops to Koweit in the event of a European war. British suspicions of Germany's intentions were well-founded. The codicil was the proof of that.

Von Bohlen had not devoted his life to the railway to see it turned into a weapon for war. The codicil made it clear that the Young Turks and the Kaiser were collaborating to create a modern system of control and suppression. For the Kaiser, it represented the chance to open up a new flank in a war against Britain, if, when, it came to that. Bad times loomed ahead for this blessed corner of the universe, von Bohlen reflected. He reached the Galata Bridge and paused for a moment to savor the glory of the Golden Horn, the Bosphorus, the city that spanned two continents. He reached into his pocket and pulled out a silver pillbox. An heirloom from his mother, God rest her soul. He wished she had lived longer. Von Bohlen's brothers had little use for him, the wayward son who had gone into permanent exile.

The banker stopped in the middle of the bridge, facing outward toward the Sea of Marmara as he leaned against the railing. He opened the pillbox and pulled out the small glass vial filled with white powder. Cyanide was standard issue to secret agents of the Reich. The embassy physician had mentioned it once to von Bohlen and did not balk when the banker said he would be curious to see one. If the enemy captured an agent, he was to bite on the pill and kill himself before he could reveal any secrets under questioning.

For von Bohlen, the matter was even simpler than that. He simply had no life left. He did not want to face Hoffenberg's men, or worse, Talaat's men, to account for the missing map and the copy of the railway agreement. Their absence had yet to be discovered, but once it was, suspicion would fall upon von Bohlen, one of the few who had free access to the ambassador's office.

Von Bohlen put the vial in his mouth. He thought of his brothers, his nieces and nephews, sweet children. He thought briefly, fleetingly of Anna, the great love of his life, unrequited because had never even had the courage to give expression to his feeling. He thought of his beloved mother, happy in heaven, soon to be separated from her son for eternity as he consigned himself to hellfire. He bit into the vial. There was the faintest odor of almonds as through his closed eyes von Bohlen saw a veil of darkness descending on him and turning all to blackness.

There was a splash as the European gentleman in the homburg hat fell over the railing into the water. A young man threw off his fez and jacket and dove skillfully into the water, swimming below the surface to retrieve the sinking man. Hands and canes reached down to pull the rescuer and the European up onto the bridge. Efforts to revive the man failed. He was not breathing and had no pulse. Observers at the railing agreed it was a sad and sudden death.

~

Morrison took the map case and satchel from Leighton and walked along the wall in the shadow. He went down the steps to the cobbled path along the tracks that ran around the Seraglio Point. He kept looking behind him to see if he was followed, but saw no sign of any pursuers before he reached the path along the shore. Rather than turn left to walk around the Topkapi Palace and toward the Galata Bridge, Morrison turned right and headed down toward the Yenikapi ferry terminal.

The map case had a strap, and Morrison slung it over his shoulder, trying to look like a tourist. The satchel was an ordinary leather case like the type used by lawyers, or bankers. Morrison wondered what they contained and how useful Leighton would find the contents. The exchange seemed to have gone off without a hitch in any case, he thought.

There was a ferry at the terminal when he arrived, but it was an outgoing ferry. Morrison went to the edge of the dock and looked southward down the coast to see if he could see an inbound ferry approaching. There was no sign of a boat, so Morrison went into the small terminal building and sat on a wooden bench. A number of people had gotten off the outbound ferry, but Morrison was now alone in the terminal.

Morrison opened the straps on the satchel and pulled out a sheaf of papers bound simply with string. The writing was in Arabic! Or perhaps Turkish, but in any case written with Arabic letters. Morrison untied the string binding the papers together and looked through them. He found a second document, this one in German. *Bagdadeisenbahn Vertrag*. He surmised this was a translation of the Turkish document. Morrison had little exposure to German but he knew that half the English language came from Germanic root words. Also, the document was typewritten with Latin letters, not Gothic, so he at least had a chance of puzzling out some of the words.

What looked to be the actual *Vertrag*, or treaty – a word Morrison *had* encountered – was followed with several annexes. Some of them had to do with loan terms. The last one was headed simply *Codizil*. It was only three pages long. One phrase leapt out at Morrison, *"europäischen Krieg"*. There was some discussion of the railway and the German Army in the event of a European war, was all Morrison could make out.

An approaching ferry sounded its horn. Morrison bound up the documents and put them back into the satchel, fastening the straps. He had a feeling Leighton would definitely find the codicil useful.

~

Leighton sat in the back of a black motor-car. The curtains in the passenger cabin, separated from the driver, were drawn so that he could not see where they were going. Two men in black suits sat on either side of him. They did not address him, and he had no questions for them. The constable had summoned several other men to take him into custody as he came out of the alley along the cistern. The motor-car with his two guards arrived a few minutes later. The car was not a police vehicle, nor were his companions in uniform, except for their identical black suits. They were Turkish in appearance, however, not European.

Leighton was not normally fatalistic. In this case, however, he had few illusions about his chances. He had engaged in activity that in most countries was punishable by summary execution, a procedure the Ottomans typically made more summary than other regimes. Because his punishment would be swift and secret, he did not expect his status as a British aristocrat to offer him much protection. At least his cable had reached London. If by some miracle Morrison eluded capture, he would be able to deliver von Bohlen's documents to the embassy. Perhaps he and Broome could fill in some details in statements that could be forwarded to Grey.

The car lurched to a stop. One of the men in the back seat with Leighton threw a black hood over his head. Leighton was surprised. Was it to keep him seeing where he was or to keep any watchers from seeing who he was? But who would be watching or would care? And if he was to die, what difference would it make if he saw where he was?

His two guards pushed him roughly along, keeping their hands on his arms as they walked across what seemed to be cobblestone pavement, up some stairs and into a building with slick floors. Perhaps not a prison, Leighton thought. This was confirmed when they stepped into a lift. No one spoke, but Leighton had a sense they went up only one floor, then down a hall that again seemed too polished to be in a prison.

Leighton's hands were not bound, but he gave no thought to flight. His escorts guided him into a room where he felt carpet underfoot. A hand reached up and yanked off his hood. Leighton found himself face to face with Talaat, standing behind a wide oak desk in a large, ornate office.

Leighton gave the faintest of bows to the Minister of the Interior, who glowered at him in return.

"Sit," Talaat said without ceremony, gesturing to a chair in front of his desk. He sat down behind his desk.

Leighton sat in the chair and his two escorts retreated from the room.

Talaat continued to stare at Leighton. He took a cigarette from a silver case on his desk, struck a match to light it, and sat smoking for several minutes before stubbing out the cigarette in a large crystal ashtray.

Leighton said nothing. He was here against his will. Talaat's presence gave him hope, though he was not sure why.

"Do you know where she is?"

Leighton was surprised. It was not the question he expected.

"Don't you?" he asked, more bewildered than provocative.

Talaat's features darkened.

"I have no knowledge of Elena's whereabouts," Leighton said. "I met her here in Constantinople before I began my journey, but I've had no contact with her since then. Has she left the city?"

"What was the purpose of your journey?"

Leighton hesitated.

"I am working on a monograph regarding some Koranic commentaries," he began. Talaat's features darkened further.

"One of the reasons for my trip was to consult with some ulemas in Baghdad, however..." Leighton raised a hand to forestall Talaat's protests, "my trip had another purpose as well.

"My friend Edward Grey has some concerns, as you are aware, about the building of the Baghdad Railway. He asked me if it would be possible to go overland to Baghdad and report any progress on the railway to him."

"You are a spy!" Talaat bellowed.

"Hardly," Leighton said. "More like a tourist with friends in high places. I used no subterfuge, broke no laws. I simply accompanied a caravan and saw things no one is making an effort to keep secret."

"We have no secrets regarding the railway," Talaat said.

"Precisely," said Leighton.

"And you have made no effort to pry into places where you have no business prying?" Talaat asked.

"None," responded Leighton, his conscience clear.

"Our German friends tell me a different story," Talaat said.

"I'm doubtful they have been able to offer any proof of anything untoward," Leighton said.

"Proof," Talaat repeated the word.

"Proof," said Leighton. "The Germans may be your friends, but so are the British. The Germans are welcome to tell stories but if they accuse your friends of some crime, they must offer proof."

"The British are our friends?"

"You know we are, of course. We have loaned you money, sold you battleships, instructed your troops."

"But you oppose our railway."

"Not at all," Leighton said, "but Grey does have some concerns – more about your German friends and what they intend to do with the railway than about the railway itself."

"They intend to build the railway and run the railway on our behalf," Talaat said. "It is a project of great benefit to our people."

"Clearly it is that," Leighton agreed. "And in peaceful times such as these, a railway can lead to prosperity. Statesmen, however, must contemplate situations that are not so peaceful and closely examine any possible threats."

"Friends pose no threats," Talaat said.

Leighton nodded in agreement.

"As you have said, we are friends with the Germans and friends with the British. We pose a threat to neither of our friends."

"The time may be coming," Leighton measured his words, "when it may be difficult to be friends with both Germany and Britain."

Talaat sat back in his chair. "What are you suggesting?"

"Talaat Bey, you are in a position to know the kinds of currents that are roiling Europe these days," Leighton said. "There is a competition to build arsenals, increase troop size, extend colonies. These can lead to conflict – a conflict that may explode in war."

"Britain is planning a war against Germany?"

"Of course not," Leighton said. "But Britain is cautious about defending itself against any threats in this environment."

Talaat lit another cigarette and blew smoke in the air. "So we are back to menace," he said, a statement rather than a question.

"Do you give me your word as a gentleman that you have no confidential information about the railway?" Talaat asked.

"As you said, Talaat Bey, you have no secrets regarding the railway," Leighton said, "and I have no reason not to believe you."

Talaat looked at him evenly for a while.

"Lord Leighton," he said at length, "you are a prominent Orientalist, you study our culture. You are a bey in your country. I must presume that you are an honorable man."

Leighton did not respond.

"You are free to go. I apologize if the manner of your invitation to come see me caused you any concern. It appears

I have been misinformed. I regret any inconvenience this may have caused."

Talaat rose from his chair and reached across the desk to shake Leighton's hand. Leighton rose to take it.

"Please, enjoy your stay in Constantinople, or wherever you visit in our realm," Talaat said, forcing a smile.

"Thank you, Talaat Bey," Leighton said. "You are most kind."

Talaat rang a bell on his desk and the two escorts reappeared. "Please see that Lord Leighton gets back to his hotel," Talaat told them.

Chapter Thirty-Two

Leighton arrived at the Pera Palace in late afternoon. His escorts doubtless knew that he had not registered at the hotel since his return to Constantinople. It was part of the cat-and-mouse game they were playing with him.

He dare not go to the American Embassy in daylight; he was sure Talaat's men were shadowing him. He was not fooled by Talaat's apparent change of heart. The Turks had observed the exchange with von Bohlen, but had missed the hand-off to Morrison, or failed to understand its meaning. They meant now to catch him with proof of his espionage. While it was a relief no longer to be officially a wanted man, Leighton had no illusions about being free.

Leighton took tea in the lobby, waiting for darkness to fall. When he felt it was dark enough, he went out of the front entrance of the hotel, and turned immediately left, towards the American Embassy. He did not look around to see if his shadows were behind him, though he thought he heard the shuffle of feet.

Leighton approached the embassy. There was a gaslight immediately in front of it, showing the front gate shut. He walked past the front gate to the corner, and there turned left onto the side street. Several yards down the street was a construction site, where the embassy was adding a wing for consular activities. The site was filled with materials for the construction and extended partially into the street. There was a fence around the site, but it was wooden, a hastily built affair of little practical use for hindering intruders. There were no gaslights on this small side street, though a half-moon enabled Leighton to make out the fence.

Without breaking his stride, Leighton walked up to the fence, put his hands on the top railing, which reached about to his chest, and hoisted himself up the fence and over quickly. Now he distinctly heard footsteps, from more than one person.

Leighton felt as much as found his way through the stacks of bricks and beams, toward the back of the embassy building. It was covered with tarpaulin. Leighton heard his pursuers at the fence. They were arguing in loud whispers about whether they should follow him onto the embassy grounds.

Leighton pulled at the tarpaulin, lifting a flap that he ducked under, as he heard the scrape of a foot on the fence. He followed a half-built brick wall towards what had been the rear portico of the embassy building. A lamp in a window provided light as Leighton came to another tarpaulin stretched across a rear entry. This, too, was loosened, so that Leighton simply had to pull it aside to step into a rear hallway in the embassy.

"Good show, old boy!" whispered Morrison, in an affected English accent. The American stood at the top of a short flight of stairs, holding another lantern. Leighton grinned despite himself, listening for sounds of further pursuit. If his shadows had actually vaulted the fence, he doubted they would stay long once they realized they had penetrated into diplomatic space protected by international law.

Morrison reach out a hand to help Leighton up the stairs and led him into the kitchen. There the two of them extinguished the lantern and sat quietly, listening for any sign of intruders.

"You were followed?" Morrison asked.

"Two or three men, I think."

"Brave enough to violate diplomatic territory?"

"I think not."

"Broome is here," Morrison said, "in the front. He was quite worried when you failed to show up here."

"I had a special audience," Leighton said, and recounted his interrogation by Talaat.

"You think he let you go so you could continue to incriminate yourself?"

Leighton nodded.

"Are you hungry?" Morrison said, with a smile and a gesture sweeping around the kitchen.

"I am, as a matter of fact," said Leighton. "I took tea at the Pera Palace but didn't eat any of their sandwiches."

Moving slowly by the dim light of the moon, Morrison found some bread and cheese in the larder. He brought them to the small wooden table where they had installed themselves, found a knife and, with a little more searching, an open bottle of wine. Morrison peered out the window.

"I think it's all right to light the lantern again," he said. He quickly lit the lantern and set it on the table. "Eat. Let me go fetch Broome."

Leighton cut himself a wedge of the fresh ewe's cheese and ate it with appreciation. He tore off a chunk of bread and poured himself a large glass of wine. Morrison came clattering down the back stairs with Broome in tow.

"Milord," said Broome.

"Broome!" exclaimed Leighton. "Sorry if I worried you – Talaat Bey decided he wanted to see me. But then he let me go, escorting me back to the hotel. I was watched, so I waited until dark to come here."

Broome bowed, acknowledging the explanation.

Morrison carried the map case and satchel from von Bohlen. "You'll be wanting to look at these," he said, placing them on the table. "Von Bohlen thought they were very important. Straus got word today that von Bohlen fell from the Galata Bridge and came out of the water dead."

"Drowned?"

"No water in his lungs. They speculate that he took cyanide."

Leighton frowned. "Let me see the papers," he said.

Morrison pulled the sheaf of papers from the satchel and handed them to Leighton. He looked first at the Turkish version of the Baghdad Railway agreement, scanning it quickly until he came to the codicil. His brow furrowed. He leafed quickly through the German version, stopping again at the codicil.

"Completely brazen," Leighton said. "I can't believe they committed this to paper."

Morrison and Broome looked at him silently. Leighton looked up. "The Turks and the Germans spell it out – in the event of a European war, Berlin will have the railway at its disposal for the transport of troops to Basra and beyond."

He looked at the codicil again. "By way of compensation, the Germans will build several secondary lines on the main railroad, so that the Turks can transport their troops to the various provinces of the empire. They're turning the railway into a military machine."

"Grey's instinct was right, it seems," said Morrison.

Leighton nodded, reaching for the map case. He extracted the map and unrolled it on the table. It was several pages of surveyors' detailed drawing of the railway route. It took several minutes for Leighton to orient himself on the pages. At length, he identified the landmarks and followed the route of the railroad. "Yes, a spur here northwards, here southwards, here off to the east as the main route veers south." Leighton shuffled the large form sheets around as he traced the rail route. "Our caravan crossed the route on two or three occasions," he said. "And here is the work site where the massacre took place." He pointed to a drawing in the center of one of the sheets.

Morrison peered over at the drawing. He saw that all the references on the map were in German. He looked at the precise pencil markings, recalling the twisted corpses they had found there. A simple drawing that plunged a knife into the heart of a culture. But that culture was ready to defend itself.

"It seems so harmless, drawings on a paper," Morrison said.

Leighton frowned. "It's markings like these that create bloodshed, though – borders that cut through tribes, railroads that invade homelands, contracts that put men into bondage." He looked at Morrison. "It sounds trite, but if everyone stayed at home, we wouldn't need drawings like these and the bloodshed they bring." He looked away. "But such is the nature of man – always looking to expand his homeland, his sphere, his wealth." What else drove a nation to empire? Leighton mused to himself.

Broome cleared his throat. "Our luggage has finally caught up with us," he said. "It was delivered to the embassy this afternoon."

"Just in time for our departure," said Leighton. He looked at Morrison. "I daren't carry these papers with me, not even as far as the embassy."

"You want Grey to see them?"

Leighton nodded slowly. So much gunpowder in the keg – would this be the spark that lit it? "I must get them to him somehow."

"We can all stay here tonight," said Morrison. "I've had some field cots installed in one of the reception rooms." Unlike its British counterpart, the American Embassy did not house the ambassador, who lived in a suite at the

Pera Palace. The entire space was given over to offices and reception rooms.

"Perhaps," Morrison said to Leighton as they made their way through the dark embassy to their temporary quarters, "perhaps, I can persuade Oscar to send the stuff in the American diplomatic pouch."

"To Washington?"

"No, our embassy in London is the headquarters for all diplomatic activity in Europe."

"That's perfect, then!" said Leighton. "None of us needs to run the risk of being caught with these treacherous papers."

"Do you think the Turks have so much respect for international law that a diplomatic pouch is inviolable?"

"More like fear of the consequences. Like it or not, the Young Turks are as dependent on Great Power support as the sultan was."

"And if they felt one of the Great Powers was ready to step in and support them against the others?"

"Germany?"

Morrison nodded.

"What if you could get them to London," Morrison said, "but not risk getting caught with them?"

Leighton looked closely at his companion. "How would you manage that?"

"I have an idea," Morrison said. "Let me check with Oscar."

~

The next morning, a slightly rumpled Leighton and Broome came out of the American Embassy at 8 a.m., just as the first employees were arriving for work. The two men conspicuously carried nothing. They walked up the street, past the Pera Palace and up to the gate of the British Embassy. Two of the black-coated men openly followed them the short distance, but made no move to stop them. At the embassy, the porter let Leighton and Broome in after a brief conversation.

It amused Leighton in a way that his great adventure to stop the Baghdad Railway, one that took him across the vastness of the Taurus mountains and the Syrian steppes, the mud flats of the Tigris, the seaways around Arabia, now ended here on a half-mile stretch of a small side street in Pera.

They had met the American ambassador, Oscar Straus, before leaving.

"I'm honored to meet you," the ambassador told Leighton in a quiet voice. "I admire the learning of a true scholar."

Leighton looked at Morrison, wondering exactly what he had told the ambassador. Straus had a beard, grown wispy with age, and the hooked nose that had drawn the attention of caricaturists during his tenure as Commerce Secretary.

"I'm grateful to you for your help," said Leighton.

Straus made a small gesture with his hand, waving away the thanks. "We must help our British friends." He paused. "Do you happen to know Lord Rothschild?"

"We have met," Leighton answered. "I see him in Parliament." Leighton paused. "He is the first person of your faith to be raised to the peerage, though his father, of course, fought a long fight to be seated in the House of Commons without having to swear his oath 'as a Christian.'"

"Yes, but you British are more tolerant than we in America," Straus said in his gentle voice. "After all, your prime minister, Disraeli, was of Jewish descent, even if he was baptized. I'll not live to see the day of a Jewish president in the United States."

Leighton appreciated the irony of Britain being considered liberal by the colony that threw off its "oppressive" rule.

"Lord Rothschild's son, Lionel, is very active in the Zionist cause," Leighton said. "He and I have often discussed Palestine."

"Ah, yes, Palestine," Straus said, shrugging his shoulders. But he said no more.

"I mustn't keep you," the ambassador said. "I delayed my own trip to meet you, and I wish you Godspeed on your return home."

Straus's hand was limp as Leighton shook it, and his smile wavered fitfully on his lips. But his eyes were bright. Leighton felt he had found an ally.

Leighton and Broome remained in the British embassy once they arrived there. Broome left only once to book their passage on the Orient Express, via the sea route leaving on Monday. Their plans would be no secret to Talaat's spies.

Broome had time to rehabilitate their luggage, much worn from the trip by caravan and the long trip back in a ship's hold. Leighton paid attention at last to his neglected Koranic commentaries, keeping his mind off their pending voyage.

Monday morning, Leighton and Broome descended with their luggage to the Galata pier, to board the ship for the trip up the Bosphorus and Black Sea to Constanta. They were not surprised when the customs official signaled to them to open their trunks. The ostensible reason for searching departing passengers was to stop the rampant theft of art objects, but it marked the first time for Leighton that his luggage was searched. The customs officer methodically went through Leighton's books and papers. Eventually, as the warning whistle blew from the deck of the ship, he waved them on. Broome quickly fastened the trunks shut and consigned them to a porter while he and Leighton walked up the passenger gangway.

Standing at the railing, Leighton watched their luggage being loaded over a separate gangway. He also observed a bulky canvas package stamped with an official seal bearing an eagle – the U.S. seal, he surmised. True to his word, Morrison had dispatched the diplomatic pouch aboard the same ship.

With two more blasts from its horn, the ship pushed off from the pier as sailors worked the winches to pull in the massive hemp ropes tethering them to the dock. The ship headed directly into the Bosphorus. Broome left to install them in their cabin, while Leighton took a seat on the deck. He never tired of the views from the Bosphorus as the city and its spires gave way to green tiers of villas and towns. Their ship threaded its way through the ferries crisscrossing the waterway as they plied their way up or downstream.

Their own trip upstream was slow going – it took several hours longer in this direction and they would not arrive at port before the next morning. In fact, Morrison was leaving on the Orient Express the next day via the land route, but their trains would be joined at Belgrade the following day.

Leighton pondered his instructions from Rashid's man to take the sea route. He had offered no explanation. Leighton wondered if he would be contacted en route. Were his secret documents safe outside his possession?

Chapter Thirty-Three

He was not really surprised to see her standing at the pier. She wore a plain brown dress and her hair up. She carried a drab, beige parasol against the sun. She was alone.

He had puzzled over the instructions from Rashid's man and given much thought to the mystery of his connection to this band of Arab revolutionaries. Finally, it came together in his mind with the mystery of Elena's marriage to Talaat and her disappearance.

The ship rocked gently against the pier as the pilot reversed the screw at just the right moment. Carriages stood at the embankment, ready to transport the passengers to the train station. There was ample time. Lunch would be served at the restaurant before the train departed.

Exchanging only the subtlest of nods, Leighton indicated to Broome he should proceed ahead with their luggage. The crew watched the passengers leaving the ship with more attention than usual. Someone had broken into the hold and slashed open the diplomatic pouch dispatched by the American embassy. It was not known if any of the contents had been taken. What was left in the canvas bag were some maps of individual states in the United States.

Leighton smiled when Broome told him of the attempted theft. He was glad he had followed Morrison's advice not to send his documents by pouch, but to have a pouch sent as a decoy. By the time Talaat's men realized the stolen maps were not in the pouch, it would be too late to discover where else they might be.

Leighton came down the gangplank and walked directly to Elena. The two of them stood there, without embrace or smile, silent, looking at each other.

"So you're my guardian angel," Leighton said at last. "You sent your comrades to rescue me at every turn, didn't you?"

Elena smiled at this, but did not reply.

"Now that we're no longer lovers, we've become allies," Leighton said.

"We've always been allies, Richard, you and I," Elena said.

She turned and walked up to the hotel at the dock. Leighton followed her. It was a ramshackle, seaside hotel, perhaps grand at one time, but now musty and faded. The room was large, however, as was the bed.

They made love, tenderly at first but then with a mounting passion. For Leighton, the months of separation vanished and the pent-up feeling he had for Elena broke through in a flood. She responded, too, with an abandon that fueled his own passion. They coupled with a fervor more intense than any before, in what had always been an intensely ardent liaison. Leighton felt more at one with Elena than he had ever felt before, with her or with any other woman. He lost himself completely in their union.

They clung to each other, together, as the passion ebbed slowly away. Leighton held her in a fierce embrace that slackened only as their breathing resumed a more regular rhythm. At length, he pulled out of her gently and rolled over onto his back, keeping his arm wrapped around hers, his fingers entwined with hers. Leighton knew he would never find words to express how he felt just now. He hoped never to forget this feeling.

When a sob escaped Elena, Leighton took her again into his arms and they embraced each other, they kissed deeply and pressed their warmth against each other.

They lay clasping to each other outside of time, lost in the moment. At length, Elena whispered, her voice hoarse, "You must catch your train."

Leighton felt a surge of resistance. For once he wanted his sense of duty to succumb to the feeling that was raging inside him. He wanted to abandon his journey, his mission, his duty and stay in this place outside of time, this bliss without measure.

He looked into Elena's eyes and saw his own desire reflected there. Then Elena turned away and rose from the bed. Leighton drew a deep breath before sitting up. They dressed quickly, wordlessly.

They stood looking at each other. Leighton had much to say but felt that words were useless.

"You will help Rashid?" Elena asked at last. "The Armenians, the Arabs, we are making a common cause against this Turkish state."

Leighton looked at her, earnest, hopeful in her desperation.

"Yes, it took me some time to figure it out," Leighton said. He smiled ruefully. "For a spy, I'm not very skilled at intrigue."

"You are not a spy, Richard," Elena said. "You are a loyal soldier." She smiled. "And a scholar. And a lover of poetry. And my wonderful lover."

Leighton smiled in return. He had not answered her question. But she knew the answer. Britain could not allow a resurgent Turkey allied with Germany. It would be hardheaded politicians like Grey and Churchill making the decision – not her gentle Orientalist. He was a soldier, not a general.

"You will be safe?" Leighton asked.

Elena shrugged. Safe, when the head of the largest spy network in the world was after her? "I – how do you English say it? – made my bed." She bit her lip at the double entendre.

"And you'll lie in it," Leighton finished for her.

Elena smiled.

The two sat for a while on the edge of the bed, gazing into each others' eyes without embarrassment, not speaking.

"I must go," Leighton said after some minutes and stood up.

"Richard," Elena said, standing as well, "thank you."

Leighton shrugged. "As Shakespeare put it, 'All the world is a stage and all the men and women merely players.' I'm playing my part."

Elena smiled at his self-deprecation. She leaned forward and kissed him gently on the lips. "Adieu, Richard."

Leighton turned and left the hotel, hailing the hansom in front to take him to the station. Elena came out to the porch and stood watching him leave, without waving. He watched her, too, until the cab pulled away and rounded the corner into town.

~

The train reached Belgrade the following morning. It was joined to the Orient Express that had left Constantinople the previous day. Morrison found Leighton in the breakfast car as the full train was pulling out of the station.

"Good morning, old man," Morrison said, affecting again his mock English accent. He sat at the table across from Leighton and motioned to the waiter for some coffee.

"And how was your trip?" Morrison asked.

Leighton paused before answering. "It was fine," he said slowly. What could he say? He looked up at his friend, and smiled. "Except for an unpleasant incident with a diplomatic pouch."

Morrison laughed. "Don't tell me – your luggage was searched at the pier before boarding."

Leighton only nodded as he ate his bacon.

"I was searched as well," Morrison said. "I can imagine some of Talaat's minions are very frustrated right now. They thought they had all their bases covered."

Leighton looked at Morrison with a blank expression on his face.

"Bases, as in baseball – if they're all covered no one gets on base," the American explained.

"Ah, baseball. Covered bases. I understand."

"We hit a home run."

Leighton shook his head and took another bite from his plate.

Morrison continued smiling. When the waiter brought his coffee, he ordered bacon and eggs as well.

"Now they have lost the scent," Morrison said. "They know you have the map and codicil from von Bohlen, and they know you will get it back to England, but they don't know how."

"They are learning the hard way how ingenious our American friends are," Leighton said.

By evening, they were in Vienna. Morrison spent the time in Leighton's cabin, where Broome served them tea. Leighton filled in his friend on the alliance between the Armenians and the Arabs, and how Elena had been the one sending his rescuers to intervene at those critical moments. He did not go into detail about his final encounter with Elena in Constanta.

Morrison smiled softly anyway. "You're a lucky man, Richard," he said.

The two sat in silence until Broome came to remove

the tea service. "I'll be getting off in Paris," Morrison said. "Teddy is coming through in a week on his grand European tour."

Leighton realized Morrison had not spent all his time in the American embassy taking care of British matters.

"First a safari in Africa, then a hunting trip in Europe?" Leighton quipped.

Morrison smiled, but said nothing. "At 51, he has a bright future ahead of him – the youngest man ever to leave the presidency –"

"Someday, Bill, you will have to come visit me in England and tell me more about your relationship with Mr. Roosevelt – unless it's a state secret," Leighton said.

"Well, I might enjoy a few weeks at an English country estate at that," Morrison said, grinning. "I may take you up on that."

The two sat looking out the window. They had left Vienna and the landscape was dim in the dusk. The train skimmed along the Danube, so that they caught occasional glimpses of the twilight reflecting off water.

"The railway will be built, you know," Morrison said at last. "They always are, sooner or later. Whenever they make sense."

"It's the 'later' that interests me now," Leighton said. "I'm sure you're right – it's inevitable that a railroad will connect the Mediterranean to the Gulf. But not while Germany is threatening war against Britain."

Morrison watched his friend. "You're sure there's not more to it? For you?"

Leighton smiled, but did not look him in the eye. "Let's say," Leighton began, "that I'm not unhappy that Britain's interests lie in delaying that railway."

"What do you think was von Bohlen's game?" Morrison asked.

"I've been giving that some thought," Leighton said. "I think underneath that homburg hat, our German friend was something of an idealist. He thought the railroad would help the region. He was appalled when he saw it turned into a machine of war."

"But at least he believed in progress," Morrison said. "You seem to cherish this desert culture, this relic of a more primitive time."

"Do you think progress and prosperity are the same? I wonder," said Leighton. "Is the Bedouin, with his meager diet, his discomfort, less happy than our urban compatriots, ensconced in luxury? He has his faith, a world he understands, that doesn't change."

"Now who's an idealist?"

"Yes, I suppose I'm romanticizing it all. And you're right, it's doomed – destined – to change."

"Richard," said Morrison, dropping his bantering tone, "don't lose that idealism. It's your greatest service to your king."

Leighton nodded. "In any event, I'm too old to change," he said.

"So the world changes, you don't," Morrison said.

"That's it – the world changes, I don't," Leighton replied.

Morrison clapped him on the shoulder. "Good night, my friend. Sleep well."

The American left to go to his own cabin. Leighton summoned the porter to prepare his bed. He read briefly, but fell asleep quickly as the train rocked its way through Austria toward Germany and the West.

The two met for breakfast as the Orient Express approached Paris.

"Here is a cable address for your order of 'equipment' for Rashid," Morrison said, handing Leighton a slip of paper. "I leave it to you to devise an entity to place the order that will not be traceable to your government."

"I'm sure Grey will be quite adept at this type of subterfuge," Leighton said.

They ate in silence. Leighton smiled. "You know, the irony of it is I never got to consult the ulemas in Baghdad about my translation. My stay was much shorter than anticipated."

"You'll just have to go back," Morrison said, smiling as well.

"Well, I know that Farnsworth will take good care of a poor scholar," Leighton said.

The two parted in the hall of the Gare de l'Est – a simple handshake, no more words. Presumably they would meet again, but the world was a hazardous place and nothing was certain. Leighton and Broome took a cab to the Gare du Nord for the train to London, and Morrison waved them on their way.

~

Two weeks after he returned to London, Leighton had lunch with Churchill in his club on Pall Mall.

"So how *did* you get the papers out of Turkey?" Churchill asked as Leighton related his adventures on the Orient Express.

"It was very simple," Leighton said. "Ambassador Straus took them in his luggage. He sailed to London via Gibraltar. It took him a week, but Talaat's men never thought to search the ambassador. I wonder if they really could have searched him."

"You mean he volunteered to take that risk for the sake of an ally?" Churchill said. "And really, only an ally of tradition, not of treaty."

"I think Morrison volunteered him," Leighton said. "I came to understand that he wields considerable weight through his relationship with Roosevelt."

"Hmmph," Churchill grunted and relit his cigar. "We are in their debt. The papers are, as the French would say, *brisantes*."

"Very sensitive, indeed," Leighton agreed. "What happens now?"

The politician smoked his cigar a moment before answering. "Grey told me your ingenious plan to supply rifles to Arab rebels," Churchill said. "That should at least slow down the railway. The maps will provide useful information to the rebels."

"And the codicil?"

"That must remain our secret for the moment," Churchill said. "It gives us some hidden leverage with the Germans, but we must not tip our hand."

"Is the situation irreconcilable?"

Churchill did not answer. He puffed reflectively on his cigar.

"Did you see any petroleum?"

Leighton told him about the bitumen fields he had traveled through with Rashid's men. He also mentioned the work on a pipeline at the mouth of the Shatt el Arab.

Churchill nodded. "The region is awash with oil. It is vital that we maintain control of it. That alone is worth fighting a war."

Leighton grimaced. My Orient, a battlefield for the 20th century, his expression said.

Churchill shrugged. "Yes, but it is inevitable. Oil is the paramount resource for our age. England must have oil to keep control of the seas."

How else maintain an empire?

"There is a new oil operation in Egypt, near Suez," Churchill said.

"Yes, our captain mentioned something about it as we entered the canal," Leighton said.

"Shell cannot be kept out of it, of course," Churchill said. "But I want Anglo-Persian involved to make sure the Germans do not become a party to it."

Shell, a British transport company, worked closely with the Royal Dutch oil company. The two had merged in 1907. The Dutch were thought to be far too friendly with the Germans, particularly with Deutsche Bank.

Leighton marveled at the range of Churchill's interest. He was Home Secretary, yet these were concerns about Britain's imperial role in the world. He clearly aimed to head the government some day.

"I could use your help, Leighton."

"My help?"

"Come now, Leighton, no false modesty," Churchill said. "You performed brilliantly for Grey. We need a man of your talents in this region. I need your help in Cairo."

Cairo, the burgeoning metropolis in North Africa, had been firmly under British control since the 1880s. For Leighton, it remained a place of study and scholarship. The city had grown increasingly European, with a huge population of Europeans and an Egyptian elite keen to imitate their ways. And yet it remained faithful in spirit to its Islamic roots.

"I am, of course, a loyal subject of His Majesty, and of His Majesty's government."

"Of course you are, Leighton," Churchill said. He reached out his hand and firmly gripped Leighton's. "Thank you, old man. Now, let me tell you what the problems are, and how you might help solve them. There will be danger, of course, but I rather think you thrive on danger, don't you?"

Leighton smiled and leaned closer to Churchill across the lunch table, curious in spite of himself to hear the details. Seeing Elena again had filled the hollowness that was in him. Losing her again, strangely, had not left him empty. Bereft, perhaps, but serene in a way that surprised him. He would take on Churchill's mission. Perhaps the young old fox was right, and he actually did thrive on danger.

www.ingramcontent.com/pod-product-compliance
Lightning Source LLC
Chambersburg PA
CBHW032154190626
46814CB00005BA/1986